MW01387854

Soul on Fire

By
Skyy Banks

UrbanEdge Publishing
Columbus, GA

Soul on Fire

Skyy Banks

ISBN: 978-0-9815326-5-3
Cover design by David Blayne and Keith Saunders

Printed in the United States of America

10 9 8 7 6 5 4 3 2 1

Soul on Fire

Acknowledgements

Admittedly, this journey has been bittersweet. However the sweet prevailed. Over the past year in penning Soul on Fire, I have been on a quest of self reflection and discovery. The most valuable lesson I've learned is that it's okay to LET GO. In accomplishing this I've authorized spiritual, emotional, and financial growth to take their respective positions within my life. I've ushered love in, because I'm loving me right now!

I want to extend my sincere gratitude to those that have been pivotal in all that has been and is yet to be:

My guardian Angel (Anna) - You left me at a time when I was just becoming a woman. I've experienced some disappointments and let downs along the way; however, your guiding spirit has never led me astray. May your light continue to shine brightly in my life in this world and the next.

My lineage - One can't fathom the importance of morals, values, and the impressions we make until we are charged with the responsibility. Thank you for being patient when I know myself I have been intolerable at times. My baby girl, you are loved and you are worth waiting for (always remember that).

Shontae Powell - Thank you for the breath of life given to Skyy Banks, for showing me that bruised does not equate to being broken and the true meaning of unconditional love. You have found your diamond in the rough.

Skyy Banks

Friends (Reason, Season, or Lifetime) - Your continued support and telling me yes when others said no has made a world of difference. You know who you are. The best is yet to come!

UrbanEdge Publishing - The creative latitude afforded me has allowed Skyy to blossom both as a writer and a person. Thank you for believing.

Dream Stealers- Must I not forget! I can't say that this would not have happened without you, whether silently or vocally, your negativity fueled the fire that burns within me.

Sherese Mays (sister, cousin, friend): Thank you for sharing your poetic prose. Just when I think I have arrived, I find myself coming full circle. Keep expecting the unexpected. The race doesn't go to the swift or strong, but the one who endures.

Survivors: You are my *OVERCOMERS* and I dedicate this book to you. Continue to not only live but thrive!!

Soul on Fire

Skyy Banks

ℴ

The four walls seemed to enclose her limp body as she sat on the edge of the bed leaning forward with disjointed thoughts racing through her mind. Her elbows propped on her knees braced her from falling face first to the floor. Dana had awakened to what had become a nightly ritual, the crimson numbers on the clock translating 3am, tears streaming down her face, and flesh in a weakened state. The vivid dreams that made their nightly social calls left her with a recurring dull ache in her heart. The remedy that Dana hungered for was only a phone call away.

Shivering as a result of the cool air from the ceiling fan, Dana stroked her arms for warmth. A fire began to rise between her legs as she thought about Andre, her Dr. Feel Good, and also her gynecologist. He knew exactly how to make the pain go away. She often thought their meeting to be kismet, but what fate causes a woman to love another one's husband? Her heart skipped a beat as she relived their first encounter.

The light bounced off his silvery specs of hair as he washed his large hands in preparation for her annual examination. She watched as he moved throughout the room with fluency. Her naked body fluttered under the sound of his voice while his sexiness intimidated. Lying on the exam table with her legs in stirrups, she awaited his grand entrance, literally.

"How are you Ms. Taylor?" he asked in a distinct tone.

Forcing her lips to part, she responded with a thick, grating. "Well."

The infallible feeling of a school girl having her first crush enveloped her. As uncomfortable as the speculum was, the movement of his fingers heedlessly tapped her g-spot, evoking an orgasm. Andre did not acknowledge her pulsating frame as he removed his latex gloves, careful to turn one inside the other.

Soul on Fire

"Get dressed and I will be back to speak with you."

Utter embarrassment prompted Dana to the door. A phone call with any unpleasant news would have to suffice. Nothing like that had ever happened to her before. Her feelings were mixed. His scripted after hours consultation ended the spectacle she had made of herself earlier. That was four months ago.

The sweat soaked baby doll dress clung to her as she dabbed at the moisture on the nape of her neck and between her breasts, anxiously anticipating Andre's return page. Barring he was in surgery the call would be made promptly. She knew he was on call at the hospital this week as she had a copy of his schedule always nearby.

"What's wrong baby? You need Daddy to make a house call?"

He was the master and she gladly served.

"Yes." Dana said like an infant.

The healing he had regardless of how temporary, served its' purpose. While they were together, she forgot about her distress.

"I'll be right over."

Whenever she called Andre he was sure to answer. That was unless wife and kid duty called first, but he seemed to have that dominion fairly under control.

Luther's woos vibrated off the walls, the candles flickered softly while permeating the room with the scent of lemon verbena, sweet grass, and white lilac. Dana lay naked atop the fresh sheets sprinkled with talcum powder, and the coolness of the shower coupled with the satin sheets induced her into a light slumber.

Andre crept into the bedroom, slid into the bed, and slowly began kissing the feathery part of her inner thighs. She woke up. He knew that was the spot, and with his tongue he touched every inch of her skin from her thigh up, continuing to tease her. Anchoring her fingers into his thick hair, she moaned, slowly massaging his scalp. The moaning grew. He flipped her onto her stomach and, bracing her body with a tight grip of her shoulders. He pushed deeper and deeper. The pain of his lovemaking hid the pain in her heart. The one he didn't know existed.

The pinnacle of their relations met with silence, one after the other, not the simultaneous crescendo they had countless times in the past. Luther serenaded them to sleep.

Seeking protection, Dana curled up in his arms, while tears rolled down her face onto his shoulders. The same tears that had awakened her two hours ago. She knew he would have to leave before dawn, but for now she was safe and that's all that mattered.

The snooze button was pressed for a third time before she crawled out of bed and dragged herself into the bathroom, and it wasn't before she caught a glimpse of a sheet of her favorite pink stationary from the corner of her eye. It was a note from Andre lying in the middle of the pillow. His writing was the typical illegible physician's writing. *To my sweet Dana. May warm thoughts and kisses carry you through your day. 'Dre.*

She smiled, then inhaled, and bringing the note to her lips she kissed it. Searching for any remnant or scent of Andre. She picked up the pillow and there it was, a touch of musk and CK. My baby, always there when I need him, she thought to herself.

A tear streaked face told the story of another sleepless night which was happening more often lately. Her body told another story of a woman always craving and yearning for the concealed.

The phone rang. It was her secretary Melinda calling to say that her 8:00 appointment was waiting and had been for thirty minutes now.

"Damn!" she said agitated.

She had recently left a group of accountants to start her own private accounting firm. Thankfully, most of the clients retained her services. Dana flipped through the appointment book to conclude who the client was and what kind of incentive she would offer as an expression of her sincere apologies... Mr. Walker. She tapped her pen on her forehead and groaned. He was a pain in the ass sometimes and today was hardly the day to deal.

"Melinda, give him a gift certificate to that little coffee shop on the end of Marietta Street. I don't know the name, but the who's who of the real estate investment community frequents that particular cyber cafe. I am sure he can meet some new contacts. Then reschedule for me. I'll be in around 10. Call Chelle to see if we can do lunch?"

Dana didn't give her a chance to respond.

"Thanks, you're a life saver."

The darkness and puffiness that encircled Dana's eyes echoed the weariness that began to manifest in her body. This is how Chelle played her position so well. She was Dana's childhood friend, the one that said what was on her mind and never worried about sparing anyone's feelings, especially Dana's. Thus, the reason for selectively sharing only the good stuff. As painful as the truth was Dana knew that's

Soul on Fire

exactly what she needed to hear. She hurried to get dressed with her number one motto in mind. People to see, things to do, and money to make.

Chelle was a bad bitch by all standards. They often joked about the mold being broken when she graced the planet. She was the brick house that the Commodores sang about - 36-24-36- she made most men wish for younger days. Chelle's man was old and filthy rich, an investment banker, and as long as he kept Chelle happy, she kept him happy.

Dana was a mini version of Chelle minus the 36 Cs, which did nothing for her self esteem. Often times when they went out, most of the men's attention was focused on Chelle and the off center mole above her lip. It had a certain kind of sex appeal.

"Hey lady," Chelle said stepping into their favorite Thai restaurant nestled on the corner of Peachtree and 14th Street, "you have become less accessible by the day. I've called you for the last two days and what? You're too good to call a sista back? Is Dre taking up all your time?"

Dana sighed. "I wish, maybe I could sleep a whole night through. I have been restless for the last couple of weeks. Crazy dreams have been haunting me. I'm a little girl and surrounded by men with no faces."

Chelle looked puzzled.

"They have faces but they are masked, the kind of masks that you would wear to a masquerade ball, in different colors and shapes."

The thought made Dana wince. She massaged the knot that began to grow in her stomach.

"What do you think it could be?"

"I don't know but it doesn't feel good."

"Excuse me ma'am." The waiter had come to the table with a bottle of wine. A closer look revealed a bottle of Amarone. "Compliments of the two gentlemen in the rear near the window." Tilting his head he nodded in their direction.

She accepted the bottle and squinted at Chelle. The waiter poured the wine and they toasted each other. Dana turned to see both men watching their every move. And a few moments later the bill came, though Dana and Chelle had not come close to finishing their meal. Chelle opened the leather jacket and on the bottom it read *paid in full*.

"Damn they're good," Dana said, copying the phone number written on the bill in her planner.

Skyy Banks

"I knew your ass was interested. Sitting over there with that nonchalant attitude." Chelle said. "You can fool some of the people some of the time, but you can't fool Chelle none of the time." They threw their heads back simultaneously in laughter. Chelle had a trite expression for everything. Things she picked up from her mother or her *old man.*

"Yeah, you see right through me. I won't call just yet." Dana said, although in her mind she knew she would do just that.

They sat and nibbled on Pad Thai with chatting at a minimal. Nibbling is exactly what Dana did. Her mind was on the other side of the room. She wanted to know who this charmer was and at that moment really didn't give a damn about what Chelle thought. Those thoughts seemed to keep her from proceeding, but Dana was going to show her this once that she wasn't always a sucker for a good looking man.

Dana laid her napkin on the table and pushed the chair back. "Watch this."

"Where are you going?" Chelle asked but her glaring eyes held the answer. "I knew you couldn't wait."

Dana snapped into defense mode. "Girl, you have Russell and I have half of a 'Dre."

"And that doesn't mean that you have to be gullible every time a man does something nice for you."

"Hold it! I am not in the mood for your pity and I definitely don't need your lecture. It's just a matter of time before Russell's old ass gives out on you or that Viagra won't cut it anymore. If you were smart you'd get up- *Miss High and Mighty*- and go with me."

Rotating her shoulders back, Chelle sat upright in the chair. She looked past Dana. Her face was marred with disappointment. Dana could not rationalize her anger and bitterness nor could she justify the insults she had hurled at Chelle. Chelle had been more than a friend, more like a sister to her and had never intentionally caused her pain. It was her honesty though that was too much at times. Right now it made Dana sick. She was not going to apologize, at least not right now.

"Wait on me girl," Dismissing the trade between them before she could respond. "I'll be right back."

Exaggerating her strut, making sure to pop her hips with every step, Dana crossed the room to the rear table. Both men stood up to greet her. She swore she was looking at twin center folds from Alaye' magazine, double the trouble and twice as nice. She gave them a quick once over. Once over the shoes and once over the thing that is supposed

Soul on Fire

to be left to the imagination. The twins had silky skin with just the right hue, a mix between olive and tan. This color reminded Dana of a past lover, who was a South of the Border native.

"Just wanted to come and personally thank you for the bottle of wine."

"Our pleasure and your friend?"

"She thanks you as well. Dana," she said extending her hand.

"Kwame , he stood , "and this is my brother Simeon, "sounding both cute and boyish.

"Pleasure to meet you and that accent?"

"Brazilian," both brothers replied in unison.

Dana's eyes continued to tease every inch of their bodies. Hairy chests peeked through the linen ensembles. Their arms were tightly sculpted. Her eyes followed every twist and curvature of the bicep. She bit her lower lip and thought to herself, now this shit should be bottled and sold. She was even more intrigued with the decision of which one to choose. They were mirror images of each other, so it really didn't matter because having one was nothing short of having the other.

"Where's your friend?"Kwame asked. Dana turned to see that Chelle had excused herself from the restaurant. She was choosing, so Chelle was an issue she would have to take up later.

"Did you enjoy the wine?" Simeon flirted. They looked so much alike even down to the identical mole on their chin, that it was hard to tell who was asking the question.

"It was pleasing to the palate." Dana flirted back with her eyes and mouth. She pushed just enough of her tongue out to lick the corner of her top lip. Retrieving a business card, she palmed it inside Simeon's hand.

"Call me and thanks again for the wine. Excuse Chelle, she had to get back to wor

The masked man beckoned the child, "Come here baby. Give daddy a hug." His voice was strong and held a certain familiarity in her life. This had been her refuge since birth that shielded her as humanly possible from life's hurts. "No sit in daddy's lap and hug me real tight." He scooped her in his arms and placed her in his lap close to his body. It was a desperate hug, not a simple display of affection from a father to a daughter. She was afraid. She felt his heart beating rapidly against hers. This uneasy feeling of being this personal with her father was foreign to her. And the mask? The mask hid his face while she called into question his identity. His hands stroked her thighs, which were exposed by summer shorts. The masked man, whose voice sounded like daddy, continued to stroke her thighs commuting his entire hand to her crotch. His movements were intense, eyes glazed, and his mouth was slightly opened.

Disillusioned and dripping with sweat Dana awakened to the blur of crimson numbers, 3am. Dana's abrupt change in posture from lying down to sitting up sent a sharp pain through her back as she sought to compose herself. Looking at the nightstand, she pondered the reality of waking at the same time every night and if there was any symbolism in this. "Maybe I need to see a shrink?" She said out loud. As *crazy* as it sounded she seriously considered the idea. Thumbing through the phone book she quickly jotted down the first name she saw that didn't appear to be urban, Dr. Johanna Mitchell. Afterwards she ran a warm bath with chamomile and lavender, to soothe the soul but the longer she soaked the worst she felt. She didn't know how to soothe the hurt in her heart, one with no known origin.

She scurried about the room getting dressed. Her new two piece pin striped suit was her attire of choice. It consisted of just enough spandex to accentuate every curve. Feeling like a train wreck on the inside was not an excuse to look like one on the outside. Applying tea bags to her puffy eyes added an additional fifteen minute delay that was well worth it. The natural astringent alleviated the swelling enough to be unnoticeable.

Her to do list was short today- call Dr.Mitchell and Chelle. Giving herself a once over in the mirror, she recited her mantra. "You are brilliant, you are beautiful, and you are loved."

That was her daily inspirational vitamin with hopes that one day she would believe it.

The office was unusually quiet this morning.

"Mornin'!"

Melinda jumped up from her desk to greet Dana. "Good morning Ms. Taylor, You know you wearing that suit."

"Thanks, I've been waiting for the weather to break to wear it."

Soul on Fire

"Wear it girl! Here are your messages and the report is ready for Mr.

Duncan. He should be here at 10."

"You're great. I need to look over this so I'll know what the hell I'm

talking about." Being on top of accounts had become second to the attack on her sanity.

"You'll do fine. You've already added three new clients and it's just

the beginning of the month."

"You noticed?" Dana asked trying not to put on airs.

Mr. Duncan was thirtyish. He had his own graphic design company and had several major contracts around the city as well as some international associations. He was well on his way to becoming a multi-millionaire. He routinely began their meetings by complaining about the fact that he needed a good woman. Dana had been quick to remind him that their relationship was strictly business, outside of that she could be of little assistance. Anyways the sight of his stomach prevented her from entertaining the thought. Besides the fact that he was aging rapidly, he looked as if he had been impregnated with twins. Dana couldn't get down with bald, barrel shaped bruthas, regardless of how long the money was and mind you, brutha's money was *llloooonnnnggg*.

She looked over her to do list and considered whom to call first. They were of equal importance, yet haughtiness crept in when it came to calling Chelle right away. Dana knew she was wrong and was tired of being wrong. They hadn't spoken since the incident at the restaurant. Dana's pride prevented her from calling. In some childish way she didn't want Chelle to have one up on her.

Forcing herself to call, Dana dialed Chelle's number. Chelle picked up the second time she called.

"Hey sweetie, are you feelin' better?" Chelle was always concerned.

She made her heart melt. Dana started to cry hysterically.

"What's wrong?"

"I'm sorry. I was a fool."

"They *were* fine. Did I see double mint?"

Skyy Banks

"Stop crazy." Dana said sniffling. "I am trying to be serious. I was wrong for the things I said and the way I behaved."

"I'm not going to beat you while you're down, but I do have some issues to take up with you and you know what about. Later though. I know you are going through some thangs and they were fine. Hell, I'd diss me too for a chance at heaven."

"I didn't diss you."

"Just kiddin'. Again what's wrong? Why are you crying?"

"I don't know what's wrong with me. I can't sleep. I can't eat. My stomach is nervous all the time. I'm having these damn dreams."

"The ones with the masked people?"

"Yes. I think I need to see a psychiatrist or something. I can't keep feeling like this."

"You have my support. But you know that already."

"I do."

"I have to get off this phone girl. I will come by tonight. We can drink some wine and you can cry all you want as long as you don't get snot all over me."

"You nasty."

"Love you girl. Bye sweetie."

She felt better, but had only 20 minutes before Mr. Duncan would arrive.

"You are brilliant, you are beautiful, and you are loved." Dana spoke boldly to the image in her compact mirror before Melinda buzzed in.

"Send him in."

"Good morning, Ms. Taylor." Carl leaned in for a hug as Dana made her away from around her desk.

"Oh, so it's Ms. Taylor now?"

"The last time I was here you were all uptight and sure to reiterate to me the boundaries of our relationship. Strictly business if I'm not mistaken?" She could tell he was undressing her with his eyes as he spoke.

"We are learning I see."

As Dana pulled the projector screen down, she attempted to ease the tension. "You can still call me Dana. I won't hurt you."

Pointing to the chart while explaining, "This was your projected or forecasted revenue. We are well above target and with the addition of Mark V, I can't see why you won't have a growth of about 20%."

Soul on Fire

"Can we go through the actual numbers line by line?"

"I was getting to that. Here's your handout."

"Permission to move?"

"Showcasing our comedic skills are we?"

The chair rolled slowly over the carpet under Carl's weight. His short stubby legs moved even slower. A tickle began to rise inside of her.

"Okay this is what I was referring to."

Carl leaned in towards her. The warmth of his breath caressed the skin behind her ear that was exposed by the up do. Dana shuddered. As much as she was unattracted to this bald thing, the subdued moisture from his mouth excited her. Dana sat impervious to the mounting sexual tension especially after the lecture she had given him about his unwanted flirtation.

"Are you following me?"

"Yes," leaning in so close this time that his lips grazed her outer ear.

Dampness filled the drought between her legs instantly. Her body contorted with embarrassment and arousal. He placed his hand inside her jacket and manipulated her breast. His touch was hypnotizing. Not uttering a rejection, she was subsequent to his lead. He swiveled her chair around to face him and parted her legs. His fingers found her scalloped thong and pulled it to the side baring a tuft of hair trimmed in a v -shape. Carl dropped to the floor and lashed her clitoris rapidly before leisurely pleasing her. The magic he worked with his tongue caused her subtle contractions throughout her body. Dana lay back in the chair powerless for what seemed like an eternity. The orgasm was unyielding and left her temporarily debilitated. She pushed off on his shoulders and the chair rolled back to the bookshelf. Her legs were still spread as though she was inviting him for seconds. Gathering her senses, Dana stood with a quickness that knocked some books off the shelf. Straightening her jacket and tugging at her skirt, she could only hope that her thong would catch the signs of pleasure that flowed from within. Carl stood up straightened his tie and dabbed at his glistening forehead. Before he left he placed an envelope on her desk.

"Just a little something to show my appreciation, I will see you next quarter or sooner if you would like?"

Dana was speechless. After he left the room, she sat in the chair took a few minutes to recover and replayed what had just happened. She touched herself actualizing she was soaked and it was real. The envelope Carl had given her had a gold seal. She popped the seal and it held several hundred dollar bills, ten to be exact.

"Hey sweetie, looks like someone could use a hug." Dana had been home 30 minutes before Chelle used her key to let herself in only to find Dana reclined on the chaise lounge drinking a glass of wine.

"I can and I am sorry."

Sitting down next to Dana, Chelle responded. "Don't worry about it. You should know by now that you don't bother me with your antics. On the other hand, you do need to get that checked out. It's not normal and that's with all seriousness."

Silence meant agreement in this case as Dana stood with a blank stare.

"Did you call the Dr.?"

"I was distracted at work. I'm going to call first thing in the morning." Dana didn't dare divulge the lascivious behavior that took place that caused her to be thrown off her pivot. Causing her to not only forget about the Dr., but who and where she was.

"Now as bad as you say your nights have been that should have been the first thing you did even before calling me."

"Yes mother. Hold that thought," Her fingers pressed against Chelle's lips while she answered the phone. Whomever it was really wanted to speak to her, they called three times consecutively without leaving a message.

"Hello," She immediately recognized the pitch.

"Simeon?"

"Surprised?"

"How are you my dear?" Dana's smiled stretched from ear to ear.

By that time Chelle was all in her face wanting in on the conversation.

"Who is that?" Whispering she asked again. "Who is that?"

Dana pulled away from her, put a finger up in pause, and walked in the kitchen for a private moment, at least for Simeon's sake because she knew she would be sharing with Chelle soon after.

"Pour the wine. I'll be in there in a minute."

"How have you been? And your brother?"

"Good! Thanks for asking. When can I see you?"

"When I......."

Soul on Fire

Her response was interrupted by a beep indicating an incoming call. It was 'Dre. He was not what she needed right now. Dana decided against answering the call.

"So when can I see you?" Simeon asked again, a little more anxious.

"Soon." It was just enough to let him know that she was interested and just enough to know that it wouldn't be that easy.

"Are we playing hard to get?"

"No, I just have a few things going on right now and I really can't introduce anything new into the mix."

"Any excuse is better than none."

Dana could hear the disappointment in his voice. "Chelle is here and we need to catch up on things. I will call you soon."

"Promise?"

"Promise."

Chelle handed her a glass of wine, perfect timing.

"So, how's my best friend doing?" Dana asked, taking a sip.

"Well, if you must know, Russell's wearing me out. Every time I turn around he's trying to get some. To be pushing 50, he can put in work. He needs to sit his old ass down."

"Ooohh, I know you didn't say that about your big daddy!"

"Yes, I did. Can he let it breathe?" Dana almost choked.

"Pour me another."

"Slow down girl. Russell wants to take me to Paris for two weeks. I think it would be good for the business. I can pick up a few ideas and shop my latest design of handbags. The ones you have not bothered to look at."

"I was supposed to be doing that, wasn't I? Bad friend!" Dana spanked herself on the hand. "I think that's a great idea. Take me with you."

"I would if I could, but you know Russell would have a fit. I think he might ask me to marry him. Enough about me, what's been going on with my Dana-pooh?"

Dana turned slightly away from Chelle, rimming her glass with her finger. She gets the man, the trip, and possibly the ring, she thought to herself with eyes half rolled in her head.

"I'm lonely and tired of being so vulnerable. I'm not sure why I am having these crazy dreams. I want to be with 'Dre but I can never be more than his trophy mistress."

"Why do you think you're so vulnerable? You have both the booty and the brains. Just kidding, I meant to say beauty and the brains."

"Hell if I knew the answer to that, I wouldn't be getting ready to pay a shrink to tell me." The wine began to have an effect on Dana. "Can I be honest with you?"

"What's stopped you before?"

"I envy you. I envy every damn thing about you and it makes me sick!"

Chelle stood, eyes wide, and shell shocked. Nothing could have ever prepared her for that.

The door bell rang. Dana avoided Chelle's eyes and stumbled to answer. She had consumed three glasses of wine on an empty stomach. Gazing through the peep hole, all she could see was a beige shirt, yet the build was recognizable from anywhere. "No he didn't." she huffed in disbelief. "I know 'Dre hasn't gotten that damn bold to just show up at my house unannounced. Did he forget I wasn't his woman?"

She opened the door slightly, just enough to show her face. 'Dre pushed his way inside. "What the hell?" Dana asked dumfounded.

Without a word he made a bee line through the family room, through the kitchen, to her bedroom and back to the foyer where he had left Dana standing.

"What the hell are you doing here 'Dre?" Dana scowled. "Have you forgotten about the *no call- no show rule*? You can't change the rules of the game. I play by yours, you will play by mine. Stepping towards him, "You don't want me waltzing my happy ass in your office like I am the Mrs. do you?"

Dana stood firmly with one hand on her hip and the glass in the other. Chelle cleared her throat. Neither party seemed to remember she was there. She gulped the last corner of wine, grabbed her sweater, and then wrapped her arms around Dana. She whispered in her ear, "Call me later. And remember, I love you, for who you are. And don't you forget it." Chelle kissed Dana on the cheek and headed for the door.

'Dre was immovable standing under the foyer lights. Dana stepped around him to enter the living room.

"You can see yourself out." She said, however his audaciousness, his strong will, the way he charged into the house, his stern looked aroused something deep within. She enticed him with subtle movements. Slowly dropping first her suit jacket and then her skirt to reveal a purple

Soul on Fire

thong - she hoped he would follow. Dimming the lights, she popped a jazz CD into the player. Standing naked in the bathroom she swayed with the music before getting into the waiting shower.

She squeezed the loofa sponge over her shoulders and let the water flow over her face into her mouth. 'Dre's stood naked before her. Stepping inside the stall, he pulled Dana into him. Embracing her, he moved with the music. It was slow and it was rhythmic. He kissed her patiently, offering a thousand apologies. His tongue outlined her lips. His lips greeted her forehead, cheeks, and chin, all the while never letting go. He stroked her breasts, one in each hand, teasing her nipples with his tongue before taking each breast into his mouth. She moaned softly. The foreplay was short and sensuous. Both dripping wet, he carried her to the bedroom. He toweled Dana dry and then himself, in absence of sound. Pulling the bed back, he pulled the covers over her nude body. He lay on top of the comforter and rubbed her back until she fell asleep.

Dana awakened the next morning to an empty bed. Her head was clanging. She rolled over searching for a piece of him. There was nothing but a brief reminder of the previous night's episode.

"You are brilliant, you are beautiful, and you are loved!" She spoke softly to the full length mirror on the opposite wall. On her way out she stepped on something, 'Dre's brown wallet. She threw it in her purse and made a mental note to call him later.

"Somebody loves you." That was the first thing Melinda asserted to Dana as she opened the door.

"And good morning to you! What are you talking about?"

"Go in your office and see!" Dana could tell she was excited, like a person bursting with a secret to tell.

Her desk was covered with three bouquets of roses, all in Swarovski crystal vases. And perched next to it a box with a neatly tied silk ribbon. Dana opened the box which held a gold, unlabeled CD.

Popping it in the disk drive. The first song that came blaring through the speakers was Rose Royce singing *I wanna get next to you*. That excluded Andre because he was already there. She took the CD and retreated to her office. Song after song was expressions of someone proclaiming their intent for Dana, for them. From *Two Occasions* by The Deele to *You are my Lady* by Freddie Jackson, she played the CD nonstop. Not having any clients today was a welcomed need, allowing Dana to work on accounts in between daydreaming. Just as Whitney belted out a classic line from *Saving all my Love,* Dana felt a lump rise in her throat followed by a steady trickle of tears. Her heart was heavy and she was missing 'Dre. As much as she disliked the thought, he had her heart. The infrequent visits only added salt to a gaping wound.

Pulling out 'Dre's wallet, she laid it on her desk. In the midst of cueing him for speed dial there was a notice indicating 10 missed calls.

She hit the intercom, "Melinda, do I have any messages?"

"Dr. Boyd has called about twelve times. He says it's an emergency but he would stop by on his lunch break."

Dana knew what it was about, but his persistence and insistence raised questions. She surveyed the wallet and then glanced at the phone, waiting for a confidence boost. Momma always said *if you look for something you will definitely find it.* She knew she was naïve in expecting 'Dre to be completely honest, the entire premise of their relationship was built on a lie. He belonged to someone else and the stars she wished upon at night could never make him hers.

Dana probed through the wallet. She had never seen his wife before. Her beauty was staggering.

"Hello, hello." 'Dre answered.

"Hey baby, you left your wallet at my house last night." Dana spoke softly while staring at the picture.

"I know." He said. "I've called you several times this morning and your receptionist would only take a message. Have you been busy with clients? We need to talk about last night. I will stop by, pick up my wallet, and call you later."

'Dre's battery of questions and statements were all a blur.

"Dana?"

"Yes?"

"You alright?"

"Yeah just thinking. I will see you in a little while."

Her chestnut skin glowed in the untouched photo. Attributes that exuded perfection was all Dana could see: skin flawless, hair flowing past her shoulders, almond eyes, a thin nose, and full lips. Not too thin and not too thick. Directly behind this masterpiece were pictures of his children, a boy and a girl. They held the same beauty as their mother. Dana thought about what their child would look like if they ever conceived.

Andre's had accumulated numerous business cards. Dana thumbed through them and studied one in particular. A card with lips

Soul on Fire

imprinted on it as a special touch. She pulled it from the stack and scrutinized it more closely. It was from a pharmaceutical sales representative. The lipstick smudge raised a red flag. Why would he have a business card in his wallet from a sales rep? Dana knew that his office saw several reps a day and the office manager handled these affairs. She carefully placed all the cards back in place, glanced at his wife once more and tucked the wallet in her top desk drawer.

Dana reclined back in the oversized leather chair and massaged her temples. She asked herself, "How could you be mad about something that's not even yours? You have been playing good little mistress all this time and this is what you get. You knew what you were getting yourself into. You've played the game before. What makes you so special? He was cheating when he got you?"

Turning the radio up, she sang along with Luther and shook her head. Who was this mysterious man with the flowers and CD? He had swept her completely off her feet. The last time this had occurred she ended up having to take out a peace bond against him........twice. Dana massaged her temples once more and searched for the number to the psychiatrist

"Dr. Mitchell's office," the voice on the other end answered.
"Yes, I would like to schedule an appointment with Dr. Mitchell."
"New patient?"
"Yes."
"Insurance?"
"Self pay."
"She doesn't have anything for another two weeks. Is that okay?"
"That's fine." Dana had mixed emotions. Relief that she wasn't going to be diagnosed as crazy immediately and anxiety over more sleepless nights.

"Melinda when Dr. Boyd arrives send him in."
"Will do!"

Dana turned the CD up a little louder and snapped her fingers. The groove was so good that it seemed to resonate through her. She stood in the middle of the room and moved her hips from side to side. Her body rolled in a circular motion, matching every tempo of the moans and groans that Teddy made.

The door opened slightly with a noticeable creak. She pretended not to see 'Dre's reflection in the mirror as he peeked through the half opened door at her. She continued to move, more seductively, more slowly with every beat. His watching turned her on. He bit his lower lip indicating his arousal as well. He opened the door and came inside closing the door gently behind him. The scrubs had their own sexual appeal. His package hung loosely in his boxer shorts. She had pointed this out to him on numerous occasions while validating her reasons for boxer briefs. He came behind her and slid his hands around her hips and down through her inner thighs, igniting a flame just above them. He pulled her into him and his manhood grew against her. They rocked together until the song finished playing.

Dana turned around and wrapped her arms around his neck. He seemed to have that affect on her, the one that caused her to cower into her own feelings of insecurity. She dared rocked the boat no matter how aggrieved.

"Feeling better Ma?"

"Yes Papi," She used her baby voice.

Girl you're as weak as they come, she thought to herself. Did you forget about the lipstick?

He pulled back and palmed her face in his hands. He didn't say a word but just stared at her.

"What?"

"Nothing."

"Why are you looking at me like that?"

Dana turned the radio down and reached for his wallet.

" Been looking for something?" She asked as she playfully waved his wallet in front of his face.

"Yes, I've been driving illegal all morning. Not to mention, starvin'. You want to take your man to get something to eat?"

"My man?"

"You've never questioned it before. What's the problem?"

Just as she formulated the appropriate response Melinda knocked at the door.

"Yes?"

Melinda walked in with a huge vase of flowers much larger than the three she received earlier that morning. The bouquet was a mixture of calla lilies, which happened to be her favorite, day lilies and roses. The array of pastels was breathtaking.

"Girl, somebody got it bad!" Melinda shrilled.

Soul on Fire

'Dre looked at Dana. His eyes said it all so she didn't have to wonder a thing. Melinda sat the vase next to the others and stood waiting by the door for some kind of reaction.

"Thanks Melinda."

All the while 'Dre's eyes didn't shift. He didn't say a word but waited for an explanation from her. One in which she couldn't offer.

"Nice flowers." He said finally.

Dana thought to herself, *player you can do better than that.* "Yes they are."

"So is this why you have not been returning my calls and the unexplained rampage you went on last night?"

"No, I have been going through some things and you have been so busy playing the good hubby these days that I couldn't tell you about it. So don't try to turn it around on me."

"Who is he?"

"Your guess is as good as mine." She said walking over to the flowers. Pulling a rose from the bouquet she held it to her nose. "But now is not the place or time. Here's your wallet."

He grabbed it and turned to leave. Dana grabbed him by the arm, but he pulled away and walked out the door. She let him leave. She buried her nose inside of the bud and hoped that she would become so intoxicated by the fresh aroma that all her thoughts would vanish, at least for the time being.

"Andre I know you have been getting my calls. Call me back." He had began to play the jealous role, ignoring Dana's calls for the last few days.

Dana lay back on the sofa and sipped on a glass of Zinfandel. Wine and men were her iniquities. She teetered between disgust and nervousness. Disgusted at how she behaved about another woman's man and nervous about the charmer. She had a secret admirer with no clue as to who he was or perhaps who she was, that's how they swung down in the south. The bottom line was she didn't know and the loving she had on the side was coming to an end.

Dana contemplated explanations to give 'Dre about the flowers. The phone rang and broke her train of thought.

"Dana," She heard her mother crying through the phone.

"What's wrong?"

Skyy Banks

"It's been a bad accident. You have to come home. Can Chelle ride with you? You have to come home!"

"I'm sure she can. Where's Mya and Jay?"

She began to sob so loudly and violently that Dana was sure something had happened to one of them. She was the baby of the three and had been estranged from her siblings for some time. Not because of some bitter family dispute but because she wanted her independence. She wanted to live and learn. What her mama called bought lessons. If Dana really had to spend money on those things she would be bankrupt. Mama's always right and she loved her so

much for that. However, she could never find herself admitting all the times she was wrong and Mama was right.

"I'm on my way!" Dana hung up the phone and scrambled around her bedroom throwing clothes into various pieces of luggage. She was in such a panic that her packing lacked the thought of coordination. She didn't bother to call Chelle to let her know that something terrible had happened. She knew she would be there for her anyway. Dana briefly replayed the countless times Chelle had either been in the passenger seat in the midst of the trouble or there to bail her out after the fact. Nonetheless Chelle was there.

Dana pulled into the driveway at Chelle and Russell's place. The long driveway was obscured by towering pines on either side and opened up to a sprawling Neo Mediterranean style home. The terracotta roof and stucco siding gave the 6 bedroom, three and half bathroom home a strong appearance. They had been playing house for about five months now and every time she visited the house seem to be more immaculate than the last time. Both cars were gone. Chelle drove a silver BMW 6 Series and Russell drove any number of luxury cars boldly tagged Grysn1, Grysn2, 3, and 4. It was late evening and no one was there.

"Damn!" She pounded the steering wheel with her forehead trying not to lose it at that moment. With Chelle in the #2 spot on speed dial, she called on her. The phone rang at least eight times before Dana hung up. She could feel a welt begin to rise in the very spot that her forehead greeted the steering wheel. Think, think she continued coaching herself. She couldn't hold it together as the tears glazed her eyes until they pooled at the lower rim and spilled over into a steady stream. Dana danced a narrow line between hysteria and sanity. Her rapid blinking

Soul on Fire

failed to halt the tears as she fumbled through the phone trying to find Chelle.

Think Dana. Think.

The drive to Hartsfield International Airport took longer than the usual fifteen minutes. As Dana pulled the luggage from the trunk her hands were stiff and hurting from gripping the steering wheel and her bottom lip was raw from chewing on it. She made her way to the ticket counter and opted for a one way flight to Ohio, she wasn't sure how long she would be staying and prayed that things weren't as bad as it sounded.

Her flight touched down in Cincinnati 2 hours later. Everything around her was amplified and the moving bodies were zombie like. The stewardess had to usher her off the plane as she sat immobilized in her seat.

"Mama?"

"No baby, this is your Aunt Lois. Your mama is resting."

"Can you send someone to the airport to pick me up?"

"We thought you were driving?"

"I was but I couldn't reach Chelle."

"Okay, just hold tight, I'll get someone. I'll call you back on this number."

A few minutes later the phone rang.

"Dana?"

"Yes Auntie."

"I've got Damien here. You remember Damien that lived up the street from your mama."

"Yes. How could I forget the man that I was going to marry at one point in my life?"

"Well he's on his way."

"Okay, see you in a little while."

Dana watched her baggage pass by three times on the moving carousel while she stood and massaged her temples, attempting to thwart the ensuing headache. She did not want to see Damien right now. The last time they had spoken was over 6 years ago was when she broke off the engagement. He was more than the person that lived up the street from Mama as she thought about what Auntie Lois had said. He had taught her a few things about life. He was one of few who told her like it was whether she wanted to hear it or not. The history between them was long. Dana had aborted his child without him knowing, vandalized his car over assumptions, and ran to his mother at least a hundred times when she wasn't acting right so he wouldn't leave her, the game that fools play. When it was all said and done his daily devotional became .....it takes a fool to learn that love don't love nobody. She had hurt him badly.

She stood curbside and waited for him to arrive while speculating on what he looked like after all this time. Did he still have that sparkling smile? What was he driving? What was his profession? When they were freshmen in college his major of choice was sports medicine. Did he pursue that? She was so caught up in the existence of Damien that momentarily she had forgotten why she was now in the Nasty Nati.

"Now didn't your mother warn you about hitchhiking?" A familiar voice called out through the passenger window of a cream colored BMW that had pulled alongside. Dana could have died. Damien was sexier than she remembered. He wore a goatee and a full head of curls. He still had that sparkling smile and smooth chocolate skin. She was fixated.

"Dana, are you okay?"

He had gotten out the car and placed one arm around her waist while the free hand pulled at her luggage. He ushered her to the passenger side door and proceeded to load the luggage into the truck's cargo area. He turned her around with one hand as though she was modeling for him.

"Girl, you haven't changed a bit. Well a little. You do have some booty now. Let me look at you."

"And you're still crazy, I see."

He reached out for Dana and cradled her for what seemed like eternity. She buried her face in his chest and cried. She cried for the old and the new. Had he forgotten all the hateful things she did to him? Had he forgotten the words she said on the last night they were together? Or was he just showing himself approved as always? Was he showing that the man he was six years ago was an even stronger man now? It was apparent his status had changed. Evident in the car he drove and the shoes he wore. Crockett and Jones if she wasn't mistaken, retailing at seven hundred and fifty dollars a pair. The antique tan leather had no scuffs or scratches and the soles were not worn.

Abruptly she pulled away, opened the passenger side door, scooted in, and closed it behind her. Damien's perplexity showed as he got behind the wheel yet he didn't utter a word while adjusting the

Soul on Fire

radio's volume via the panel on the steering wheel. He was listening to jazz. The alto sax edged its way through the speakers and through her. She closed her eyes to keep the looming tears from falling. Although unaware of the details of the accident, Dana was immersed in sadness. Damien slid his hand in between hers and stroked it.

As they approached the old neighborhood a dark cloud seemed to envelope Dana. It was very unsettling to return to a place that she had made a distant memory.

Obviously Damien knew about the accident yet he played his role of being helpful and supportive, leaving the family to be the bearer of the bad news. He pulled in the driveway behind five other cars Dana didn't recognize. She was petrified and her eyes were hard as stone. Damien opened the truck door and helped her out, escorting her weak and numb body to the door. Opening the door, he disregarded the door bell and led her inside. The living room was crowded and quiet. She saw her aunts, uncles, cousins, a few of her classmates, and more of Jay and Mya's classmates. Everyone was in a somber mood and most had tear stained faces. Dana searched the crowd for Mama. Dana ran to her room and found her in bed awake and under the covers. She was still oblivious to what was going on. Lying across her lap, she stroked her face.

Indistinctly she greeted her, "Hey baby."

"Mama, where is Mya?" Mya was the first born child, Jay was in the middle, and Dana was the baby.

"She was in a terrible car accident this morning. She died on impact, so she didn't suffer." Mama must have been all cried out or the strongest woman Dana had ever seen.

She turned to find Damien standing composed behind her. "Mama, you need anything?" He still called her Mama after all these years.

"Is that you Nuke? She asked through swollen eyes. " I didn't know you were here?"

"My mom called and I drove home. Actually we are in spring training so I was here already, just not a few doors down."

"Are you still working for the Bengal's?"

"You remembered?"

"Well, you know you just like my son and I keep up with all my children." That statement ripped like a serrated knife.

"I know but enough about me. We can catch up on all that later. Do you need anything?"

"I'm fine baby. Dana, you see Nuke?"

"Yes Mama, he gave me a ride home from the airport. Aunt Lois called him. Get your rest. I am going out to speak to everyone and talk to Damien for a bit."

Jay had made his way into the room as well. They hadn't seen each other in about three years but spoke regularly. He had been away at medical school.

"It's good seeing you sis, not on these terms but it's good seeing you." His wide physique engulfed her body as he hugged her.

Dana walked through the living room, Damien was on her heels. She was sure to chat with some of Jay and Mya's friends and thanked them for being there. Her uncle Willie grabbed her by the arm just as she made it to the far corner of the room.

"Who loves ya baby?"

Something was jarred loose inside her from that one question.

"Who loves ya baby?" he asked again.

"You Uncle Willie." Her voice had taken a firm tone and she was immediately on the offense.

"Give me a hug. Let me look at you."

A chill went through Dana's body causing her to pull away with nervousness. Willie wasn't her blood uncle. He was married to her Aunt Lois. She was her favorite aunt. The kind of aunt that would get you out of trouble and in the same breath help you get into trouble. She was Dana's alibi on many nights always warning not to get herself caught up. What she meant by that was getting herself pregnant. Dana smiled inwardly as she thought about the times they shared, good and bad.

"Hey Auntie Lois." Dana called out across the room just loud enough to get her attention. Once they made eye contact she gave her the look and Aunt Lois knew that it meant to clear house. Dana was exhausted and needed private time with her family. She reserved getting up to speed about Mr. Damien for later. He was in the big leagues now, literally and figuratively speaking. She also knew another bit of important information. He was single in the aspect of not being married. Dana noticed that on the drive home.

Soul on Fire

Auntie Lois cleared the house. Dana gave out more hugs and kisses and checked in on Mama one last time before calling it a night. She found Mama resting after being given a sedative and Jay watching over her as she slept. He would make some woman a helluva husband one day. They say you can determine the way a man will treat his wife based on how he treats his mama. He truly adored Mama. He treated her like a queen, always at her beck and call, rubbing her feet, and planning his next move after med school with Mama in mind.

"I'm going to lie down."

"Okay sis."

Dana caught a glimpse of Damien sitting in the living room as she made her way down the hall to her bedroom.

"What are you still doing here stranger?"

"Just making sure everyone's okay. How are you doing? You've hardly said three words to me. *You still crazy*," he said mimicking her voice.

"Just a lot for a girl in a day."

"I understand. Well, the home number is the same. Call me sometime tomorrow."

"I will." She could feel the emotions rising as she locked the door behind him.

Her bedroom was the same way she had left it years ago. The walls were painted mint green with a splash of gold. Mya enjoyed decorating and this was a weekend project that lasted for a month but it turned out beautifully. The matching unfinished wooden end tables and canopy bed were all in place. She laid on top of the comforter in a fetal position and rocked herself to sleep.

"Who loves ya baby?"

Dana's restlessness must have stirred Mama because she awakened to her standing at the side of the bed calling her name and shaking her until she woke up. Dana sat up and grabbed her around the waist and cried.

"I know, I know, but everything is going to be alright." Her words accompanied rubbing and patting of the back.

"It's just too much right now! I am so lonely. I am holding on to a married man that will never love me like I deserve to be loved. I can't sleep anymore. I am being haunted by different men in my dreams. I am going to see a doctor that will probably tell me I am hallucinating. My sister is gone and I didn't get to tell her bye."

The rambling came to an abrupt halt. It finally had hit her- the reason why she was back in Cincinnati. Dana had spent an entire evening *just there*, not actualizing what was occurring around her until that very moment. It was truly disproportionate in comparison to what she felt on the inside.

"Dana, it's okay baby. Just call on the Lord. Look to the hills."

She marveled at her Mama's strength and resolve. Now someone that was supposed to bear a burden of greater grief from losing a child is now consoling the other. Dana didn't know how to be strong for her because she couldn't be for herself.

"It's okay just let it out baby. This won't be the last time you cry. You've got to get right with God. I have raised all of you with the fear of God and when you don't do the right things sometimes things happen. You won't have inner peace. You can't sleep at night. Did I tell you Mya got saved? I have the peace and strength to know that my baby is alright."

Dana peeked up at Mama through distended and inflamed eyes and gave her a slight smile. That was her Mama's careful way of not be judgmental and she appreciated every word.

"She did? I know you are proud and that makes me feel better."

"Take yourself a warm shower and I will get you some warm milk. Or are you too old for that now?" She laughed.

"That would be good." Warm milk was a childhood favorite and cured the most unpleasant days.

Mama headed towards the kitchen and Dana combed through her bags to find some fresh clothes. As she opened the larger bag she noticed a white envelope with her name on the face. It was from Damien. She recognized his handwriting after all those years. He must have put it there when he brought the bags in from the truck. Seeing him made her yearn for him all over again. And she didn't know whether to love it or hate it, accept it or leave it.

Dana let the water run over her head, into her mouth and down her back. She adjusted the nozzle to flow at a higher pressure to relieve the tension in her shoulders. She felt weak and powerless.

"Black women are not supposed to get tired. We take life as it comes and we have multifaceted lives. I don't think we have mastered the relationship thing. Dominance outweighed submissiveness." She vocalized her thoughts hoping to make better sense of things.

She increased the temperature in the shower. Hot as she could stand it, determined not to cry anymore, at least not tonight. The water began to run cold. The shower left Dana feeling emotionally drained but somewhat refreshed.

"Dana?" Mama called from the kitchen.

"Ma'am?"

"You alright? I've been calling you for about fifteen minutes."

"Yes, I couldn't hear you over the water."

Dana toweled dry and dressed quickly, she didn't want Mama waiting any longer. Jay was sitting at the table sipping a cup of warm milk as well. He lifted the cup to Dana and motioned for her to sit beside him. Mama poured the milk and kissed her on the forehead. Dana nestled into the round back chair at the table and looked around the kitchen. It was just as antiquated as it was before she left. The wallpaper was smoky from all the cooking, wood knots and knick knacks adorned every available space. Mama was old fashioned. She made sure they had a hot meal every night and if she couldn't get to it she made sure Auntie Lois did.

Sitting in the chair uneasy and unguarded, Dana peered over her shoulders discreetly for the ghost she felt lurking. She proclaimed to not be one that believed in the supernatural, yet she was on a constant lookout for a shadow that was not there. From time to time she thought she could hear faint laughter. The voice wasn't unfamiliar although childlike. It was hers.

"Dana, what you thinkin' about li'l sis?"

"Oh Nothing! Just admiring the scenery."

"You got jokes I see."

"A few."

"How's life been treating you? The last time we spoke you were this independent black woman who didn't need a man. Is that still the case or you got someone waxing that bootie now?"

"Did you hear your son?"

"Yes, I did and you better watch yo mouth boy. Talk to your sister better than that. I am going to lie back down. You two talk a while and be nice to each other. I think it'd be good for both of you." As soon as Mama was out of hearing range the conversation ensued.

"I'm just playing. But you shouldn't let that body go to waste. If you weren't my sista I'd holla at you."

"Thanks for the compliment. I guess?" That whole statement made Dana's stomach turn. "Next."

"Next what?"

"Next topic. Now why are you still single?"

"Mr. Do Right must be doing something wrong."

"That's not a new topic anyways I am just being patient because the next woman I date I plan on making her my wife. Proceeding with caution is what I call it."

"I can't be mad at that. Whoa! Listen to my brother. I am proud of you. You know you are a rare breed. I've always said you would be a damn good catch for any woman. How was Mya doing? Mama told me she had gotten saved."

"She did. She was finally beginning to be happy with herself."

"Happy with herself?" Dana asked puzzled.

"Well, I don't know. She just seemed to not be herself. Her emotions were all over the place. I didn't want to call her most of the time because I didn't know where her head would be."

The table became a momentary reflection respite, her thoughts were disjointed. The whirlwind that had blown through and upset the stability of her life caused her to almost forget who she was and where she was until Mama intervened. The vibrating phone disharmonized the flow of making sense of things. Remembering how she couldn't reach Chelle earlier, she didn't hesitate to answer but was too late. The phone beeped indicating she had a message. Dana's thoughts continued to wane and wax between 'Dre and him ignoring her calls and the fact she was a successful business owner yet all these things that were an intricate part of her life fit nowhere. Kissing Jay on the forehead, she excused herself from the table.

"It's 4 am but I need to return that call."

"Go ahead, we have time."

Clutching the phone, Dana went to Mya's room. Her room was just as she had left it before she went to college. Dana mused over the many evenings spent in there, trying on her clothes, snooping through her letters, or talking on the phone. It was exactly the same. She liked dark colors so it wasn't much like a girl's room at all. Her trophies, plaques, and dolls bedecked the four walls. Dana felt a feeling of warmth. Running her hand alongside the desk top, she traced her name in the

Soul on Fire

dust that had accumulated. Mya was very athletic and involved in most high school activities that were acknowledged by the trophies and plaques. Dana smiled at a picture of the two when they were small, both

dressed in there Sunday's best. Dana sat on the bed and let out a sigh. Looking at the phone she had 48 missed calls. Strolling through the list, there was not one call from 'Dre. Was he that mad? Most were from Chelle, a few from Simeon, and surprisingly Evan. Dana thought Evan was very attractive, he cut hair near an Art gallery she frequented. He was a master barber and had asked her out a few times. She had a thing about dating younger men. She always thought of them as looking for another mama or wanting somebody to take care of them. Plus there is also the inability to have a thought provoking conversation, and without shame not being able to conquer her sexual prowess. The pillow crumpled behind the force of her fist as she lashed out in anguish. Nestling in the bed, she went down the list returning phone calls disregarding the 5am that was on the display screen.

"Hello," Melinda answered with the frog still in her throat.

"Sorry sweetie. This is Dana. I didn't mean to wake you but I've had a family emergency. My sister was killed in a car accident. I will be away for about a week or two. Business as usual at the office, go on and generate reports and reschedule all the clients. I am not looking at my planner, but I think I had a meeting with a new company this week. Check it out and let me know and then I can decide how to handle it." Although Dana had given her an ear full, the only thing she probably heard was that Mya was killed.

"Your sister was killed?" She responded now wide awake, throat clear, and probably sitting straight up in the bed.

"Yes."

"How's your mom and brother holding up?"

Irritated, Dana responded. "They are fine. Thanks for asking. Now did you get everything? Reschedule, reschedule, reschedule. I will check in with you tomorrow afternoon." She continued asking questions as Dana hung up the phone.

"Chelle?"

"Dana? What's wrong? I saw all the calls but you didn't leave any messages. I was out looking at some new fabric just imported from Africa and then Russell.... Her voice trailed off. Where are you?"

"Cincinnati."

Skyy Banks

"Cincinnati? Is Mama okay?" We were just like family and she never called Mama by any other name as long as Dana had known her.

"She's fine. It's Mya. She was killed in a car accident today."

The phone was quiet. Then it dropped to the floor. Shortly after, Russell was on the phone.

"Dana, what's going on? Chelle you okay baby? Dana!" Russell was back and forth between the two of them trying to figure out what was going on. The growing concern could be heard in his voice.

"My sister was killed today. You know how close we were."

"Oh, Dana. I'm sorry to hear that. Let me take care of Chelle. I will get her on a plane to you right away. I am sure she wants to be there for you all."

"Thanks Russell. Call me as soon as you know something."

The last call was placed to 'Dre. Dana had paged him several times already because she knew he was at home with the wife. She hurt even more at the thought of him lying in bed with *that* woman. She was beautiful and Dana envied her. She had the man, the house, the car, the kids, and probably the dog. She had heard this before and it was starting to sound like a broken record that just needed to be gotten rid of. She hit #1 on the speed dial and put her number in as an urgent callback. Lying in the bed, the ceiling stared back offering no answers. She tried to think about something else while retrieving the voice messages.

"Dana, this is Simeon. I really would like to see you. Call a brother." *next message...............................*

"Hey Ma! I haven't seen you at the gal' lately. You know I told you I would get that piece for you for your new office. Guess what? I got it. You thought I was flexin' didn't ya? You know who it be. Holla at yo boy."

That damn Evan, the "corporate thug." He did manage to elicit a smile. *next message..................................*

"Dana, where yo ass at?"

Dana came to the conclusion that she would have to wait and speak to anyone else. She jumped out of the bed pretending she was that nosey little girl again. She quietly snooped through Mya's drawers. In the bottom drawer she came across lingerie, sex toys, and some nude pictures. Dana laughed when she saw who it was, Joey. Joey was Mya's high school sweet heart and he was packing. She looked under some other things and found several neatly bounded journals. Pulling them all out she laid them on the bed briefly contemplating if she should read

Soul on Fire

them. She proceeded to read and share in Mya's innermost thoughts. This was the only time Dana could see how Mya really felt.

"Good morning, sunshine."

The whites of Dana's eyes could barely be seen through the puffiness. The lids appeared to kiss each other as she struggled to open them. She had fallen asleep in Mya's bed with a journal in hand. Damien towered over her with a bouquet of fresh flowers. He bent down and kissed her forehead with a lingering kiss.

"Nuke what are you doing?"

"So I'm Nuke now?"

"What time is it?"

"It's after twelve."

"What?"

"You're okay. Your mom wanted you to get some rest. Jay and Aunt Lois took her to the funeral home to make arrangements. They were leaving as I was coming in. You hungry?"

"I could eat something."

"Hold on. I'll be right back." He pulled the cover up to Dana's chin and handed her the remote control. Kissing her on the forehead again, he left the room.

The clanking of pots and pans could be heard from the kitchen. Dana jumped out of bed and ran into her room to get her bags. She brushed her teeth, pulled the scarf off her head, and shook her wrap loose before raking the comb through her hair. She had a thing about the morning look. The glowing in the morning thing just didn't do it for her. There was nothing glowing about a stinky breath and unkempt hair. That was one thing Nuke never understood about her. After years of being together, she still insisted on looking good at all times. If it weren't for the healthy hair thing she wouldn't dare sleep with a scarf on looking like Aunt Jemima. The thought provoked Dana to laugh. Looking around the room for something to do she decided against any thoughts and snuggled back into the comfortable place Nuke had left her. The scent of blueberry muffins and bacon drifted into the room. This brought back memories of when they shared their first apartment. It was almost guaranteed that she would be having breakfast in bed on Saturday mornings and if there was a thing as dessert after breakfast, she was getting that too.

Skyy Banks

Dana ignored her growling stomach and flipped through Mya's journal. She couldn't remember the last time she had eaten and began to rub the hollow spot to stave off the rumbling. Most of the pages in the journal were poems Mya had written. The one that stood out was titled, *I'm Just Lovin' Me for a Moment....*

Pardon Me...I'm just lovin' me for a moment this morning. I woke up this
morning to the smell of my conditioned hair.
As I lay in my satin sheets, I noticed the beautiful outline of my Vessel.
It came to me...
I am a resurrected vessel...Beautiful
Moving into another level of wholeness.
I think I ought to love me this morning,

This poem was deep in every sense of the word. Dana paused to allow what she had read thus far sink in. These words seem to weave themselves into her inner most thoughts. This surpassed her morning ritual of looking into the mirror and trying to convince or condition herself to believe that she was beautiful and loved, the feelings that arise from a depth within. These feelings were of an intrinsic nature. Dana never stopped to think about the minute things, the things that may appear trivial to others? She never stopped to appreciate the smell of her hair? She laid the journal on her stomach and wished for the words to miraculously jump off the page into the depths of her belly. Like a consuming fire. She lay with her eyes closed yet the tears found an escape route down the sides of her face. Dana wanted so much to be "lovin' herself" for not only this moment but always and forever.

Damien came quietly into the room. He knelt down beside the bed and kissed the trail of tears on Dana's face. He kissed from one side to the other and again on her forehead and nose. It was soothing. Dana didn't open her eyes just yet.

"Oh baby. It tears me up to see you like this."

"I'm okay." Responding with her eyes still closed.

Dana could feel him take the journal from her stomach. "Sit up."

She opened her eyes to an amazing breakfast tray. There were muffins, eggs, bacon, orange juice, and fruit.

"Eat with me?"

"I was thinking the same thing." Damien pulled an extra fork from behind his back and they laughed together. The food was so good. Dana had forgotten how bad Damien was in the kitchen. Had she been a fool? Harping on the past was one of her weaknesses. She had too many

Soul on Fire

regrets and shoulda, woulda, couldas that she couldn't do a damn thing about, yet they all seemed to have a strong hold on her.

Dana's eyes watched Damien's every move after breakfast, trying to make sense of things. He was the same man she had left for no apparent reason. He had met 8 out of the 10 criteria she had outlined for the man she wanted to spend forever with, he exceeded the tall, dark, and handsome. The specs for her future husband included the ability to knock it out the park and only 8 to 9 inches could achieve this feat as well as having good hair, she'd be damned if their offspring had nappy hair. When she compared notes with Chelle she felt foolish. Her requirements were short and included such things as good credit, spiritually sound, and the ability to satisfy her intellect. The things she desired eluded the flesh.

After cleaning the kitchen Damien climbed into bed with Dana and snuggled against her warm body. He knew spooning had always been her favorite position. His heart beat strong against her back. His slow breathing was unmatched to his racing heart. The arrhythmia stemmed not from nervousness from not seeing each other in years but more so anticipation of what could happen.

"What's on your mind? You want to talk about something?"

"Not really. I'm good."

"I don't think so. Something's bothering you and I think it's more than Mya."

"You think you know me." Dana smiled as she turned to face him.

"The only woman I have ever loved, you think otherwise?"

"Really I'm fine. Just trying to sort through some things not only here but in my personal life. How long do you have off?"

"As long as you need me."

"I'm serious. How long?"

"And I am serious. As long as you need me. We have several trainers and you know you all are my family. Even though you walked out on me. I am here for all of you."

"I knew you were going to throw that in there. Will you ever forgive me?"

"I forgave you a long time ago. That was the best thing for me. Especially if I was to move on with my life."

"Well why are you single?"

"Who says?"

"The finger without the cheerio."

"That's what you call it?"

"Yes, that's what I call it."

"So you've been checking me out? What's your excuse?"

"Excuse for what?"

"Not having that rock on your finger? That is what you called it?"

"You got me. To be honest Damien, I haven't had much luck in the dating arena. I have been spending much of my time building my own business. Now I'm not saying that I've not dated at all, not just any keepers."

Dana dared to tell him the whole truth, that her pastime was pole hopping. She had countless short term dating stints. Never serious because most of them were either out of her league, yes she had been guilty of lowering her standards sometimes for some memorable sex and not to mention bedding the married man. What would he think if he knew his Dana was more daring and dirty than dainty? Maybe this would be a skeleton or two that she would leave in the closet.

Damien's eyes pierced Dana's with intensity. "My career has kept me busy. You know being in my profession you have women literally throwing themselves at ya, the pussy, the thongs, and a few platinum cards. But that doesn't appeal to me. You should know that. I have on the other hand thought about *Hotlanta*, where the women outnumber the men 4 to 1. That must be a playa's heaven?"

Dana was so sick of hearing that shit. Yeah, the women outnumbered the men and yes they were like predators looking for any available prey. However, the caliber of man that she sought to marry and procreate with was slim to none. Being educated, employed with benefits, and no baggage made any man a hot commodity. Just when her thoughts peaked at 10 with rage, her cell phone rang. Dana reached for the phone and the caller ID flashed Dre's name across the screen. She paused for a quick second, not wanting to spoil the moment with Damien, she ignored the call. She didn't realize how much she had missed him but was also torn, she missed 'Dre just as much. She never explained that she didn't know the anonymous pursuer. At the time it didn't matter because she wanted 'Dre to be jealous. It all backfired. She hit the ignore button again and rolled back into Damien's arms.

Twirling his curls around her fingers, she wondered if he cared who was on the phone. If he did he didn't indicate otherwise. His hair was soft and silky with the top long and the sides faded just right. The phone interrupted dreamland once again. This time it was Russell.

Soul on Fire

"Hey D. How ya feelin'?"

"I'm fine. Thanks for asking Russell."

"I just put Chelle on a flight to Cincinnati. She should be there in the next couple of hours. She's feeling better. Call me if you need anything and I will be out there by week's end."

"Sure, see ya soon."

"Dana, before you go. I just wanted to say that I know I have not been the kindest person over the years. We are both in love with a beautiful woman. You love her dearly as your lifelong friend and I love her as my soul mate. You do know that I am planning to ask her to marry me?"

"I kind of figured it would be soon and I think it's great. You too deserve each other and all the happiness that comes along."

"It's good to hear you say that."

"And I mean it."

"Well I said all that to say that I admire the friendship that you have and us getting married won't change that."

"Ask her first Russell." They laughed together. Something they hadn't done in a while. "Talk to ya soon."

"I think it's time I got up and did a little cleaning. I am sure we will have lots of visitors these next few days and Chelle will be here in a few hours."

"Tell me what you need me to do. I'm at your service."

Damien jumped out the bed and bowed. The perverted side of Dana wanted him to be at her service alright. She wanted to know if he had lost his touch. Brother was just like King Midas, turning everything he touched into gold. Dana wanted him to know that she still had the P-funk and had picked up a few tricks of her own over the years.

The ride to the airport was long. Damien spent much of the ride on the phone, about business and a few other calls that left him in silence. Dana could hear a woman's voice on the phone in one of the conversations. She bobbed her head to the music and pretended she wasn't eaves dropping. She almost got a crook in her neck from listening so hard. All he kept saying was. "I will call you when I get back in town. I will call you when I get back in town." He was insistent and that confirmed that it was a woman on the other end. Dana didn't worry because whoever was there and she was here.

Skyy Banks

Chelle was coming out of the terminal as they approached curbside. That girl was bad. Every time Dana saw her she marveled at her beauty.

"Hey sweetie." Dana couldn't wait for the car to be placed in park before she leapt out to greet her. Damien walked around the car as he had done the day before to retrieve her bags.

"Hell naw. Hell naw. I know this ain't who I think it is!" Chelle's excitement startled the passerbys. They had done some serious hanging back in the day and when Dana broke it off with Nuke, so had Chelle. Some child's play, but what was a friend to do but remain loyal? Dana hoped this was a time that they all would reconnect with a fresh start. She understood that time didn't allow any hands to be turned back so a fresh start would be the only option. If Damien had truly forgiven her, it was a possibility.

"Yes, it's me baby girl, the one and only. You're as beautiful as ever."

"You don't look too bad yourself," Chelle replied with a nudge in the side.

"Okay, can I have my friend back now?" Dana pulled her by the arm and looked at her anxiously. "We have some catching up to do."

Damien had gotten in the truck without them noticing. "Ladies, I am ready when you are." He continued with his phone calls on the drive back while the two chatted and giggled as they rode in the backseat together.

"Where's Mama?" Chelle inquired as this was the woman she had grown to know and love as a second mother.

"Jay and Aunt Lois took her to make the arrangements for Mya. They left me in the bed sleeping. I needed it anyway."

"Have you gotten everything taken care of at the office?"

"Yeah, I need to call and check in though."

"Please do! You know how crazy Melinda is."

"Leave her alone."

"As long as you know," Chelle snickered.

The conversation was a distracting pleasure that found them pulling into the driveway with no thought of time. "Ladies, I have a few errands to run, but if it's not asking too much I would like to take you out for dinner. Make sure Mama is straight and I will be back around 8ish. Tell Jay to come too."

"Big baller!"

Soul on Fire

"Naw Chelle, just want to help get you alls mind off things for a little while. The road ahead may be long. We know that it is sad when we lose loved ones. But hey heaven's got to be better than this place." They shook their heads in agreement.

"See ya then," Dana winked and headed in the house carrying three of Chelle's bags. That girl packed like she would be gone for months.

"I need a drink."

"You know this is a dry house. Want some warm milk?" Dana teased.

"Not the warm milk."

"Yeah she got me early this morning. It helped though."

"Well, I need something a little stronger. That damn Russell. He worked my nerves girl. What ya want? What ya need? What ya need me to do? Do I need to feed ya? You need some money? Damn, I'm grieving not helpless!"

Dana fell off the couch to the floor laughing. Chelle had that man marked to the tee. "Girl, Damien's been the same way. Very attentive, but he didn't ask me about no money. You can never have enough of that."

"He is still super fine. Super freak did you screw him? I know you did! You were home alone, and I know you never pass up the thunder. I remember all the times you told me about Damien beating it up so bad you couldn't pee for days."

"Heifer, you need to quit. You know I am not that bad!"

"But you are bad!"

"For your info we had breakfast, cuddled, and had pillow talk. I was more interested in getting in his business than his drawls."

"You forget who you talking to? I know you like the back of my hand."

"Yeah but you are wrong this time. I am grieving and his ass better not try to take advantage of me while I am so vulnerable."

Chelle was making the wanh wanh wanh sound like on Charlie Brown. She threw one of the pillows that had fallen to the floor at Dana's head. "Damn, I don't have any Oscars to give out tonight. But that was ggrreaatt!"

"Oh you trippin' now!" Dana jumped up in her pillow fight stance and they went at it. They were laughing and crying so hard by the time they had finished, an audience had formed around them.

"Just like old days. Look at them Lois. Y'all better straighten this livin' room up."

"Mama! Chelle almost knocked her down in sheer delight of seeing her."

"Hey baby. Let me look at you. Ain't changed a bit. I told Dana y'all ain't too grown that you can't come home every once in a while."

Aunt Lois interjected. "Yeah, we worry about you two down in that big city by yourselves. It's been about three years since you all came home. Don't wait until a funeral to come again."

"Amen, tell them Lois."

Chelle went around the room hugging everybody. "It's so good to see you all."

Jay squeezed her butt on the sly. He always had it in for her and swore that if she wasn't like a sister, he would have hit it five or six times.

"Ma, Nuke wants to take me, Chelle, and Jay to dinner tonight. Do you need us to do anything? Did you get everything taken care of? What are you doing for the rest of the evening? I'll stay here if you need me."

"Slow down girl. I see you excited about going out." Dana couldn't believe it was that obvious. "I'll be fine. I know we will have people visiting this evening, paying their respects and checking on us: some of Mya's friends, coworkers, and the like. Lois and I will work on the programs. She'll keep me company. Go on and enjoy yourselves. Jay, you behave. I saw what you did a minute ago."

They all let out a whoop or two. The doorbell rang with the local florist delivering several bouquets of flowers and a few plants. Two were for Dana, a beautiful spray of lilies and a huge green plant with a purple bow. One was from 'Dre and the other Simeon. How did they know? Where did they get the address? With a melting heart, Dana handed Chelle the cards. Overwhelmed with emotion, she was unable to read them.

"Melinda, how is everything going?"

"Fine, it's like a flower shop in here girl. I called to reschedule your appointments and ever since then flowers have been coming. A couple of people wanted your mom's address. Other than that all is well. Do you still need me to come in for the rest of the week?"

"But you don't know who called for the address?"

"No, I didn't ask but it sounded like Dr. Boyd."

Soul on Fire

"And yes you need to work if you want to get paid. It's business as usual. Talk to ya later and call me if you need anything or have questions."

Before Dana could end the call, "She asked if she could be off, didn't she? I told ya she was crazy." Chelle smirked.

"Mind your business, CRAZY!"

Skyy Banks

ℒ

Googling the phrase "dressed to the nines" turned up Damien's name every time. At least that was the inside joke Chelle and Dana had. He walked into the house and the fragrance inspired all kinds of memories. *Pleasures* was just what it was, an aphrodisiac. Chelle and Dana decided to both wear neutral tones. Dana's dress was designed with a cowl neck that flaunted just the right amount of cleavage. Chelle had spaghetti straps with a scooped back. They knew well enough that they had to come with it when stepping out for a night on the town with Damien.

"Jay, bring your slow ass on. Yeah you really look the part so staring at the mirror ain't gone change that."

"Okay, Chelle. That's my brother."

"Mine too!"

"Ladies, ladies no need to argue the Prince has arrived!"

Jay was looking fine as hell. He wore a chocolate linen suit. It was a perfect match against his creamy skin. Dana anticipated the moves she and Chelle would have to pull to keep the skanks off him. It was implicit that no matter how upscale a venue was, the rift raft seemed to always slip through the cracks. Promises of after hour favors or flashing tits seem to get the job done time and time again.

"Ready?" Damien asked with restlessness.

"Yeah let's go. I haven't eaten since brunch." Chelle hoped Damien caught the appreciation in her voice.

The valet section was located in the rear of the restaurant. Damien opened Dana's door as well as Chelle's even though it was the job of the valet. There was gold signage in the rear of the building that read Welcome to the Bankers Club. It looked like money and it sounded like money. The towering building was oval shaped with exquisite architectural designs. Dana gazed in admiration for a brief moment. She pinched Chelle to see if she was feeling the same way. Graciousness covered their faces as Damien opened the door. He escorted Dana in and Jay, Chelle.

The maitre d' led them to a square table in front of a built in saltwater aquarium that ran the length of the floor to the ceiling. It extended clear through the next level. Sade's *Sweetest Taboo* played softly in the background. The lighting was paradisiacal and the ambiance was soothing to the soul. Damien had definitely commensurated in status and had become the true epitome of class.

Dana stood and politely spoke, "Please excuse us." Nodding a Chelle she continued. "We are going to the ladies room."

"We are?"

"Yes." She pulled Chelle out of her seat before she could continue with her act.

Both the bathroom floor and countertop were made of Royal White marble. A lounge area opened up just off the entrance. The overstuffed red sofa circled a small fountain. A few women sat comfortably chatting and smoking cigarettes. Dana had dabbled in the finer things here and there but knew this was something she could get use to.

"Girl, I was sweating so hard that I needed to do the test." She lifted up her arm and Chelle sniffed.

"Good but a little wet!"

"Breath mint?"

"Check."

Dana pushed her breasts together to give life to the fading cleavage followed by a once over in the mirror. She was ready for the vanquishment of Damien.

"Hell, I haven't seen you do this much primping for 'Dre, the love of your life."

"He's not the love of my life and yes I have, right before he punished this."

"You are bad." They walked out of the bathroom laughing and arms locked as girlfriends do. Their playfulness caused them to carelessly bump into Mr. 4th of July as they left the bathroom. He would have been wearing a drink if he had one in his hand which could have only complemented his red, white, and blue suit.

After dinner they all moved upstairs to mix and mingle. Dana was on her fourth martini and feeling kind of woozy and lustful, wanting someone or something. Damien was very attentive and blocked anyone that moved her way. She was sure Jay would be getting a ride home and possibly Chelle who looked like she wasn't going to make it if things kept going in the direction they were. Chelle was definitely over indulging as she stayed on the straight and narrow for Russell. Dana giggled all night, sometimes uncontrollably. Around 2 o'clock things were winding down. Jay was lost but had sent a text message telling Dana not to wait on him.

She knew her brother and knew he wasn't for any one night stands but would probably hit a burger joint to satisfy his late night cravings while trying to get to know whomever he just met. Chelle was all in somebody's face but was too in love with Russell to do anything.

"You ready babe?" Dana intruded.

"Oh! She with you? Well, I can dig it. I have a room at the Hilton. You two down?"

"Sorry boo, I don't share." Dana kissed her on the lips and mouthed the words bye-bye leaving the cunt hound with a hard on.

Chelle and Dana had played a many a trick before but never to the extent of sharing a kiss. The uncanny thing about the exchange was that Dana liked it. Chelle was too drunk to notice or comment. Damien asked Dana to stay in the car while he helped a half sleep and drunken Chelle in the house. Dana's insobriety did not circumvent where the night would end. She was a willing and consenting partner without the influence of alcohol.

Chelle's head hung low and she made gurgling sounds as Damien nearly carried her inside the house. The feat of getting her clothes off would be her own or as most drunkards do, she would be sleeping in them and in hope she didn't' pee on herself.

"I know this is awkward, but I want you to spend the night with me. It has been quite some time but I do believe time does heal all wounds. Look at me."

Dana's fingers brushed his lips ushering him not to speak. "We can talk about that later. Just drive."

His high rise luxury building appeared to be at least 15 stories or more. As they entered the covered garage, Damien began to lightly stroke Dana's arm. She squeezed her thighs together to fight back the mounting urge. He held her close to his body until they reached the door. Dana stepped over the threshold before him and was immediately enveloped with the scent of Patchouli and Lavender. These were essential oils blended for a harmonious inspired combination of balance and inner calm. The thin straps fell to the sides of her arms as Damien slowly slid them off her shoulders synchronously. The shoes were removed in the same fashion, strap over heel, however one at a time for stability. One click of a button illuminated the room in a soft glow of orange, quite different from dim lights. Dana yearned for a physical connection between the two, but allowed Damien to actuate. Dana reached for his extended hand and was guided to the bathroom. A marble encased

Soul on Fire

fireplace was built adjacent to the vintage, oversized claw foot bath tub. Damien drew the bath water and added bubble beads and dried Rose petals. His fully clothed body towered above hers. The unzipping of Dana's dress was so slow and provocative that no sound could be heard besides the wet kisses being planted on her shoulders. Damien lifted her out of the dress that had fallen and crumpled around her ankles. Bubbles rose with the water as Dana sank her body in the tub.

"Relax baby. I'll be right back." Damien stopped to prop a neck roll behind her before he left.

A weakened Dana mumbled. "Un huh."

Lavender saturated her nostrils with every inhalation, there was no light penetrating her closed eyes. Damien walked back into the bathroom only this time with sounds of Maxwell trailing in the background. The champagne sparkled in the long stemmed flutes he carried. An etching of his well-defined body showed against the fireplace. He leaned over the tub to refill Dana's already half empty glass, her eyes affirmed he was naked and a growing manhood extended before him. Damien quietly stepped into the glass shower stall. The shower steam distorted his body and only a blur could be seen yet Dana noticed the contour and curves. He had been taking full advantage of his profession. The water flowed over his head while he braced himself with one arm. Steam surged over the top of the shower into other parts of the bathroom soon adding condensation to the mirrors. His muscles flexed as he shampooed his head. Dana waited patiently for him to join her in the tub and soon after he obliged. The water splashed over the sides as he slid in behind her. She could feel *him* against her back. This facile movement ignited a fire within Dana, from deep within. Damien continued to plant kisses on her shoulders and the nape of her neck.

"I have missed you so much."

The water was beginning to cool. A nudge in the back indicated it was time to move on to something else. Damien handed her a warm towel from the microwave size warmer which kept her in the zone. The master bedroom's wall had a hidden compartment and another click of a button unmasked a built in fireplace. In front of the fireplace was a plush white rug that Damien had laced with bottles of massage oils, more champagne, and candles. With the towel stretched across the area rug, Dana laid on top of it.

Shuddering from the oil that Damien drizzled on her stomach, Dana expended a single forceful breath. It was warm and sensuous.

Damien's hands kneaded her body from head to toe with just the right amount of pressure. He continued to delight in her pleasure by providing each one of her toes with its own session of special attention. His warm mouth took each toe in and sucked it slowly, one by one. He had taken her to a place that momentarily erased all the hurt and pain.

Dana was eager to give as much gratification as she was receiving, the red light special. Grasping the nape of his neck, Dana pulled Damien down and straddled him. A trail of wetness lingered from his neck to his navel. Her tongue moved provocatively across his flesh. His manhood stood stark and inviting. Dana continued to make her way to the very thing that was calling her, taking it all in. Damien fought back the urge to let any sounds escape his mouth. Yet his trembling spoke volumes. Subtle movements of her hips continued to taunt him while she gave him a dose of her head game. The night subsided with back to back sessions of lovemaking from the floor to the bed. Exhausted and sweaty they clung to each other until morning. The scent of sex and lavender lulled Dana to sleep.

Soul on Fire

ও

"Hey girl come and give your uncle Willie a hug."

Chelle and Dana had gone over to Aunt Lois' to help prepare some food. Dana's house was full of family, as well as Aunt Lois'. The decision to spend the rest of her nights at Damien's had been made. She invited Chelle to come along.

Chelle spoke before Dana. "Hi Unc."

He had been like a father to them all. Dana's father had passed away when she was a little girl and Willie stepped right in. Being in the house gave her an eerie feeling. She couldn't put her finger on it but was very unnerved. Still tired and sore, she curled up in Uncle Willie's lazy boy to catch a quick cat nap.

"Come on baby girl. Sit up here." The masked man patted his thigh. A fragment of light passed through the half opened door that led to outside, otherwise leaving the room dim. "You know what I like. Come on make me happy." He gyrated his hips in the chair as he beckoned for the girl. The dark mask became more visible upon approach, yet obscured any recognizable image. The eyes were exaggerated from the small holes. He gyrated his hips more. A bulge grew in his pants. She had seen this before. She was obedient and retardate in her movements, after all, the girl knew she was supposed to do what adults asked of her. Aggravated by her reluctance, the masked man yanked her closer. He subjected her hand to his protruding crotch and began to move vigorously upon contact.

"Dana! Wake up! What are you afraid of? Who are you afraid of?"

A trembling and dazed Dana muttered, "I don't know." She sat up and looked around as to gather her senses. Her outbursts drew attention from the kitchen, however Chelle was the only one to acknowledge them. Dana stood hurriedly and pulled Chelle to the door with one hand and a finger to her lips with the other as to ensure an unnoticed exit.

"I don't know what the fuck is going on with me!" They were barely clear of the living room before Dana exploded. "It's like I am trapped in a time zone, at least in the dreams. But the catch is the dream takes place here, in Ohio. Nobody has a face or least one that can be seen. I have been here for only two nights and I feel like I am going fuckin' crazy. My stomach is crazy nervous and just now........"

Skyy Banks

Chelle stood with boundless eyes fixed upon Dana. She looked at her mouth as she spoke, attempting to decipher what was being spoken. Her ears were amplified with listening.

Dana rambled on, "Like when I was balled up in Uncle Willie's chair. It was something so unpleasantly familiar about this place from the smell, to the squeaky sound his chair makes when someone sits in it, to the lighting."

"What was going on in the dream that caused you to cry out like that?"

"I don't know."

"Let me guess. He had a masked face?"

"A red one."

"Man or woman?"

"Man, his voice, his build, his penis?"

"Penis, now you talking real crazy girl."

"No, he had a penis and wanted the girl to touch it."

Dana was too embarrassed to say she did.

Nodding."Okay, okay." Chelle's eyes wandered from Dana towards the front door. Someone was there watching. She smiled and waved. Dana turned to see Uncle Willie.

"You girls alright?"

"Yeah just talking."

Chelle reached over Dana's shoulder and turned her around to face her. "We'll talk later. Did you ever make that appointment to see your shrink?"

"Therapist! And yes. Oh shit!"

Dana had forgotten about Dr. Mitchell in the midst of the bedlam. She knew it would be in a couple of weeks, but rather than cancel decided to play it by ear not knowing how long she would be up there.

The attempt to leave behind her thoughts about the dream was transient. Stepping over the threshold the same ominous feeling befell Dana. The feeling was so enduring that Dan knew she wouldn't be able to stay. The smell of the food intensified the nausea. Dana knew she wasn't pregnant and she knew that Aunt Lois could throw down when it came to cooking so the only other cause must have been an inner disturbance.

Soul on Fire

Dana convinced Chelle to accompany her to the bookstore in search of a book on dreams. She didn't know if it would present any understanding but knew that with the number of believers in zodiac signs and dreams that some things must be accepted as true.

"You know when you try to interpret dreams, it becomes unnatural. I'm not with that voodoo or superstitious shit and you know it. Step on a crack and break yo momma's back. Break a mirror and seven years of bad luck."

"Oh! I got one. My hand is itching. I'm gonna have some money. My eye twitchin' someone is talking about me. Pee outside, get a sty on your eye. Hell, something like that." Dana threw out anything to lighten the mood.

"Yeah and you know that ain't me. Next you'll be trying to make voodoo dolls to kill all those masked people."

"Ha, Ha. I'm for real girl. I need to find out what is going on with me."

"I know sweetie and I'm here for ya, just don't have me doing no crazy shit."

Chelle was very afraid of anything remotely close to *black magic*. Her family was from New Orleans and had not strayed from their roots even after moving from the bayou. Her aunt was believed to have hexed her uncle with an egg. Whatever she did, when she finished with him, he couldn't tell if he was coming or going and all the women he was running around with was sick as hell soon after. They were stricken with some kind of body illness that turned any man off from touching them. Dana's visits at what her mama called the devil's house were limited. Colorful ornaments, bottles, candles, stuffed dolls, and other what nots filled a small room, what was believed to be the practicing room. This is where all the spell casting took place. Dana stayed away as much she could at least on days that there was no cooking. She was drawn to that Creole style of cookin' and she couldn't get enough of it. Her mama would be yellin' and threatening to beat her behind if she ever caught her eating at Chelle's. She laughed at herself at the thought of the countless times Aunt Lois had covered for her. Somehow those ways escaped Chelle.

"TeTe, can I have some gumbo?" Dana mimicked her little girl voice.

"Don't start that shit or I'm gone tell Mama 'bout all those times you didn't eat at Aunt Lois'. You probably got some of that Bayou magic working in ya now."

Cracking up together, Chelle rubbed Dana's shoulder. "You gone be alright."

"I know."

"Do you really know?"

"Yeah."

"Well why we going to this damn store."

"Shut up and ride."

"What's going on?"

Enthralled by the book she bought on dream interpretation, Dana answered the phone without looking at the caller ID. She instinctively knew it was 'Dre before recognizing his voice. Without an immediate acknowledgement, Dana laid the phone on her chest and sighed. Her heart beat wildly in her chest for reasons unknown. This was a man that had seen her pee. That was the sure thing that took a relationship to another level besides being able to pass gas in front of your man without shame.

Taking deep breaths to shake the nervousness in her voice, Dana mustered up an uncertain "Hey."

"I've been calling you for two days now. I called the office and Melinda shared the news with me about your sister. How are you holding up?"

"As well as to be expected." She hadn't tried to come off brusque and short yet her response sounded as such.

"What's wrong? You don't feel like talking? I thought you would be happy to hear from me." These were her sentiments as well and rightfully so considering he was the only man in her life, so he assumed. Simeon and maybe Evan were close by on the sidelines despite the fact they hadn't even sniffed the panties. That assumption however true was just another slap of reality. She was single and the comfort that she had gotten acquainted with was that of another woman's. These points of existence ushered Dana back into present day time.

"I'm fine baby. I received the flowers on yesterday. They are beautiful. I'm not sure when I will be home, a week or two, maybe longer. As long as Mama needs me or until we start to get on each other's nerves, whichever comes first." A faint laugh could be heard on the other end the phone.

Soul on Fire

"You never cease to amaze me beautiful. You are so strong. I'm covering at the hospital for someone else this week. So you can call anytime."

"I won't be calling you as much. You know with the funeral and all. We have lots of family and friends here as well. Chelle is here taking good care of me too. Maybe after things settle." That entire statement was predicated on the actuality that Damien was here and if she had to choose her armor bearer for this season, it would be him. Saying that she would call him later on in the week meant that she really planned to free up time to be with Damien as well as dispelled any thoughts of him coming up there. If he indeed dared to be that bold.

"Just know that I am a phone call away."

"Thanks again." Avoiding the urge to utter *I love you*.

The services would be in two days and Dana had to mentally prepare herself. She had skipped two stages in the grieving cycle already and seemed to be, in her mind, at the acceptance stage. The exhaustion of living gave her temporary leeway to feel so. They had experienced a wonderful childhood and there were no immediate regrets, although her communication in recent years was without effort. An area she admits could have been better. Impelled by her thoughts, Dana decided to spend the rest of the day loving on her family and the night would be spent loving on Nuke.

With Dre' being a constant in her forethoughts, Dana immersed herself in family and skimming through the dream book to divert feelings of guilt. Melinda hadn't called so she was inclined to think everything was well. Every corner Dana turned someone was badgering her about not being married yet and when she was going to add to the family. Her superwoman façade cloaked the truth while she attributed her busy life and growing business as to reasons why she didn't have time to seriously date. Deep down inside these were two things she wanted most. Russell coming to support Chelle would definitely add insult to injury.

The color red continued to cause agitation. The surreal feelings arose due to the relation to Aunt Lois's house which was repressed in Dana's memory. "Red," Dana continued to murmur the word until she found the section devoted to deciphering colors in the dream book. Red was said to be an indication of raw energy, force, and aggression. It was also a color of danger, shame, sexual impulses and urges. The line that read sexual impulses caused Dana to inadvertently drop the book. It was more than surreal and the dream instantly began to replay itself, from the point where the little girl's hands were guided to his bulging penis.

Dana hadn't seen nor heard from Damien all day. She called his cell phone several times and no answer. This was the time she wanted to be in his presence. Chelle was waiting for Russell's flight to arrive and would soon be kidnapped. Dana had become so unnerved that she was seemingly eating every time she walked by food. She was on her third round of peach cobbler.

"I know you just gained about 20 lbs!"

"You probably right girl."

"What time does Russell's plane get here? I was thinking we should head down to *the spot* for old times sake."

"Hell naw! That place is a swingers club now."

The spot Dana was referencing was an old strip club that she and Chelle liked to hang out at back in the day. At one point the strip club had become a fetish she couldn't shake. The scent of sex, musk, and smoke became her daily high. Chelle came along for the ride but never got into it. She was ignorant about the many times Dana had gone alone.

"You plan on screwin' somebody?" Chelle asked.

"Who knows?"

Dana waited for a moment to see her reaction. "I'm saving the goodies for D and I know you ain't giving nobody nothing. Russell old ass got you on lock. I don't mind spectatin' though."

"You a freak to your heart and you damn right Russell treats me like a queen and this is his pussy. You want to see his name?" She slipped her hand under the split in her skirt and revealed the cherries she had tattooed on her inner thigh. The stems were curled to form the letters RG, Russell Grayson. "Stamped, branded, however you want it, but it's his for as long as they make that little blue pill. After that RG stands for *real good*."

"Now that's my girl! I was starting to wonder about you."

"I think they have one of those swingin' spots in the A. We can hit it up when we get back if that's still your fantasy, but I can't meet my man smelling like bodussy."

"Booty, dick, and pussy. You so damn old school. I had forgotten all about that one. I gotcha, I definitely don't want to get on Russell's bad side. I know he talks shit about me."

"Don't start that jealousy shit."

Soul on Fire

The old superstition about ears burning must have been true. Dana's attention was directed to the family room when she heard her name. A conversation was going on about her but not with her. The nerve of some people, family was the worst, always concerned with other folk business instead of sweeping around their own front door.

"Am I complaining?" Heads turned and necks rolled.

"Again, am I complaining about being single and having no kids?" It was so quiet you could hear a pin drop.

"All we were saying was that a girl like you…"

Before her distant cousin could finish, Dana cut her off. "Save it and mind your own damn business. I hardly doubt I will be 45 and lonely." It was an indirect mockery of her life and a low blow.

"Dana that was not called for." Mama was scolding her in a childlike manner.

She glared at the distant cousin with no name and walked back into the other room.

"Girl, don't let them bother you. You and I both know that we got it going on in the A and it's just a matter of time before we hook, line, and sink 'em."

"A matter of time, huh?" Dana's smile or laugh wasn't as convincing. Chelles's was already hooked. She opened the dream book and started thumbing through the pages, hoping Chelle would see she was no longer in the mood for talking and leave her alone. Dialing Damien again to no avail, the worrying started to border anger. He had screwed her till the break of dawn and now he was nowhere to be found. It reminded her of the one night stand that occurred when she first moved to Atlanta. Dana was all into the brother and the only thing he wanted to be into was her drawls. She had been foolish and hasty again. Repulsed by her behavior, she shrugged. Wasn't the first and doubt it to be the last. Her track record had proven that.

Skyy Banks

⌀

"Ma'am, would you like a beverage?"

Dana turned from gazing into the clouds towards the stewardess. "No thanks." It had been a week since the service and Mama was doing what appeared to be fine. Jay would be staying for another week. Mama insisted that Dana get back home. There was no need for both of them to be dragging around the house she insisted. Dana knew a pile of accounts were waiting to be updated. The misery and sadness she felt resonated through every word and move she made. Her only consolation in leaving for Atlanta was that Auntie Lois would take care of Mama. Catching a glimpse of Damien at the service was the only thing she saw or heard of him since their tryst. She wanted closure to a wound that he had reopened and abruptly left to heal on its own. Everything had happened so fast. Staring out the window again, she questioned the decisions she had made. Her thoughts changed as rapid as the shape of the clouds with no definitive answers. The pilot's announcement of the arrival to Hartsfield International could not be soon enough. Chelle would pick her up. They had spoken almost every day and the rift that had been was starting to mend. "Seventy eight degrees, clear blue skies......" That was the last thing Dana remembered hearing. The ride home was a blur. Dana's living room had been transformed into a botanical garden, filled with orange, white, purple, yellow, and green flowers and plants. She kicked off her shoes, dug her feet into the plush Berber carpet and took in the awe inspiring scene. Melinda definitely had a green thumb. The blinds were slanted at the exact angle to allow just enough sunlight to pass through. All the leaves were fresh and green. Her efforts would be compensated nicely. Files with sticky notes were piled high on the desk, a task that Dana avoided undertaking. Looking past them she reached for the stack of sympathy cards bound together with a purple ribbon. The radio and wine was a temporary asylum from the real world. The retrieval of a week's messages would have to be on pause as well.

In your time of sorrow, look to the hills, earth has no sorrow, the underlying themes of the cards were indistinguishable, however beautiful. The card from Simeon caused an interruption in swallowing. She held the wine in her mouth and stared at the name scribbled on the envelope's flap. Damien had relegated him to the back of her mind.

Soul on Fire

Seeing his name had suddenly reinvigorated her with the thought of getting to know him. He had written his number in the card so he was right at her fingertips. The voice mail picked up after the first ring.

"Hi Simeon, this is Dana. I am back in town and was wondering if you would stop by later and keep me company."

She hung up the phone and thought for a moment, she had forgotten the cardinal rule.

"Call before you come." She said on the second message.

The cards were heart warming to read through, she basked in the love. News traveled fast. There were cards from old clients as well as her previous firm. Albeit beautiful and emitting the sweetest aromas the botanical garden had to go. The living space felt cramped so Dana found a new spot on the patio until she could give them away to the neighbors. Mid transfer of the flowers, the phone rang. Preoccupation with the task caused Dana to become addled. She didn't recognize the number she had dialed only five minutes before. After the fourth or fifth ring she opted to take her chances.

"Hello," Her voice guised as sleepy to thwart off any unwanted caller.

"Dana?"

"Yes."

"You sleeping? This is Simeon. I was in the neighborhood and wanted to know if it was still cool to stop by."

This was a pleasant surprise. She wasn't expecting him to call back so soon and was unprepared for the occasion.

"Give me a minute to straighten up the place."

"Half an hour?"

"Yeah that's good."

"See ya then."

Hanging up the phone, bubbling with excitement, Dana skirted through the house in such a frenzy an accident was waiting to happen. The drawer became dislodged from its track as she extracted it with force. Lace things, boy shorts, camisoles and stockings littered the floor while she flung one piece to the next in search of some sexy, yet comfortable lounge wear. She usually had it organized by occasion, but what Dana called her naughty wear was mixed in with the other things. The naughty wear began to stir some intense naughty thoughts. However intense, she dismissed the self destructing thoughts. After a steaming shower, she finished her second glass of wine and brushed the pearly whites. The shower was hot and relaxing yet the anticipation of seeing Simeon again wouldn't allow her to enjoy it. Thirty minutes seemed like five. Dana hurriedly dried off, applied lotion and slipped into her soft pink, Egyptian cotton lounge wear. The bottoms fit low and snug around her hips and hung loosely over her feet. She pulled the matching cami over her head. Her erect nipples were visible through the form fitting fabric. Candles were lit to both hide some of the clutter from the past few weeks and soften the mood. Dana pulled the scrunch from her head and shook the hair loose to fall over her shoulders. The tousled look heightened her sexy. She was very inviting in a subliminal way.

Only 25 minutes had passed from the time she had spoken to Simeon. To avoid clock watching Dana began unpacking and putting away clothes. In the absence of time, she had cleaned both bathrooms, her bedroom, and what she could of the living room, started on thank you cards and a fourth glass of wine. The little daylight that was left over an hour ago had disappeared. The orange light that glowed from the setting sun began to fill her disappointment. Giving the benefit of the doubt to men was a constant pitfall. Surely, he was not like the other brothers, being at least a man of his word. Dana opened Mya's journal and plunged into her thoughts. Mya appeared to have been all over the place, one minute she wanted to do this with her life and the next she wanted to do that, yet one thing could not be taken from her, the girl was poetic and deep. Turning to the page with the folded over corner, Dana recited a line or two aloud from her *favorite* poem.

"It came to me. I am a resurrected vessel...Beautiful. Moving into another level of wholeness. I think I ought to love me this morning."

Those few lines cleared the negativity that was arising in the air. Dana stood in front of the mirror which reflected an even toned brown skinned being that was amazing in form. The ugly scars from her past couldn't express the wiser. She leaned in and kissed the reflection. She kissed it one more time before turning to answer the door. The doorbell had buzzed three times already. Her internal mood was being set and she was reveling in the moment. A cautious look through the peep hole assured her it wasn't 'Dre. She wasn't sure if he had gotten the message from last time he arrived unannounced. If it was, all he was getting was a glimpse of her ass as she told him to kiss it. Initially all she could see were flowers through the hole, the same calla lilies that surprised her at the office weeks before. A tell-tell sign that it wasn't 'Dre because he was just

Soul on Fire

as surprised as she was when he saw them. Inching the door open with a tad of uncertainty, a familiar accent emerged.

"Hey baby. Long time no see."

"Hi yourself stranger."

Opening the door wide she wanted to give him a full view. She looked around and down the street to see if anyone was watching before she locked up although being unattached gave her full reign to do as she pleased. Simeon was just as stunning as the last time she saw him. He carried a brown bag in one arm and flowers in the other, the typical movie seen.

"What do we have here?" Standing on her tiptoes to peek inside the bag, Dana inquired.

Pulling away. "Nosey aren't we?" Simeon chastised. "Where's the kitchen?"

Pointing in the direction of the kitchen, she followed behind him.

"For you." Simeon extended the flowers. "Not that you need or have room for any more but I think a gentleman should never come to a woman empty handed."

"Mama or Playa school?"

"You cold blooded."

"No just wise." She had fallen for those bullshit lines all the time but refused to acknowledge how naïve she could be at her age. He settled the bag on the counter and turned towards her. Placing his arms on each one of her shoulders he pulled Dana into his chest. She was intoxicated with the smell of Weekend by Burberry.

"I am sorry to hear about your sister. I thought about you every day. How have you been?"

Immovable she mumbled into his chest. "That is very sweet of you. I have had my days."

"Well I am here for you now, that's if you'll let me."

Dana blinked in disbelief. Was she hearing this brother plain? He had skipped completely over first, second, and third base with those exact words.

"I appreciate the offer and we'll see." Her tone spoke doubt. He pulled back and reached in the bag. Leaning on the counter, Dana attempted to peek inside again. She could see three take out trays. The bagel she had eaten for breakfast was long gone, yet another brownie point for him.

"Jamaican?"

Skyy Banks

"Yes." He was even more on time. Dana grabbed some plates from the cabinet and another wine glass. They made a cozy little spot on the floor, ate, drank wine, laughed, and talked while music played in the background. The wine had taken Dana to a somber place, beyond tipsy and tired. By this time her speech was slow and slurred. She laid back on the throw pillow and wriggled her shoulders to mold her head and neck into it. Sitting at her feet, Simeon pulled them onto his lap. She could feel his manhood under her feet but she was too gone to become aroused. Dana drifted in and out of sleep as Simeon massaged her feet. He hit every pressure point on her sole as he stroked in circular motions.

"Ummmmm." she moaned. Simeon squeezed harder. The wall clock read 2 am.

Soul on Fire

Pain radiated from Dana's back. She reached behind to put a finger on the aching spot. "Damn."

"Morning sleepy head."

"Simeon, what are you still doing here?" she winced.

"Watching you, making sure you were- are okay."

"Coffee?"

"Don't drink coffee but will have some warm tea."

"Gotcha."

"Can you help me up first? I'm going to get a quick shower."

"Okay, is it cool if I jump in after you? I have my overnight bag in the car."

"Mama or playa school?......"Cold blooded." Dana mocked with his usual phrase and they laughed together.

A smile appeared on her face as she headed towards the shower. It was Saturday and she was taking it easy. Dana realized she was breaking one of the cardinal rules of love and relationships she had learned years ago, *don't question the love embrace it.* Yet she found herself scrutinizing, probing into the life of Simeon. He had charm, intellect, and was always one step ahead of her. That shit was good but scary. The phone rang while she was in the shower. When 'Dre's voice came through the speaker, she turned the shower completely off to hear.

"Sweetheart, I thought you were coming back in town yesterday. I haven't heard from you and I've been calling. We need to talk. I've been thinking about you. Call me."

She was unaware of Simeon's current location. Did he hear the voice mail? Turning the shower back, Dana sponged her body with lavender oil and mentally prepared herself for any possible fallbacks to the phone call she just missed.

Simeon was sitting quietly on the sofa, standing like a gentleman when she entered the room.

"Are you ready for your tea? All I could find was orange tea."

"Yeah that's it. Towels are in the hall closet."

Now something was wrong with the picture. Maybe he didn't hear the message or maybe he was waiting on Dana to say something or maybe he was thinking hell I'm the one here with her and have been since last night so all that other shit was irrelevant. Whatever the case was Dana was baffled. Dismissing her thoughts, she snuggled in the corner of the couch and sipped on the tea. As soon as she heard the bathroom door close, she reached for the phone to call Chelle.

"Hey girl."

"Hey sweetie. How are you? What did you do last night?"

"Simeon is here."

"The twin?"

"Yeah."

"You fucked him?"

"You know me better than that."

"Yeah I do. How was it?"

"Heifer when I find out I'll let you know. He is the sweetest thing."

"Yo ass didn't give him none?"

"No! I'm still grieving. My foot grazed his dick and I didn't even get wet. You know something is wrong with me."

"Get the hell out of here!"

"Hell yeah. Just wanted to call and give you a heads up. He's in the shower and I'm going to be in most of the day. I need a favor though."

"I'm listening."

"If 'Dre calls."

"Thank you Jesus, you finally realized it was no future in fuckin' a married man."

"Go to hell!"

"Just kidding. I'll take care of it."

"Tootles."

"Smooches."

"Excuse me." Dana looked to see Simeon standing in the hallway. "What's up?"

"What's on your agenda today?"

"Relaxing and getting ready for the week. And yours?"

"I have to meet one of my business partners later on and that's about it."

"Business? And what business is that?"

"We talked about that last night."

"Now you know how I was last night."

"Hold that thought. Can a brother get some breakfast?"

Dana was more than eager to show her skills off in the kitchen but more so in the bedroom. Both would have to wait. She hadn't been

Soul on Fire

home in a few weeks so the fridge was on empty and guilt wouldn't let her see the other through fruition.

"Sorry boo no groceries."

"Says who?"

With a curious look on her face, she walked to the refrigerator and opened the door.

"What?"

"I made a run to the store early this morning while you were in your deep intoxicated sleep. I kind of knew what you liked from the old stuff and I just replaced it with the new stuff and a little more. Now can a brother get some vittles?"

Pancakes, bacon, potato frittatas, and fresh fruit topped with whip cream were the items on the menu. Simeon had made himself at home and was watching ESPN.

"Baby, that smells good."

Dana placed the breakfast tray in front of him and lingered long enough for him to survey her breast.

"Apple, orange, or coffee?"

"Don't serve me baby. You sit here and I'll get the food."

She didn't say a word and sat in the space he once occupied while waiting on her Prince Charming. They sat beside each other and let the television watch them indulge in brunch. Dana secretly wished it was each other. She didn't doubt her cooking ability but was reaffirmed when Simeon said, "Mama can stop cooking."

"What crazy?"

"Nothing baby the food was great and the omelets?"

"That just wasn't any omelet- a frittata."

"That was good too." Dana giggled. "I have to get ready for my meeting, but I would like to see you later if that's okay?"

"Sure. I need to get up and be productive anyways. Thanks for the attention. I needed it but can I get a rain check. I need to get caught up on things and get ready for Monday." The true *no* came from a little thing called intuition. She knew without a doubt that a little more time in this man's presence would be nothing but trouble. Trouble for her because she could not allow anyone else to get in that place again, the place where her soul met her heart. It was so fragile these days that any wrong move would probably leave her forever scorned. She didn't want to invoke that fury on anyone.

"I respect that. Call me if you change your mind or if you get lonely."

"I will."

"Promise?"

"Promise." She noticed that he asked that quite frequently when seeking solidarity on a commitment. Had he not heard that promises were made to be broken? Simeon pulled Dana close to him. Again she buried her head in his chest and inhaled. Lifting her chin, he kissed each one of her eye lids. Her insides fluttered along with her eyelashes. They walked to the door, her hands inside his. Standing in the doorway, she watched his car until she couldn't see it anymore.

Soul on Fire

10:30 a.m. Dana looked down at her watch for a third time. She paced the floor of the lobby for another 5 minutes. Her appointment wasn't until 11:00 to see Dr. Mitchell and she had contemplated turning around at least four or five times. She pushed the button to the second floor. The elevator ride was slow and steady...very slow from 1 to 2. Holding her breath she stood quietly and as instinct would have it her hand found its place at her temples and she massaged in small circular motions.

The office was indeed beautiful and inviting. The bold and eclectic artwork drew on her apprehensions, unwinding the knot in her stomach. Richly painted walls melted into each other exhibiting earth tones that mingled in a perfect ratio. The space gave the slightest hint of being a doctor's office. The waiting area was small and private to comfortably accommodate no more than three or four patients at a time. Being the only patient in the waiting room eased Dana. She flipped through the new patient forms and filled out the simplest parts first and saved the big one for last. The big one was some kind of test for mood disorders and depression, similar to the Myer's Briggs personality test. There were statements that read: I am more irritable than usual. I feel miserable and sad. I have crying spells or feel like it. The choices ranged from no-not at all or yes-definitely. It was scary because all of her responses fell along the lines of yes-definitely or most of the time.

"Dana." A white woman with a pixie cropped haircut stood with the door open off side of the waiting area.

"Yes," Dana responded with an uneasy smile. Gathering all her things, she walked towards her extended hand. The woman had a firm grip and a closer look revealed more lesbian characteristics. The rainbow necklace that hung around her neck put any questions Dana had to rest. Damn a dyke and a white woman. Not that she had anything against white people but that was the last thing she wanted, for one of them to label her as crazy or deranged.

Dana's expectations of the typical shrink's office as seen on TV were debunked, so far so good. Instead of the recliner or dingy sofa there were two overstuffed chairs facing each other and a beverage bar area in the corner of the room. A nice expresso machine, coffee maker, and tea maker were lined in a row. The room was quiet and although no candles were burning, the smell of aromatherapy lingered in the air. Dana continued observing her surroundings while Dr. Mitchell reviewed her file.

"Would you like anything to drink, coffee, tea, water?"

"No thank you." A dry, cotton mouth was not enough to accept the offer. Dana was out of her comfort zone and guarded.

"Dana let me tell you a little bit about myself and what I do............ Do you have any questions?"

She had missed the last five minutes of what Dr. Mitchell said. "No, I don't have any questions."

"Now tell me something about you."

She opened up like Pandora's Box and released everything, going through the whole spiel about her occupation, what had been going on with the dreams, irritability, emotions, and many irrelevant things in between.

"To sum it all up I feel like an emotional train wreck!" Tears started rolling. Dr. Mitchell handed her a box of tissues and let her cry it all out without interruption.

"We need to look for triggers. Triggers are things that might spark a certain emotion. For example, you could be watching a show on television and something stirs an emotion inside of you. Once we find out some common links that cause you to exhibit these kinds of emotions, we then can get to the root of the issue. Another thing I want you to do is start journaling. Journaling is an effective way to channel your emotions. You can put it all down on paper and it's done. You have released it and then it won't be on your mind. When you are awakened at night from a nightmare the first thing you do is write. We can then discuss those thoughts at subsequent appointments. I can give you something mild to help you sleep in the interim."

"I think I'll try the strategies you proposed first before trying meds." This was the last thing Dana wanted.

"I am here to help you, so whatever you think is best for you."

The hour long session had flown by. Although Dana was leaving with some strategies, she felt worse, leaving with no answers.

Soul on Fire

Ƨ

"Just do like I showed you." Squirting baby oil on his penis, the mask man commanded the little girl. It was big and shiny and she was afraid. "Here, put your hand here." He guided her hand to his penis. With his hand on top of mine hers, he groped his enlarged penis and moved her hands in an up and down motion over it. The oil combined with the stroking made a squishing sound and seeped through her fingers. "Just like that, keep going." He moved his hand away from hers. The girl squatting in front of him continued stroking. The red eyes glared back at her through the gray mask. His mouth was parted slightly as his hot breath escaped through the mouth of the mask. The masked man moved his hips up and down with force and the heavy breathing turned into moaning. He pushed her away and grabbed his own penis and began to stroke it violently. She was petrified.

Dana sat up in the bed shaking and dripping wet in her own sweat. "It's not right." She screamed out in anguish. Anguish is what she felt in every inch of her body. *When you wake up from a nightmare – Journal!* Dr. Mitchell's voice was the one she heard in her ear. Retrieving a notepad from her nightstand, she began to write, at first illegibly. Dana wrote everything she could remember being careful not to omit any of the details, no matter how horrible and disgusting they were. This was the first time she could actualize the dream and recall details so vividly. The mystery of the mask man or men still haunted her. The dream guide was the next thing she consulted.

"Gray." she mumbled while skimming the pages looking for the color and its interpretation. The excerpt read: Gray indicates fear, fright, depression, and ill health. It went on to read that one may feel emotionally distant or detached. Dana began to think about the men in her life, there wasn't that many that had significant roles, but many lovers. Was the description referring to the masked man's feelings or hers? Who was emotionally distant or detached? These were questions that needed to be answered.

"It's just not right!" She yelled out one more time in anguish. Tea would be her only comfort this time of night. She elected for a cup of tea instead of 'Dre, her usual solace. She would read herself to sleep with some of Mya's poetry. The indicator light on the phone blinked, message waiting. The tea kettle whistled as she hit the play button.

Skyy Banks

2:14 am. The wall clock read 4:20 am. The call was 2 hours before.

"D. I know you are not still busy. Are you avoiding me? I'm not upset about the flowers anymore. I just don't like to be the last one to find out." 'Dre went on for as long as the recorder would allow him and the next message rolled on with a continuation of him declaring his feelings for Dana and how he really needed to see her.

Dana spoke to herself aloud, "Excuse the hell out of me. You're not upset about the flowers anymore. Did I forget something? I have as much right to be upset with you. Don't think I don't know about the lipstick card and your ass fairly needs checking. I chose to give you the pussy knowing you are married. But I refuse to sleep with you, your wife, and the sales rep." Dana acted as she was speaking directly to 'Dre. Hands on her hip, arms crossed, she rolled her eyes to the back of her head and moaned. She couldn't deny he was always what she wanted but not always what she needed. After all he was another woman's man. They needed to talk and she needed to let go. Maybe something could blossom with Simeon. Pulling his schedule from her desk, his availability read on call in bold, red letters. Dana paged him, sipped tea, and waited on his return call. The pager couldn't have finished vibrating before he called back.

"Hello."

"Hey baby. I've missed you. How are you feeling?"

"I'm fine and you." Dana was purposely cold and dry. If she put a wall up, maybe it would soften the blow when she broke it off.

Dismissive of her tone, "You have perfect timing. I just saw my last patient. You need daddy to come over."

"I don't need you, but you know the way." That was a yes and no in the same sentence. Dana sat on the edge of the sofa and played the break off out in her head. She went through several scenarios. Him begging, him crying, him being pissed off, as well as him trying to get some. She was prepared for anything.

The door chime had suddenly unnerved her. She felt weak. The peephole held a visual of a familiar frame. 'Dre looked finer than ever. The place between her legs began to grow warm. She opened the door and immediately walked over to the sofa.

"Can a brotha get some love?" He didn't wait for an answer but sat beside Dana and embraced her. He pulled her so close she was almost in his lap. The scent of CK and work was hypnotizing.

Soul on Fire

She turned and put her arms around his neck. Forgetting the sole purpose of his visit, she was relegated to a state of helplessness. "Yes he can. Did you miss me?"

"You know I did."

Hugging him tighter, he kissed her on the neck. In a matter of seconds, Dana was tonguing him down. She didn't reject any of his advances. This booty tapping was long overdue. The last time she had any was with Damien. 'Dre's tongue was soft and wet. His kisses were like a baby's cry. They meant something. The force and rhythm behind them was always a good indicator of what kind of sex that was to come. Slow and passionate meant that he was going to take his time and make love. The foreplay on those nights lasted as long as the love making. Fast and forceful meant that he wanted to fuck, hard, rough, and raw. This was one of those nights. They tore at each other's clothes. They were all over one another and he pressed against her hard. He was ready, but Dana couldn't give in. She pushed him back. Through heavy breathing, she yelled.

"We need to talk."

"Okay afterwards. I'm all ears."

"It won't be an afterwards we need to talk." The throbbing between her legs was as intense as that in her chest but Dana was going to stand firm.

"What are we doing? I mean we both know that you are not going to leave your family."

"We put all this on the table from the beginning. I was going to fill a void in your life and you in mine. It was up to you to keep your feelings in check. I care for you, more than you know, but baby, my family is my family. They don't deserve me but..."

Dana put her fingers to his lip. "And on that note you know how intimacy takes a relationship to another level. There is an emotional attachment. You have said many times that you wouldn't continue to see me if I started dating someone else. Now tell me the fairness in that bullshit? You know we are not going to have a future but I am supposed to wait and only give the pussy to you?" This signaled the direction the conversation was headed.

"No, what I said was that if you decided to see someone else let me know and I would step aside. I don't want any more confusion than it has to be. I am not down with you, me, and the he thing."

"Same difference."

Skyy Banks

"What do you want from me? I have done all that you have asked. I treat you like my woman. I spend on you like you my woman. Who is he? I wasn't going to mention it, but is it the same person that sent the flowers?"

"You can't assume that it's somebody else. Maybe I am just tired. Tired of not having someone to talk, tired of having scheduled sex, tired of eating dinner alone, hell tired of being tired."

"Come on now. I am available most times when you call. You know my schedule better than I do. Scheduled sex? You and I both know we get it when we get it. What's scheduled about that? Unless the definition has changed. What's really wrong?"

"Nothing. I just don't want to be second anymore."

"Which one is it? Nothing or you don't want to be second? D, I care about you but I can't and I won't do what you want. You knew that from the beginning. So don't go changing the rules."

"I am not asking you to leave your wife. Most of you niggas whine about being unhappy but that's about it."

"What are you asking then and I never said I was unhappy. You complement the part of woman she's not in my life and in some strange way that completes my circle. You know like yen and yang?"

"Try that shit on someone else. She is a beautiful woman and she has given you two beautiful children. She's educated and from the little bit I heard she didn't come with the baggage a lot of us black women do. Hell, she still slim and trim after the kids. Need I say more? You know you are a hot commodity in the African American community, black, educated, no record, kids not scattered all over the world, and fine as hell. I can't knock her for keeping tabs. I can't knock her for having the life I yearn for."

"Baby, be patient. You are a prize any man would be blessed to have." 'Dre sat back on the couch at that moment and reflected on those things Dana had said about himself and his wife. He couldn't help but feel bad. He looked over at Dana, sulking with a tear streaked face and fresh ones streaming down. He took her face in his hands and kissed the tears in mid stream, from one cheek to the other. "Do what's best for you." He really didn't mean it but knew she was too emotional right now to see it any other way. "I'll let myself out."

Soul on Fire

ℒ

'Dre

7'oclock stared back at him from the Rolex that his wife had given him on their 10th wedding anniversary. 'Dre had driven around town for at least two hours thinking and hoping that Dana would call. The sun had just begun to rise and he knew he would be expected home soon. His stomach was weak and head hurt slightly, needless to say he was stuck between a rock and hard place which made for an even more uncomfortable feeling. 'Dre cared for Dana more than he thought he did, but at the same time he knew in his heart of hearts he wasn't going to leave what was near and dear to him. Replaying all that Dana had said, he couldn't help but admit she was right, right about everything. With no reason to step out, 'Dre journeyed into unchartered territory anyway. Dana deserved better yet the selfish part of him couldn't see her with another man. Checking his phone and pager once again before he pulled into the driveway, there was nothing but a hollow space in his heart. He'd give it a few days and see what happened.

Skyy Banks

Ø

Leaving a message for Melinda to let her know she wouldn't be in until noon, Dana crawled back into bed and tried to get whatever sleep she could. Her next appointment with Dr. Mitchell wasn't for another week. She was falling apart literally. Before closing her eyes she reconsidered the advice on a prescription to help her sleep. Anything would do at this point.

"Do it like I showed you."

The dream was abruptly interrupted before it could play itself out. Dana tossed and turned so violently that she was awakened by her body crashing to the floor.

"What is it? Dammit!" Why was she being cursed? It was only 9'oclock. Her clients had been scheduled and rescheduled so she knew it was not an option to call off for the entire day. The shower was turned on as hot as she could stand it then as cold as she could stand it. A cream cheese bagel and tea was all she could stomach. Witch hazel cotton balls rested on her eyes. Everything she could think of to calm her nerves was going on from candles to jazz. The slow motion movements her body made coincided with how she was feeling. Gradually, she began to regain feeling in the numb parts of her body, mainly her heart.

Shuffling through the closet she dug out a sexy two piece set, slacks and a cropped jacket. The weather was warm enough for a cowl neck silk blouse instead of the traditional cotton. It hung just right in the front and the peak of cleavage made her feel sexy.

"You are brilliant, you are beautiful, and you are loved!" The mirror frowned at her this morning or least her subconscious made her believe.

"Hey lady." Melinda greeted Dana with a chipper voice. Dana put on a façade to desperately try and blur how annoyed and agitated she was.

"Good morning sweetie. What's on the agenda?"

"You alright?"

"I'm fine. Why?"

"I don't know. You seem kind of spaced out this morning."

"I just walked in so how you can deduce that is beyond me." The tension was mounting in her voice. "I'm okay. Just a little tired. So who do we have scheduled?"

Soul on Fire

"Two clients that were rescheduled from when you were in Ohio and then you have a meeting with the Osaki brothers but that's at their office."

"Is everything ready?"

"You know I got this!" Cheesing from ear to ear, Melinda handed her a stack of files. "Tea's brewing."

"Thanks."

Standing behind her desk, Melinda stared at Dana. She could feel a question coming on, but Dana was going to beat her to the punch. Just as she turned to leave....

"Did you ever find out who those flowers and that bad ass CD was from?"

"Not yet." She lied. Dana had an idea that they were from Simeon but it wasn't Melinda's business. She was also sure Melinda was wondering if she was fucking Dr. Boyd too. Dana was going to have to create a fake client profile to throw her off track. Just in case, but after last night it probably would be far fetched. A depressed feeling came over her all over again just thinking about it.

"Will you make me a cup of tea? I'm going to look over these reports for a while. Buzz me fifteen minutes before my first client."

"Sure thing."

Sitting at the desk, Dana popped in the CD from her secret admirer. Her mind was too bogged down with relationship issues to focus on business. The few thoughts she was mulling over were interrupted by the buzz of the intercom.

"Ms. Taylor you have a visitor. They don't have an appointment but he says that it will be a welcomed surprise. He also says to tell you that he has a picnic basket and a CD. He won't give his name."

She didn't immediately respond but rushed to the door to have a peek. Not to be so obvious, she peered through the blinds and saw Simeon. Her heart skipped a beat.

"Just a moment." Glancing at her watch, it was ten after one. Was he spying on her? How in the hell did he know she was at work and not out to lunch? Giving herself a once over in the mirror, she made sure everything was in place. She tugged at the blouse slightly to make sure it hung in all the right places. Dana paused all but two more seconds before responding to Melinda.

Skyy Banks

"Melinda, send him in." She was right on his heels with Dana's tea in hand. Nodding towards the door, she took the tea. Melinda continued to stand and look around the room.

"Whoever made that CD is a real lover. I would not mind meeting him."

A smile came across Simeon's face.

"Thank ya. Hold all calls and buzz me ten minutes before my first client."

To go on and get busy with Simeon, Dana held the door open for Melinda to leave. She was cutting' into her time. Dana had some business to attend to or should she say he had some business to attend. Simeon carried on as though the ladies weren't there. Dana turned around to see a small blanket spread out in the corner, the wicker basket opened, and Simeon laying out a small breakfast regale. He greeted her as she closed the door. In one swoop she was in his arms. Holding her close, he kissed her forehead and then gave her a butterfly kiss on each eyelash. Dana pulled out all stops and took his face in her hands and slowly circled his lips with her tongue, before engaging in full saliva swapping. He didn't resist. His mouth was wet, warm, and soft. Even more arousing was the unusual sweetness of his breath. After about a minute or what seemed like a long time, they pulled back from each other. Simeon led her to the blanket. Jazz was now playing in the background which indicated he had changed CDs. In front of Dana were strawberries, grapes, and cheese cubes. He had a small warming plate on the desk and prepared plates from there.

"Need any help?"

"No baby, I am here to cater to you. Spinach, cheese, and ham frittatas, grits, and raisin toast."

She was overwhelmingly impressed. He had really been listening to her and brought all her favorites.

Pouring sparking apple cider, he asked "So this is you?"

"Yes," her mouth watered as she took a bite of the frittata.

"Ummmm!" It was delicious, just the right blends of cheese and not too much spinach. "Who do I owe the honors?"

"I can't tell you all my secrets just yet. Just know I have the right connections."

"Is that right?"

"That's right. So how have you been doing?"

Soul on Fire

"I'm still pulling it together." Simeon stared at Dana. "You are so beautiful."

"Thank you." She replied humbly.

They continued to talk and eat. He fed her strawberries and she fed him grapes. He fed her frittata and she fed him cheese. Dana was full, full of food and full of Simeon. She took in all his mannerisms, the way he carefully chewed his food, the way he held his glass, the cute little way he bit his bottom lip as he listened when she spoke. He was genuinely interested in knowing her.

"We better start cleaning up." Dana couldn't have spoken a minute too soon, Melinda had just given her the ten minute warning.

"Baby, can you pick up while I brush my teeth and freshen up? I would hate to be talking to my clients with spinach stuck between my teeth."

"Sure, but I would have told you if you had spinach bling." Dana gave him a peck on the lips before heading to the bathroom. When she reappeared he was gone, but not without leaving a note on her desk. She would have to read it later. She lit a candle and sprayed Lysol to rid the air of the smell of food.

"Melinda, send in Ms. Chandler."

"Good morning sweetie. I was sorry to hear about your loss."

"Thank you Charlene. I received your card. I still haven't gotten around to sending out all the thank yous yet, but it was heart warming."

"Here is your portfolio and as you can see business has been good. There has been thirty-three percent growth. Even with your proposed salary increases you'll be fine."

"I really wanted to stop by and bring you these two new contracts so you can input them and start the necessary accounting work for them, not too much on that side. I know I'm in good hands."

"Great. You look different. How's life been treating you?"

Ms. Chandler started to blush. "Since you asked, it's been good. Well, I'm being modest. It's been great! I'm dating again. You know I've been divorced for 4 years now and been attending those support meetings."

"I remember."

"Well, I met David at a support meeting. I'm starting to believe that saying, once you go black, you never go back."

Dana's eyes said it all. They got big as hell. She had met a brother and he had her nose wide ass open. They both giggled like school girls and slapped each other a high five. Dana knew when she first met Charlene that she had a little soul in her.

"You know I love my black brother, but you be smart girl. If he doesn't have a job, a car, good credit, and has baby mama drama.....R-U-N!!!" They laughed again. Charlene had a great sense of humor and Dana simply adored that about her.

"BMW- Black man working. I've heard them all. I know them all. I got this, girl!"

"I see. I'm thrilled that you're happy and doing well. I guess you don't need that support group anymore?"

"I really don't but David does, so I will keep going to support him."

"That's sweet. Well, I will get to work on this and I'll see you at the end of the year."

"I got something for you."

"Yes?"

"Two tickets to see Maxwell at the park."

"You bad girl! Thanks so much!" Dana hugged her in appreciation.

She knew exactly who she would be taking. Could the morning get any better? Simeon and then Maxwell tickets. After Charlene left she sat at her desk and turned the volume up on the stereo. The jazz CD Simeon had brought was definitely music for her soul. The tempos resonated through her body. She was the trumpet blowing out all the various emotions she was experiencing from highs to lows to lows to highs. It was a therapeutic release. Swiveling in her chair only now had she remembered the card she had delayed to read.

Dana Taylor, I request the honor of your presence. I will send a car for you at 8p. I can't wait to see that beautiful smile. Hugs and kisses.

Simeon

The note was short and sweet, but held all the right words. Dana's mind was now in overdrive with all kinds of thoughts racing through. A car would pick her up? What was she going to wear? She needed to call Chelle and give her the latest and greatest update as well as to see what was going on with her and Russell. Had he proposed? All must have been well because she and Chelle weren't seeing much of each other lately. She knew Chelle would be so proud of the fact she called it off with 'Dre. She had been right, there was no future in fuckin' a married man. Maybe Simeon was the person God had placed into her life

Soul on Fire

at this moment to pull her away from the situation. Anyways who in the hell was 'Dre foolin'? She wasn't his only side pussy or at least that's what her gut feeling told her. Dana couldn't ignore the lipstick embellished business card. She was sure he got quite a few of those.

Skyy Banks

Ø

"Damn, 7 o'clock!" Dana must have spent the last three hours trying to find the perfect attire for the evening. She couldn't wait to see what Simeon had planned for them. Her only concern was having the kind of night that had her calling off the next day. Actually that's exactly what she hoped. Rushing to get dressed, she knocked over things, had clothes strewn everywhere, and ignored the ringing phone. That was the beauty of having caller ID and an answering machine. She could return those calls tomorrow while at work.

Simeon was truly a man of his word. Dana looked out the window five minutes before eight to see a white Rolls Royce pull in front of the house. Not allowing the chauffer time to ring the doorbell, she flung the door open like a desperate woman or a school girl going on her first date.

"Madame Taylor." Extending his arm towards her the chauffer motioned as to escort her to the car.

She almost lost it, on the verge of breaking into one of those Southern Baptist Hallelujah shouts. Her head was so damn big she could hardly hold it up. Walking on cloud nine was understating how she felt just at that moment. The inside of the car was brimming with calla lilies.

"Madame Taylor please focus your eyes on the screen." A small flat screen dropped from the ceiling. It was Simeon with a message. The only thing that was clearly visible were candles and what appeared to be a flow of water reflecting off a wall. There was indistinct, soft music playing in the background. Dana knew one thing for certain, the only feasting she wanted to be doing was her on Simeon and vice versa. Nervous tension increased with the long ride, which was out of Dana's character. A man was the very last thing she feared. The car pulled into the drive and drove around a towering granite fountain facing a set of wooden French doors that led to the entrance of the mansion. The fountain center piece was that of two figurines entwined with each other illuminated by an aqua blue light. The exquisite sight held Dana's attention for a while. Her eyes traced the basin which was constructed with small pieces of multicolored stones that fit together like a puzzle. Each shape was chiseled perfectly and varied in size. She wished this symbolized her life in some odd way. All the events in her life were marked by the different pieces of stone and the figurines were she and

Soul on Fire

Simeon. The fountain represented the full circle that had come or was yet to come. She was beginning to believe Simeon might be the King she had been waiting for. He had been evasive about the kind of work he did, but all the grandeur heightened her curiosity. She would save the small talk for later, but it was definitely a talk to be had. She had come too far to get caught up with a drug dealer or someone partaking in any other kind of illegal activity. Right now the only talking she wanted to hear was the whispering of sweet nothings perhaps moaning and groaning. However and whatever Simeon wanted.

"Madame Taylor, Madame Taylor." Dana was so engrossed with all that she was seeing that her name fell on deaf ears when the chauffeur called. Looking up only when he placed a card in her lap. "I was instructed to give you that upon arrival along with this basket." It was an empty wooden basket draped with a teal satin cloth. She was clueless as to what she was going to do with an empty basket. Her entire body shook with eagerness. The words from the The Bar Kays' song *Anticipation* played in her head.

The slow opening of the envelope alluded to the beginning of a scavenger hunt.

#1 - A little light often helps you see things clearer. The white soft glow accented with a touch of rosemary and jasmine warms the spirit.

Yet to see Simeon, she was bursting with excitement that she hardly could contain. Understanding now the purpose of the empty basket, Dana rushed inside the house and stopped dead in her tracks when she stepped over the threshold into the foyer. A sparkling crystal chandelier hung from the vaulted ceiling and displayed a beauty that surpassed even that of Helen of Troy, the woman's beauty in ancient Greek times that launched 1000 ships to sea resulting in the Trojan War. Hell, Halle Berry's beauty couldn't floor a person like the exquisite compass viewed before Dana's eyes. The basket brought her back to the task at hand. She knew that the hunt would lead her to Simeon.

First impulse led her to the great room. The fireplace mantle was lined with assorted white candles. Some were in votives and others were meticulously arranged. A card was placed in the middle, her second clue.

#2 – It gets better with age. Best when served chilled by candlelight.

She knew without a doubt that this clue was wine. Heading towards the kitchen, she looked in the refrigerator but there was no wine. On the counter was a mini wine rack entangled with faux grapes and vines. The bottle she assumed that was to be added to the basket was dressed with a teal bow with a card attached.

#3- Slip into something comfortable before and after......

Before and after what she questioned aloud. These were items that could only be found in a closet or armoire. The stairway seemed to meander and swerve for miles. Needing to catch her breath, she paused when she reached the top of them. The carpet was covered with rose petals, pastels of yellows, pink, and whites. Dana kicked her shoes off and did a two step in the thickness of the petals. Absolutely elated, she felt as she had died and gone to heaven two or three times. The petals were cool and refreshing under her feet. The trail led her to a room with another set of towering wooden French doors. Music escaped from under the door. Dana opened the door and could see the bottom of a white satin dress hanging over the side of a California King bed. Climbing the side step she was able to see the dress in full length surrounded by even more flowers. She picked up the dress and held it close to her body. The only other thing to do was put it on. Changing into the dress immediately, her body was inflamed with wanting. The dress hung low in the front and even lower in the back. There was no card attached, she had arrived at her destination. She lie on top of the down comforter and let the music form a sheath around her while she awaited Simeon.

Soul on Fire

ℒ

Simeon had set the alarm to prevent Dana from oversleeping. The morning found her refreshed with a sense of clarity. Or did it? She prayed that she wasn't falling for the okey doke, finding herself repeating the cycle of falling hard for every man that showed a little interest, not taking the time to see if it was a genuine interest in her or genuinely trying to hit it with no strings attached. Nowadays that's just what men preferred, no strings because they were already attached elsewhere.

Simeon was gone. He left a note saying that he had to pick up a business partner from the private airport out in Peachtree City. This friend was particular and only wanted to be picked up by him. His note however was loving. Breakfast was served with all her favorites and prepared by the mystery chef.

Her body felt like she had been through a storm. Grimacing, she looked at her breast in the mirror. They were so tender that she couldn't stand the touch of her shirt against them. Simeon was a passionate lover and it showed. He made sure that he had signed his name, sealed it, and delivered whatever he intended to. Dana rushed home to get ready for work. The message light flashed on the answering machine. She was tempted to check the answering machine, but decided it best not to, avoiding the possibility of being removed from her euphoric state. Her mind was at peace, the pain in her heart from 'Dre was a memory. Not quite distant, but getting there.

"You got that glow girl!"

"What's that?" Dana blushed.

"Like you had a good night and an even better morning."

"That I did." They laughed together. Dana was sure to keep it moving. She wasn't into telling her business, although Melinda's ear burned to hear every juicy detail. Stroke by stroke and she meant that literally.

"You know you can't leave me hanging!"

"And you know I don't kiss and tell, so you can hang that up."

"Do I have any messages?"

"Yes." Melinda couldn't hide the irritation in her voice.

Skimming through her messages, Dana proceeded to walk into her office. With no clients to be seen, she had the full day to meditate in silence.

"Call on line one."

"Ms. Taylor." Dana answered the phone before knowing who it was.

"Good morning beautiful." She had heard Simeon's voice over the phone only a few times but his accent was so mesmerizing that she recognized it instantly.

"I missed you this morning."

"So did I."

"I need to talk to you about some business. Are you available for lunch today?"

"You name the place and time. I'll be there."

"I'll pick you up at noon. Is that cool?"

"Sounds good to me. See you then." She wanted nothing more but to spend as much time as possible with him and let this thing develop into something special. Hell who was she kidding, having wanted that for all her previous relationships or involvements, 'Dre, Todd, Matt, and Osaze. Osaze the African Prince, from Africa yes, a Prince not. The bastard was broke as hell. Dana had gotten tired of picking up the check or him calling asking to borrow money for gas, light bills, whatever he could. It had gotten so bad that he started asking to wash his clothes at her house. She had become his one stop shop. The thing about African and Jamaican men being well hung kept her hooked. After his car was repossessed, she retired his ass and turned to Chocolate Thunder. That's one thing about a battery operated friend, you are in total control. She smiled at the thought of the sessions they had, two and three times a day.

"Hey Chelle." Dana decided to bring her up to speed while she had time.

"Stranger. It's good to hear your voice. You sound good girl. What's been going on? I called you yesterday and the day before. You know we are leaving next week for our trip."

"I am doing great. I have been seeing Simeon. He is too good to be true and I mean that in more ways than one." Dana howled.

"Is he packing?"

"I couldn't help myself. I think I need to go to a therapist or something for this. My twat don't feel right if I don't have a dick in it."

"You need prayer, crazy."

"On a serious note, I am doing as good as to be expected. I am missing 'Dre off and on, but calling it off was best for us both. We need

Soul on Fire

to get together in the next few days for dinner so we can catch up on things. I have a lunch date with Simeon, but I'll call you tonight."

"Okay, sweetie. I thought you had sunk into one of those depression modes. I was going to have the APD come over there and bomb rush the place if I hadn't heard from you by today."

"I know and I'm going to do better. Talk to you soon."

Chelle always knew what to say and when to say it. Dana realized how difficult it was to find friends like that especially amongst black women. Hell when a woman walks into the room black women checkin' her out faster than a man. African American women seem to be embodied with a sense of insecurity when it comes to bonding with other women. She too had been foolish enough to be sucked into that mentality from time to time when it came to Chelle. Dana knew she had her back, always had and always would.

Skyy Banks

Ø

Simeon arrived promptly at noon. Dana felt somewhat embarrassed about the night before. Her horniness caused her to reveal the uninhibited side a little early in the game. She did everything except swing from the chandelier and was sure if Simeon hadn't tapped out after his third climax she would have.

Staying true to the man he was, he exited the car, greeted her at the door, and hugged her tight, unknowing how swollen her breast was. They mutually agreed upon dining at the same Thai restaurant where they first met. The radio was the only communication being exchanged all the way there. Dana was too preoccupied playing the guessing game, what did Simeon need to talk about? She knew it couldn't be anything too serious on the line of relationship issues. They weren't in one per se.

After ordering wine, he got straight to business.

"Dana, I really never told you what my business was, but I am a commercial real estate investor. The market has opened up substantially in the metro area. I also have investments in the telecommunications industry. Most of my partners in that field are in India, but I am trying to expand."

Dana sat across from him with eyes and ears wide open. Wondering where this was headed and what exactly it had to do with her.

"I'm listening," Simeon's cue to continue.

"Well, it's going to take a considerable amount of money to launch these new ventures and most of my assets are tied up in some ongoing deals."

Dana looked at him with intensity. By now she was positive Simeon could discern the blank look that had come across her face.

"Okay. Have you spoken with your accountant to see how you can free up some of that money? Or can't you wait until those deals have cleared?"

"Yeah, but time is of the utmost importance. I can stand to make a million dollars if I jump on this."

"And you need what from me?"

"You are an accountant, right? You handle millions of dollars for several major clients, right?"

Dana had already solved the mystery. The question alone answered everything she needed to know. She couldn't believe this nigga. She knew damn well he wasn't asking her to funnel some of her client's money into whatever he was doing. He was good but not that damn good.

"Baby, what I need you to consider doing for me is diverting half a mil into my business account and once the deal is clear, I'll re-route the money back to you."

"What?"

"I know it sounds farfetched, but I need you baby. I'm going to take care of you."

So many thoughts were running through Dana's head that her vision became temporarily distorted. Had he had this shit planned from the moment he found out what she did? He's gonna take care of her? He was going to have to do more than wine, dine, and fuck her bowlegged to jeopardize all she'd built. They weren't even together and even if they were how the hell did he fix his mouth to ask her to embezzle funds, risk going to jail, and God knows what else. She was on a wild ass tangent, a mental tangent, by now.

"Dana, you following me? At least consider it. I need you to do me this one."

"This one?" She was speechless. He acted as though he was asking her to pick up some beer from the store or run him some bath water when she was dog ass tired. This one?

"Simeon, I can't even get my thoughts together. Can you just take me back to the office?"

"What's wrong?"

Was this mother fucker serious? "Nothing's wrong, I forgot I have a client coming and I need to review the files beforehand." Her voice was shaky and nervous. Dana was on the verge of crying and she knew it. Was this nigga crazy, a con artist, working for the feds, or all of the above?

"Okay, but let me know so I can start working on other connects."

She wanted to say that's what the fuck you should have been doing in the first place instead of bringing the bullshit to me. When they returned to the office she gave him a fake ass peck on the cheek, as much as she could stomach. Not waiting for him to open the door, she jumped out the car and didn't look back.

"Dana, you had a client stop by. Her only message was to be expecting her call."

Skyy Banks

"Did you get her name?"

"Last name Boyd. I asked her if she knew a Dr. Boyd."

"What?"

"Yeah, just having small talk while she waited."

"No you didn't! You know about the confidentiality clause as it relates to my clients and my business." If Melinda didn't know she was fucking the good doctor then she definitely knew now. "What did she look like?"

"Stunning. She had the prettiest hair and almond shaped eyes." This is exactly how Dana described her.

She had an immediate flashback of the picture in 'Dre's wallet. "What did she say when you asked her if she knew a Dr. Boyd?"

"No Dr.'s by that last name. You're back early. What's up and what's all this confidentiality talk?" Melinda blurted in that annoying ghetto tone.

That was his wife. She just knew it was.

"I'm going to work from home. I'll forward all calls from my direct line there and take messages on this line." Dana ignored Melinda's questions because anything else would only open a floodgate of more questions. Getting the hell out of dodge was her best option. She couldn't have the Mrs. coming up in her place of business cutting a fool about her husband. Besides that was over.

Soul on Fire

Everything whizzed by like a roller coaster. Dana was speeding home and trying to get Chelle on the phone at the same time. Chelle was down for whatever and just in case the wifey knew where she stayed and wanted to pay an unexpected visit, they were going to be a force to reckon with. At this point, the fact that Dana was in the wrong for fucking her husband was not a rational defense. The Mrs. needed to be checking 'Dre's ass and leaving her the hell alone.

After about the fifth call Chelle answered the phone.

"Damn girl, where's the fire?"

"You ain't gone believe this shit. I need you at my house ASAP."

"What's up?"

"Forget all the talking, come on girl. It's some serious shit."

"On my way!" The urgency in Dana's voice canceled the questions. Before she could hang up the phone good Melinda was calling.

"Mrs. Boyd came by again. This time she wasn't as nice and wanted you to know that you could run but you couldn't hide, whatever that meant. I know you too honest to be messing' with somebody's money so it must be somebody's man?"

That remark really lit a fire under Dana. "You must forget who signs your paycheck! I pay your ass to answer the phone, take messages, file and draft reports, and sometimes make tea. I don't think anywhere in that description it says to keep tabs on who I'm fuckin', if I am fuckin' somebody." Dana slammed the phone closed so hard she cracked the side. Melinda called back. Dana didn't feel like her shit and didn't give a damn if she was calling to say she had quit. She really didn't know who these motherfuckers thought she was, Simeon, Melinda, Dre's wife, Damien and whomever else who kept hitting her with the nonsense. When she was upset and this was putting it lightly, the choice words rolled like thunder.

Chelle had made it to Dana's fist. She must have been somewhere nearby.

"What's going on? Dre' just called me talking about his wife and asking me to talk to you so you wouldn't tell her anything and something about your ass going crazy on him the other night."

Skyy Banks

Dana hadn't even gotten in the door good before Chelle started her barrage of questions.

"Girl, Dre's wife found out about us and she came by the job, not once but twice. Can you believe that bitch?"

"And you called me over here like the FBI was on your ass for that? I know you don't want to hear this but I'm gonna have to come out the bag for this one. We are getting too old for this shit. I am pregnant and am on my way to marriage. We have discussed this shit time and time again. You can't get mad when you crossed the line. 'Dre wasn't yours from the beginning. I can't ride with you this time. I suggest you talk to him and stay clear of his wife. To be honest I'd be mad at you too but that's where we fail, we want to kick the woman's ass. He knew better because he stepped out the marriage but you are just as much to blame. This is your mess and you're going to have to deal with it. You know I love you but I can't sweetie."

Dana stood with her mouth open. Chelle had come from left field with the voice of reason bullshit. That hurt worse than how dirty Damien did her. That hurt worse than being lonely. That shit hurt worse than wanting somebody to love you, knowing they never would. Tears rolled down her face. Chelle reached to hug her and Dana pushed back.

"Get the fuck outta my house. I can't believe you! As many times as I have rode with you, been there when you needed me, cried with your ass. Don't get me started!"

"It's not about that." By then Chelle was crying too. It's not about that."

"Get the fuck out and don't let me ask you again." Dana held the door open. When Chelle left, she sank to the floor and cried out in a way she never had. "It's all falling apart! It's all falling apart!"

She lay in the same position on the floor until the entire house was dark. Drinking wouldn't solve anything but it would help her forget for a while. She opted to call Mama. She always had the right answers and the way she told them to Dana weren't as hard to accept as with Chelle. She knew this would ease her pain, but didn't know how to say she was screwing a married man and now his wife was looking for her, probably with a 22 caliber. That's how they handled infidelity back in Cincinnati and had the nerve to want to call it a crime of passion. She definitely didn't want to burden her but her options were slim to none.

"Hey Auntie Lois!" It was impossible for her to disguise the hurt in her voice.

Soul on Fire

"Dana?"

"It's me. How are you doing? I haven't heard from you in a while. I thought you were going to do better about keepin' in touch?"

"Child, you know how busy things can get with the job, church, and your old uncle trying to act like he thirty five." Dana couldn't muster a smile.

"I've been checking on your mama. She's doing just fine. Your brother's still here but he says he's going back at the end of the month. They've been working with him over at that school real good. Now what about you baby? What do I owe the pleasure of this call?"

Dana wished it was a pleasure call. "I was just thinking about you and wanted to call."

"I know you better than that? Talk to Auntie."

She couldn't even talk, the lump in her throat was so big Dana thought she would suffocate and the tears streamed down her face nonstop.

"Let it out baby. I got all the time you need."

She cried and cried and cried. "Where do I begin?"

"Anywhere you want. Right now it seems like you need more listenin' than talkin'."

"Well, the reason I'm not married yet is because I keep picking the wrong ones or letting the wrong ones pick me. Either they married, already with someone, or sorry as hell. This last one was married and now his wife is looking for me. I cussed Chelle out because she wouldn't come over and have my back if the woman came to my house. This other nigga had the nerve to ask me to steal from my clients so he could do a business deal. I think I am going crazy. I keep having these weird dreams and now I'm seeing a shrink. Do I need to go on?"

"Not unless you want to."

Dana paused and cried some more.

"Let it all out baby. Go on."

"I'm lonely. I don't know what it feels like to wake up beside a man more than two nights in a row and it makes me sick."

"I know you don't want to hear any practical advice right now so I'm not going to give any. Pick yourself up, take a hot shower, get you some warm milk and lay down. Calm down baby. I just buried one niece and ain't quite ready to bury another. You gone give yourself a heart attack or have a nervous breakdown one. Calm down now and do what Auntie says. I'll call you later on and check on you."

Skyy Banks

Dana continued to cry but she felt better to get it all out or at least what she thought was all of it. "Okay."

"Do what Auntie says now."

"I will."

She willed herself up, moving in slow motion. Her body was heavy and tired. Even a good lay wouldn't do it this time.

Soul on Fire

ℒ

Dana didn't claim to be the knockout queen but at the same time, she didn't have a problem putting anyone in their place albeit man or woman, verbally or physically. Nowadays a verbal lashing was just as harsh as a physical one. Looking over her shoulder was never an issue either, even though she dealt with a number of married men. It was their duty to make sure wifey was out of the loop. Today the infamous Mrs. Boyd had her unnerved, unnerved because she was bold enough to show up at her job.

The answering machine indicated seven messages waiting. Tempted to ignore them until after work, her inner voice insisted she listened. Her fate could have lied in one of them.

Beep...Beep. The first two were hang ups but the number was from Chelle. Beep...Beep. "D. We need to talk. You already know about what. My wife is on a rampage and we need to be on the same page before you talk to her. I have a lot of shit to lose. Call me."

She rolled her eyes to the back of her head. Speaking aloud had become a habit. It seemed to make more sense to hear herself verbalize what she was thinking. "You got some nerve bastard. You want me to corroborate your damn story? If the Mrs. is as smart as I think she is, she had her ducks in a row before proceeding, pictures, recorded phone messages, bank statements, and then some. I'd be damn if I get drug into divorce court as the mistress. You gone have to work this shit out solo, Boo."

Beep...Beep... "Dana, I know you probably think I am some kind of con artist but I do have a business plan that you can look at and please don't think I did all those things to try and swindle you for money. It is legit. Call me baby."

"Can this shit get any more stupid?" She questioned. "Simeon ass is a trip. Legit? And you want me to steal from my clients? Then you have the audacity to call me and try and sugar coat the whole situation?" Dana would have to check his ass at some point as well. Her shit list was getting longer by the minute.

Beep...Beep... "I got your number from your Mama. You know who this is?"

"No Mama didn't, liar!" She knew Aunt Lois had called Damien. That's the only explanation for him calling her after all this time. He had basically pulled a fuck and flee deal. If it was more than that Dana's anger definitely wasn't permitting her to give him the benefit of the doubt.

Beep...Beep... "This Auntie checking on you."

Beep...Beep... dial tone.

A slight sigh of relief came over knowing that Mrs. Boyd hadn't just nutted up and called her house. Her second point of unreliable security was the peephole. One could only see someone if they were directly in front of it. Everything else was a blur. Dana was going to have to take her chances after seeing nothing.

The office was unusually dark and quiet. Mail was piled in front of the door. "Hell naw!" Dana grunted. Melinda hadn't shown up for work nor had she called. A recap of the exchange played in her head. Dana wouldn't work for herself either after that foolishness. Shoving the mail in her bag, she fumbled with the door, repeatedly looking behind her. She didn't have a clue as to what Mrs. Boyd drove. There was some consolation in knowing what she looked like. Who could forget that beauty? For all Dana knew she could have been staking the damn office out.

Dear Ms. Taylor,

I've been nothing but a loyal employee. I do answer the phone, take messages, and prepare reports and even some tea sometimes. I do everything that my job requires and then some. Even a dog will bite after being kicked too many times. I cannot and will not continue to work in a hostile work environment. Here's a piece of advice for your next door mat. Lighten up and don't take your personal problems out on them. I knew you was fuckin' Dr. Boyd all along. I could easily just give his wife all those phone messages and copies of the cards from the flowers he sent and invoices from the trips you took. I bet they will match the same time he was out of town. But that would be dirty. Don't bother to call.

Melinda

That note totally caught Dana off guard. She stood with emotion holding the note when the office door flew open. Flawless beauty stood before her.

Towering over her, Mrs. Boyd spoke slow and steady. "No need for introductions. I know who you are."

"Do you?" Dana asked.

"Yeah, you've been a part of my life for a while now. You see I usually can tell when Andre has a new one because I change."

Soul on Fire

"You know you shouldn't even be here. Any issues you have should be discussed with Andre. You are both adults, so let him answer any questions you have about me." Dana struggled to maintain her calm.

"I understand that but, woman to woman, hear me out."

Something about that whole woman to woman phrase took her down a couple of notches. "I'm listening."

"The change I'm speaking of is attitude, feelings, and the whole nine. I believe in personality, vibes, spirits and whatever else you want to call it. Most of the time the spirits of other women are different than mine. These are imparted upon me every time I make love to my husband."

That was astonishing and deep, it took Dana a minute to wrap her mind around what Mrs. Boyd was saying. She heard Auntie Lois speak about this same phenomenon before. Not saying a word, a curious look conveyed that Dana wanted more.

"What I'm saying is that if the woman has a nasty attitude and just bad vibes, my being has been poisoned. I start snapping on the kids, acting a fool for no apparent reason other than Andre has been messing around and brought that back to me. So you see men can bring more than just an STD home."

"What do you want from me?"

"I don't know what I want. I guess just to see what it was all about. To see if he came up. You know most men who cheat on their wives either get gutter women, if they're not ugly or fat they're usually another color."

"I guess," However true, it was no alleviation to Dana that the Mrs. was only concerned with what she looked like, what she drove, and her occupation. As she was about to bring a close to the impromptu meeting Andre walked through the door.

"Baby," he called out with a weak voice. Either he was a ventriloquist or Dana was going crazy. She swore for a split second that he was looking at his wife but talking to her.

"You, me, and he. What cha gone do baby?" Mrs. Boyd spoke facetiously. Dana thought she was about to go crazy and kill both of them.

"We need to go home and talk. There is nothing she can tell you that I won't." 'Dre pleaded.

Dana's mind was rolling. The little red thing appeared on her shoulder. Oh really! What about the weekend getaways? What about all those late night emergencies? What about? The devil wanted Dana to tell all the secrets as she watched 'Dre damn near in tears beg his wife to leave with him peacefully.

She was unwilling to watch the drama unfold to another scene. With keys in hand, Dana fought the tears. She stood not feeling much like *a woman* but the other woman, the mistress, and all the titles that she loathed. Holding Dre's attention via eye contact Dana stated firmly, "lock the door behind you."

"Have you lost her mind? You should have kicked their asses out." Dana scorned herself. She had bypassed her car and began a brisk walk down the street. Breathing hard, walking fast, and tasting the salt of her tears, she continued trying to sort things out. A little more than 24 hours ago she was being pampered and adored by fake ass Mr. Prince Charming. Heart racing and head swirling, she attempted to call Dr. Mitchell. The numbers were all a blur.

"Dr. Mitchell's, please hold."

Please hold, this is a life or death situation and this bitch says please hold. Dana knew that the receptionist on the other end of the phone was doing her job but at this moment didn't a damn thing matter but the ensuing crisis.

After what seemed like eternity she was back on the line, "Can I help you?"

"Yes, I need to come in and see Dr. Mitchell. It's an emergency!"

"Are you thinking about hurting yourself?"

"No, I am just really upset!"

"Well, her first opening isn't until Tuesday of next week."

"Tuesday?"

"Yes, if it is not a life or death situation and you don't need to call 911 or a crisis hot line. I suggest you use some of the de-stressing techniques and remove yourself from the situation. If we have any cancellations I can put you on the waiting list."

The calmness in the receptionist's voice immediately began to clear her head. How could she argue or be insanely upset with someone who was this nice or was this rational. Dana answered her own question. *Easily*, as she thought back to the times she had mistreated Chelle for being just as sane and civilized as the receptionist, one who she had no connection with other than patronizing the office in which she worked.

"Dana?"

Soul on Fire

Disillusioned and disheveled it was just as hard for Evan to recognize her as it was for her to recognize him. Dana shied away in embarrassment. Her frustrations had led her to walk at least four blocks before she realized it. Feet hurting and wondering how she was to make it back to the office she still tried to play it cool.

"Dana, did you get my message?"

"You were next in line for a return call." She smirked.

"Oh! So a brotha has to take a number and wait? You got it like that?" Evan responded jokingly.

She could not believe that she'd walked that far and wound up in front of the barbershop and ran into Evan. Of course, this fine young thing crossed her mind a few times. But that was the extent of it, just a thought.

"No, I've been busy trying to get caught up with things since returning from out of town. That's all."

"You aight?"

Dana groaned again. "Hell no. My feet are killin' me!"

"You want me to carry you?"

"You always playin'."

"I'm for real because you look a little crazy right now. That body and hair is still banging but you look sad. You been cryin'?"

Trying to avoid his probing, "Turn around so I can get on your back!" They both cracked up.

"Now you playin'. I'm about to get some coffee across the street. Want to join me? That's the least you can do since you haven't returned my call, and I do still have that gift for ya."

Looking down at her watch, she really needed to get back to her unmanned office. Hopefully the air was clear.

"You can give me a ride back to my office and I'll call you later."

"That's wuzzup."

He was young and fully immersed in the hip hop era, the era of cool and what's happening. Yet she couldn't fight the attraction. The flesh is an awful thing. Apart from the situation at hand, Dana reflected on a previous Sunday's sermon about yielding to temptation and wrestling against flesh and blood. Despite all that had transpired over the last 48 hours, she imagined herself being on top of E. What the hell? She concluded she would give him a call and worry about straightening all the other out tomorrow. Or the next day or better yet....as it came.

Skyy Banks

The office was empty and in one piece. She wasn't sure what to expect upon return: broken glass, toppled furniture, the works, but all was left just as it was. The phone rang off the hook. She sent every call to voice mail and flipped through Melinda's scheduler. E had so graciously gotten her tea before the ride back to the office. Avoiding the urge to get pissed off all over again, Dana channeled her thoughts to the future. She pulled reports and files for the two meetings scheduled for the afternoon. Shifting between massaging her temples and her feet, jazz comforted her. The phone had finally quieted.

Soul on Fire

♨

Walking in three inch heels over a few blocks was murder on her feet. They still ached, especially her toes. Dana would forego being cute and wear comfortable shoes when she met Evan later on.

She went on with her usual routine of listening to messages, going through mail, then unwinding with a glass of wine while the sweet sound of Lionel Hampton on the vibraphone restored her soul. Not true restoration but some much needed temporary peace of mind.

The names she had scribbled on the note pad would have to wait for a return call. She didn't want anything to change her mood and any venting would have to wait until she saw Dr. Mitchell. Looking over the short list of names, a pang hit her in my heart. Out of the names, the one that mattered the most was missing. Nonetheless, her pride wouldn't give way to call Chelle.

Skyy Banks

Evan had decided that after a long day at work he still wanted to see her even if it was for a quiet movie at his house. Dana didn't argue. She wasn't feeling the dressing up thing or the going through the motions thing of a night on the town.

Evan's apartment was south of the city and deep in the cut. She called a few times for directions only to discover that she had passed the entrance at least three times.

"If it was a snake it woulda bit ya!"

No he didn't, she thought to herself. He was too new school for such an old school saying. "I'm here now!"

The smell of the pizza persisted to the bottom of the stairs. Evan's apartment had stairs at the entrance that led to a layout on the upper level. A dim light on the wall lit the way. Pizza was served by candles. It wasn't what she was quite use to but sweet.

"I got Boomerang for us to watch. That's cool?"

"Yeah, it's actually one of my favorite movies." Dana tried to hide her girlish grin. "Which character are you might I ask?"

"I'm gonna let you figure that one out. I do like pretty toes though, but that don't mean I'm Marcus."

"Oh really?"

"Yeah, really!"

"And I don't take no bullshit, but that don't mean that I am crazy like Yvonne or hard nose like Jacqueline either."

"I hear ya."

They ate pizza. Dana passed on the salad and drank wine. The combination wasn't too bad, different but not bad. She snuggled close to Evan while they watched the movie. Dana couldn't resist wondering how he could afford such a trendy but swank apartment on a barber's salary. Maybe he was a drug dealer perpetrating as a barber. The walls were covered with expensive art. Not the prints dressed up in expensive frames, the real deal. Various pieces of sculpted art peeked out of corners and rested on table tops. She was very impressed but pretended not to notice.

"Come here." He pulled her into him, barely missing her sore breast. "So you gone tell me what took you so long to holla at the kid? You know I been tryin' to get at you for a minute now."

Soul on Fire

"I didn't think you were serious." she lied. The truth was #1- she wasn't into young men. #2- she wasn't trying' to date someone that didn't have some kind of status in main stream society or shall I say the corporate world. #3 He had small feet and everyone knew what that meant. Dana laughed inwardly when she thought about the reasons she had avoided him, childish to some degree.

"It's all good. You're here now like you said." He pulled her closer. "Why you so quiet?"

"Just watchin' the movie." Damn he smelled good. Evan pulled a blanket from the basket beside the couch and spread it over them. She had somehow changed positions and was laying back on him between his legs. It felt good. Evan began a slow scalp massage and then worked his way to her neck. Dana shuddered between her legs. This ain't happening she thought. Her mind was saying one thing but the other part of her was saying something else. "I gotta go."

"What's wrong?"

"Nothing, I just need to get ready for tomorrow. It is a weeknight remember? Thanks for the food and company."

"No problem." Dana was shocked that he wasn't pressuring her to stay. She looked back up from the bottom of the stairs at him. To be young he had a nice ass body. He stood in his wife beater and gym shorts, smiling down at her. In one motion he pulled his penis out of his shorts. He knew that he was packin'. She could tell by the confident way he exposed himself. Dana caught herself before letting out a gasp. He could have been a porn star. The head on that thing was more than a mouthful.

"I know you crazy for real."

"Holla at ya boy!"

She turned and closed the door behind her. Walking slowly to her car, she contemplated going back. That thing was so big and she had to have it. But was she going to give in that easy? She couldn't let that young boy have a hold on her or even a thought that he had that kind of pull. Her feet were heavy but she made her way to the car. Driving around the complex a few times to pass time, she called.

"I'm on my way back."

"The door is open." He spoke brashly. She was sure he watched the clock and timed how long it took her to call him back. At least that's the game she and Chelle played when they were his age. Timing how long it took men to call them after they got the digits, usually within an hour.

The door was indeed open and the aura was better than before. The glow of candles was accentuated by the sound of water falling. Dana almost toppled down the stairs when she bumped into a waiting Evan. He wasn't nude but she was wishing he was. She grabbed the full wine glass that had been extended her and gulped it down, dribbling the last corner down her chin. Before she could wipe it away, Evan's mouth cleaned it up. To describe his tongue as soft and wet would not be doing any justice. It was more like gushy and warm. The way a man would describe a woman's vagina. When one was described like that it meant the stuff was *real* good.

The sucking of the chin, led to the sucking of the neck, then to the sucking of toes and every body part in between. The bed rocked and her body shook throughout the night. Her hair was drenched. The wet sheets were cool under her body. The last thing Dana remembered was H-Town bellowing out, *Emotions make you sad sometimes, Emotions make you cry sometimes.* Tears streamed down her face as she lay there on her stomach. She didn't know if she was crying because she had just finished an intense session of love making that was so good it made me cry or that she was so emotional and vulnerable, whatever the case was Evan didn't say a word. He sat for a while at the head of the bed watching her before he lay down beside her. Their bodies didn't touch but were close enough that she could feel the warmth from his.

"I don't want to," the little girl cried out. *"It's okay. I won't hurt you. Open up."* The mask glowed a yellowish green similar to that of a boiled egg yolk. *"Don't start this shit!"* The voice behind the mask was growing angrier. The girl looked a little older than before, but she was the same person.

Dana woke up to Evan rocking her in his arms.

"Shhhh. It's okay Mommy." He didn't ask any questions, just held her like she needed.

Soul on Fire

Work was as much a struggle today as it was yesterday. Dana had to admit that Melinda was an invaluable asset to the firm, but she'd be damn if she let anyone she signed a check for run her. It wasn't that she didn't know how to prepare reports, answer the phone, schedule clients, or make her own tea, all that was tedious and time consuming.

In between number crunching Dana journaled. So much had taken place in a short period of time and the only outlet that was safe to feel anyway she wanted was through pen and paper. The dream that had awakened her to Evan was fresh on her mind. The guide to dreams was a close companion these days. The dreams were more distorted but the color of the masks stood out. Two descriptions were listed for yellow: a bright yellow represented sunniness, joy and optimism. Muddier shades of yellow represented treachery, betrayal, and blocked intuition. She decided that the latter was a stark interpretation of what was going on. The mystery that seemed to eat at her more was the face behind the mask. Dana needed to replay the dreams over again. No matter how painful to dissect every piece. She needed to examine the surroundings, the smells, the tones, the features of the masked man, the one who she now had come to call *public enemy number one*. Unstirred, she remained quiet in the chair determined to pull something from the dark into the light. The ringing phone jarred her back to reality.

"Dana Taylor."

"Ms. Taylor. This is Dr. Mitchell's office. There has been a 3:45 cancellation for today. Would you like to come in at that time?"

"Sure." She responded with the slightest apprehension. Answering the phone still had her on edge. She was unsure who had her personal number, but nothing had jumped off beyond an unexpected visitor.

Skyy Banks

⌀

1. I am concerned with what other people think although I pretend that I'm not.
2. I have trouble articulating my feelings.

Dana's assignment was unfinished from the first visit. She didn't like to admit when she was wrong. #3 and was the last person to see any flaws within herself #4. The more she thought about the assignment the longer her list became. Crumpling the paper inside her hand, she reclined in the chair.

"Come on Dana, and bring that paper with you."

Dr. Taylor had witnessed the song and dance of her trying to put her thoughts onto paper. Dana almost felt like a kid getting caught with their hand in the cookie jar and was embarrassed, which was a rarity.

"How are you?"

"I'm good."

"If you were good then you wouldn't need me. Now let's cut to the chase. Let's start with that paper in your hand. I saw you writing. It must have been pretty intense because you almost chewed a whole in your bottom lip."

"I started on the list of things that bothered me about me. Before we get into that I want to talk about what's been going on. I was sleeping with a married man and his wife found out. She confronted me. My administrative assistant quit. I cursed out my best friend because she basically told me that it was my fault and that she was too old to get caught up in my bullshit. I had another dream last night."

"Okay let's take one issue at a time. Which one is the most pressing?"

"The reoccurring dreams, I think if I knew why I was having them then maybe my personal life would be better."

"Personal life?"

"Well, my whole being. I am barely functional after a sleepless night, waking up in sweats, crying, and afraid for a reason that is not apparent to me. I don't even know what significance the dreams have in my life."

"So, have you been journaling afterwards?"

Soul on Fire

This back and forth went on for more than an hour. The resolution was to try a form of hypnotic therapy. This was supposed to allow Dana to see within the dreams, hopefully behind the masks and reveal what was haunting her. Skepticism weighed heavily on her but at this point she was willing or better yet desperate to try anything. Dr. Mitchell made a few phone calls and arranged for another doctor to actually complete the process.

Skyy Banks

$\mathscr{D}$

The hypnotherapist arrived a few hours later. The purpose of this treatment was to enable an artificial trance of sleep, semi-consciousness. This state would give her the ability to choose new ways of doing, being and thinking, without being controlled by past experiences. Textbook theory working at its best is what the pessimistic side of her kept saying. Within ten minutes Dana was reclined and on her way to that deep relaxing place in her mind.

"Sit up here." The girl was pulled onto the mask man's lap. The red glow was extremely intense similar to a fiery furnace. His hips began to roll under the girl. Her body lunged forward as she was taken by surprise by sudden movements. In a low whisper, the voice said "open your legs." "Open up so I can feel that pretty little thing."

At this moment the therapist's voice not Dr. Mitchell interjected. "What are you seeing, who is speaking, and what they were saying? Is there anything you recognize? furniture? Sounds? smells?"

Squirming in the chair, Dana struggled to make a clear picture of her surroundings. The voices were just as hazy.

"Relax, Ms. Taylor. Fighting it will only make it more difficult. Just relax. Everything should be as vivid as if you were there in the natural. Take a few slow, deep breaths for me."

Dana took two deep breaths followed by slow breathing. Slower, slower, slower, so slow that she could no longer feel the rise and fall of her chest. This was the onset of panic and confusion.

"Sit up here." Dana's body experienced an episode of astro-projection. She stood in the corner and watched the assault unravel.

"Sit up here." The mask man asked again. The little girl, who was Dana, was wearing a blue and orange halter that tied around the neck. She had matching shorts and sandals. As the man lifted her on his lap one of the sandals fell to the floor. She could see the bulge growing in his pants. His hips began to rotate as he placed her strategically on top of the bulge. "Open your legs." He wanted to feel her innocence as he dry humped her. "Open your legs." Dana continued to watch from the corner, frozen in fear. Her eyes were fixed on the one sandal on the floor and the other one that was dangling off the girl's foot..... Her foot. The voice that first appeared muffled became discernable. "It can't be!" She yelled out in utter disbelief.

Soul on Fire

"Can't be? Can't be what Dana? Who's there?" the therapist asked.

She willed herself to shut down and continued to watch from the corner in silence, instead of words, tears flowed.

"Ms. Taylor? Ms.Taylor?"

Dana was brought back to a level of consciousness to find herself balled into a fetal position on the sofa.

"Can you explain to us what just occurred?"

"Me explain?" she asked with a mix of attitude and sarcasm.

"I was the one under hypnosis. I am sure you heard and saw everything."

Dr. Mitchell responded by saying, "Yes we did, we saw that you saw something or someone. Whatever or whomever this something or someone was it caused you to shut completely down. Shut you down to the point of you resorting to infantile behavior."

Dana couldn't argue that because she saw herself in that state. The masked man's face flashed before her eyes and she flinched. She couldn't tell, she wouldn't tell, too embarrassed and too hurt to reveal the perpetrator of this heinous act.

"I don't know what you all are talking about. All I saw was a little girl." She couldn't allude to the fact that the little girl was her. "And I saw the masked man but I couldn't see his face or really understand his voice."

"We're not going to push you but we know that if it really wasn't anything the reaction would not be as the one we saw."

"Okay Dr. Hogue. I appreciate that." No matter how brutal that truth was.

"Dr. Mitchell, can I come in and see you next week?" Dana really needed to stay and sort some things out, the pain from what she saw was unbearable. The suffocating lump grew.

"That's fine. Stop at the front desk. Would you like to see Dr. Hogue again?"

"Yes." Dana's body felt as if an additional 50 or 60 pounds had been added within the last few hours.

Skyy Banks

♉

The darkest part of my soul no one will ever know. I wonder if he did the same thing to Dana? I am too afraid to ask and too embarrassed to tell. Will I ever be able to tell?

It began with light brushes against my body or more frequent lap visits. At every opportunity he would ask me to crawl onto his lap and pat my behind. I really didn't think anything was wrong or obscene about his gestures because he was Daddy and had been Daddy all my life. Daddies are caretakers, breadwinners, protectors, they make boos-boos better, not make boo-boos. The first time I laid with my father was nothing short of a living nightmare. We were home alone not often but every chance he had he took advantage. I stepped out of the shower to him standing outside the stall handing me a towel. His eyes seem to pierce my body as they gazed my newly budding breasts down to the little tuft of hair that covered my vagina. I was paralyzed were I stood. His eyes conveyed to me some kind of code or secret creed between father and daughter. It was as though I was in a hypnotic state and that my silence instantly entered me into a covenant with a man that for all intent and purposes was to give his life for mine and not take mine. I followed his lead as he toweled me dry. He planted kisses on my naked body in the process. I didn't feel. I was numb. He led me to the bedroom and sat me on the bed. I can remember thinking if this was how Celie from the Color Purple felt when her father came to her and said "she would do the things her momma wouldn't do." The room was deathly quiet. I couldn't even muster up tears. I was numb. My father then placed my hands to unbuckle his belt. I think I did it automatically as though I was welcoming what was taking place and was about to take place. He pulled his shirt over his head. I could see his stiff penis bulge through his boxers. He laid me back on the bed and began oral sex on me. Tears did begin to stream down my face into my ears. Yet, I didn't utter a word. My father was breathing hard and his eyes looked wild. He positioned himself on top of me ready for actual penetration. He stroked my vagina with his penis and tried countless number of times to enter me and I cringed. It hurt so badly and the only thing I remember doing was whimpering like a puppy. He got up after what seemed like eternity and pulled his pants from around his ankles. I turned my head to look at the wall. He said, "Clean yourself up" before leaving the room. His tone was soft and caring. I laid there in the midst of my own blood and

Soul on Fire

tears and his semen. This was years ago, but my inner person is so raw and exposed that it seems like yesterday.

I have been so imprisoned by shame that I often question my reluctance to seek counseling or to prosecute my father. I question if my silence was agreement. I allowed my father to have his way with me when and how he wanted. My legs seemed to open to him as though I was accepting my own rite of passage to womanhood. I couldn't trust my own perceptions of what was happening to me. The reality or possibility of not having my own mother believe such a terrible thing was too painful. It seemed as though I made excuses for my father or somehow, in a warped since of thinking, believed that I had some responsibility in being assaulted. Did I convey a hidden message in the things I said, the way I dressed, talked, or acted around my father? As a child I could not rationalize how a mother couldn't, didn't know, so I retreated into disgraced shadows.

Mya's journal hit the floor with a thud. The pericope of text that Dana had randomly stumbled upon debilitated her entire body. She couldn't move. The act was cruel enough for Dana to wish her heart to stop beating in the very chest that it occupied.

"Not daddy. Not Mya" Her thoughts wavered back and forth as she agonized over who to feel more sympathy for, the victim or the villain. She knew villain was a harsh word. It literally meant an evil or wicked person. Her father was a pastor.

"Not daddy." Turning back through the pages, she was directed to the line that read: *Daddies are caretakers, breadwinners, protectors, they make boos-boos better, not make boo-boos. The first time I laid with my father was nothing short of a living nightmare.*

Dana's head throbbed badly, massaging her temples offered not an ounce of relief. To try and mull over every detail was sickening. She felt powerless reading a story that literally was being told from the grave. The first time is what she read not the only time. The abuse was ongoing. "But for how long?" "Why didn't she say anything, even after daddy died?" Questions inundated her mind. She wanted to die.

The doorbell chimed. The thoughts didn't dissipate immediately, but made her a little nervous. After all how coincidental was it that someone would be ringing her doorbell at the same time she was having suicidal thoughts? Before the thought could fully re-enter her mind, the doorbell chimed again. She moved towards it with a swollen face. If it weren't for the fact that she was a single woman with no man, live in or part time whoever on the other side would have sworn she was a battered woman.

"Just a moment." Dana spoke barely above a whisper. The man in the brown truck obviously from UPS was walking down the steps when she finally answered.

"Yes."

"Excuse me ma'am. I have a delivery for a Ms. Dana Taylor."

"This is she."

"Did I catch you at a bad time?"

"No, I look like this all the time." She hadn't lost the sarcasm.

"You're beautiful."

She wasn't in the mood for the game spitting. "Thanks, package please."

When he did come back from the truck, Dana immediately recognized why he hadn't carried the package to the door with him. It was square and huge. She stepped aside to allow him room to bring the package inside.

"Where would you like it?"

"On that wall." Pointing to an empty space near the kitchen.

"Sign here."

"Thanks."

"No problem and you are beautiful. I can see that clearly through the swollen eyes." Sure to hand her a business card before he left.

She didn't know UPS drivers had business cards, thinking as she glanced over it.

The phone rang. God was really making sure she didn't do anything stupid. The answering machine picked up as she wanted.

"Dana, I was wondering if you would like to go on a date with me. Yeah a real date not watchin' movies and eatin' pizza. Although we was really vibin'. Anyways, Maxwell is going to be at the park next Saturday and I would like to request the pleasure of your company." Laughing, he went on to say, "Let me know what's good, holla at cha boy."

That tone and the familiar play on words had Evan written all over it. The moniker also fit him perfectly. Dana was lost, numb, and everything around was a haze. Searching the room, she looked around for answers, answers that held the key to her future. If she was to survive both physically and mentally, she had to have answers. Her eyes, at least the little bit she could see through stopped at the brown parcel recently

Soul on Fire

delivered. At first sight it was just another piece of African American art. A closer look unveiled an oil painting, not a print. The same painting she had marveled at months back. This was the surprise Evan had told her about. It was beautiful. She stood back in awe of the painting. She had memorized every detail, from the way the woman's hand held a golden key in one and a silhouette of a man standing behind a closed door. What was the picture saying? Did she hold the key to her future of love? It was beautiful and momentarily gave her solace.   Turning the radio on her favorite jazz station, she poured a glass of wine, and cleaned house as a distraction. Every candle in the house was lit and the smell was captivating. She was exhibiting some serious bipolar behavior. She had gone from being a suicidal nervous wreck to at peace, from one phone call and a picture. This is how she had been living her life, repressing and bottling up all things negative. Remembering she had been given Maxwell tickets a few weeks before, she thought about bribing Melinda to come back by giving her the tickets and a pay increase. The latter would have to be discussed with her accountant but knowing black folk, fifty cents raise would go a long way. Her better judgment kicked in. She would have to do something else besides the Maxwell concert. The biggest reason for Melinda quitting was being blasted for being in Dana's business. The last thing she needed or wanted was to bump into her at the concert with a man on her arm. The chances were slim to none but she'd rather have none.

ℒ

"Dana, this is Dr. Mitchell. We are very close to a breakthrough I believe. With that being said, Dr. Hogue and I would like to see you as soon as possible, tomorrow afternoon if at all possible. Call me if this is feasible. We would like to try a new technique. I look forward to hearing from you."

This was the first message she heard when she made it to the office. Still nothing from Chelle and she needed Melinda or someone else terribly. Dana flipped through the Rolodex to call one of the temp agencies she had as a client to get some hired help fast. If just to answer the phone, take messages, and make tea while she thought of a way to get Melinda back that didn't require ass kissing, which was definitely something she wasn't good at.

The day was filled with rescheduled appointments from her time out of the office. Thankfully, Melinda had all the reports ready. The phone would have to just roll over to voice mail as it had been doing all week. She would listen just in case Chelle called. Dana doubted that she'd call the front office anyway, but instead directly to her cell. Around lunch time, she called Dr. Mitchell and confirmed the appointment for the next evening. By that time the temp agency had sent over an administrative assistance. She wasn't exactly fair skinned, more of what my kinfolk from the south would call mulatto. Her features of full lips and wide hips definitely led her to believe that she had some black in her. Dana laughed at her stereotypical thoughts. That was a peeve of hers, yet these days she was all over the place in contradictions. She hoped the new girl had the brains to match the beauty. If she did she was a keeper, Dana could only imagine what this would do for her male clientele.

"Ms. Taylor, I am here from A-1 Professional Solutions. Alexia Towns," she extended her hand in formal greeting.

Dana was very impressed with her poise and tone. "Nice to meet you." Spending the better half of the afternoon between clients and training Alexia, Dana's mind was at ease and she felt a burden lifted immediately. She was going to try her out for the remainder of the week and possibly offer her the position. She already had one up, the girl knew how to make tea. She even brought her own tea bags tucked in a cute little canister. She suggested a new system of filing for the office and didn't ask a lot of questions. The more she thought about it Dana found herself saying, "Damn, Melinda. I guess it's true what they say, when God closes one door He opens another. Something like that anyway."

Skyy Banks

⌀

Sitting in Dr. Mitchell's office, Dana wrestled with the idea of being completely honest in this session. This would be the only way she could heal. Keepin' it real meant not hiding the things she saw, facing the realities of it all no matter how painful and seriously meshing what she had read in Mya's journal with her haunting dreams. The other election would be to continue repressing everything with the possibility of one day completely losing her mind. The latter seemed easier but the former was definitely more realistic. That's if she wanted to be healthy, have a thriving business, and salvage what was left of her friendship, or perhaps be intimate with someone because she loved them not because she needed to fill a void.

"Ms. Taylor, Ms. Taylor." Dr. Mitchell tapped Dana's shoulder light enough to not startle her but get her attention. "Are you ready?"

"Good evening, Dr. Mitchell." Dana dragged the cement blocks that were once her feet back to the consulting area.

"Dr. Hogue will be in shortly. Tell me how you've been feeling in the past few days."

"I've been up and down with my emotions. At one point I felt so bad that I wanted to just give up."

"Give up? What do you mean?"

"I felt so bad. I-I-I-I don't know. Like I wanted to die."

"Was it after the session?"

"Yes." The room was still, feeling boxed in Dana could not bring herself to open up and say anymore. Not without Dr. Mitchell's open ended questions.

"What happened in that session that caused you to feel that way?"

"It was something I saw when I was under hypnosis and then something I read when I made it home."

"Something? What were those somethings?"

"More like someones. My dad and my uncle."

Dr. Hogue had entered the room. She stood quietly in the corner and listened. Dana and Dr. Mitchell continued their conversation.

"Your uncle and your dad?"

"Yes, they did horrible, horrible things." Dana's voice trailed off.

Soul on Fire

Dr. Hogue interjected, "We are at such a critical moment, let's begin our session."

Moving to the next room, Dana found a comfortable position in the recliner and closed her eyes. Her body was tense, uncertain at this juncture if she wanted to know the facts.

"Relax. This is just like last time, except this time we are going to visually record the session. Just relax. Listen to the waterfall.........."

"Hey Willie, that girl is really growing up!"

"Yeah look at her. Nice huh? Dana baby, go get your Uncle Willie some sweet tea."

He slapped her on the behind before she left the room. She could hear the two men talking, about her. The blue mask concealed who the other man was. His voice was that of a burly man yet he had a small stature. The ice rattled in the glass as she walked back to the living room. Dana had been waiting for Aunt Lois to come home to take her to piano lessons.

"Come sit in your Unc's lap." *He had stepped out of his comfort zone to expose his dark side to this strange man, obviously, no stranger to him. Dana had not encountered this before, she stood scared stiff. The ice rocked so hard against the sides of the glass that the tea started to spill over. Uncle Willie pulled Dana onto his lap while grabbing the glass simultaneously. She could feel the hardness in his pants. Her squirming to get away seemed to arouse him more.*

"She's feisty Willie."

"Yeah, but she knows what I like. Feel it girl. Put your hand down there."

She was terrified. It wasn't like he hadn't touched her before, but she had no idea what both men would do to her. She looked at the man with the blue mask and then back at Uncle Willie. This went on for a few minutes. The man with the blue mask began to stroke himself. The diamond from his ring glared at her.

"The ring!"

"What about the ring?" asked Dr. Hogue.

"The ring!"

Jumping from Uncle Willie's lap, she knocked the glass of tea over and ran outside. She ran and ran and ran. It couldn't have been too far because the sound of Aunt Lois' horn blowing in her direction found her at the corner of Lee and Vine Streets. These streets were only a few blocks over.

Skyy Banks

"Child, where you going? Running all wild and looking wilder by the eyes. What's wrong?"

"Hey Auntie Lois, some girls were bothering me after school that's all. Then Uncle Willie was teasing me."

"Dry them eyes up and get yo'self in the car. How about we get some ice cream before you go to piano practice?"

"Don't want none."

"Who, you don't want no ice cream?"

"No, I just feel bad." Dana could tell Aunt Lois most anything, but couldn't bring bare to tell what Uncle Willie was doing.

"What about the ring, Dana?"

"Enough! Enough! I've had enough," Dana screamed.

Dr. Mitchell put her arms around her. It was useless trying to console the inconsolable. "Dana, if you are going to get pass this and start seeing a glimpse of the light at the end of the tunnel... and sweetheart there is light at the end of the tunnel....you have to push ahead. Regardless of how painful the situation or memories are. You cannot change or undo what has already been done."

"The ring?" Dr. Hogue broke the monotony of her reactions. She was going to push Dana to that breakthrough one way or the other.

Straining to speak, "The diamond ring belongs to one of Uncle Willie's friends." Dana forced a sentence.

"Where do you see the diamond?"

"It's on his finger. He is watching while Uncle Willie is touching me."

"Is he touching you?"

"No touching himself and watching."

"Is he saying anything?"

"No just touching himself and watching."

"Do you remember his name and his exact relationship to your Uncle Willie?"

"No I don't." She lied again. It was already too embarrassing to acknowledge the awful things at the hands of Uncle Willie therefore, she dare say that his friend, the preacher did the same things. Even if he didn't actually touch her, silence meant agreement.

Soul on Fire

⌀

A week had passed and Dana had yet to speak to Chelle. She desired to talk to her badly but could not bring herself to call. She felt an ultimate sense of betrayal. She had quickly turned her career into a work from home one. Dragging out of bed to complete a file or two, a few follow-up phone calls, snacking while in pajamas all day, a shower maybe, sleeping pill, warm tea and bed, had become her daily protocol.

"Hey chic! Get your behind out of bed." Almost knocking Dana over she forced her way inside past her. "The office is too quiet without you and apparently you haven't been answering your calls because they keep calling the office for you. Besides how am I s'pose to be bonding with my new boss lady if you ain't there?"

Dana suddenly had a flashback of loud, nosey Melinda. "Well, who's answering the phone while you are here?"

"Did you forget today is Saturday and you need to get out. Where is the teapot?" Alexia shook an orange tin can at Dana?

"It's on the stove. Give me a sec while I jump in the shower." Alexia found her way to the kitchen while Dana headed to the bedroom picking up clothes and straightening things on the way. She could hear Alexia busying around in the living room. Maybe this was what she needed, a burst of fresh energy. That energy had just plunged into overdrive when Dana heard Alexia screaming and hollering from the living room.

"What's wrong girl?"

"No, what's right? You were just about to let these go to waste." Fanning her face with two tickets.

The puzzled look on Dana's face must have given clue that she didn't remotely know what Alexia was talking about or what the tickets were for.

"Maxwell! Today! At the Park! Is it a date?"

Dana had forgotten that she had been given the tickets a while back nor where she had placed them. With nothing else to do and over due for fresh air and sunlight, she responded. "What the hell. It's a date."

"We are going to have so much fun. Get dressed, the tea is almost ready. I'll keep cleaning up in here. Maybe next time I'll find some money."

"You nosey girl, but it's okay!" Shaking her head, Dana was beginning to feel better.

Soul on Fire

∅

"What's your story?" Dana probed. She and Alexia elected to do lunch at Milan's Bistro. The weather was more than a typical spring day. Breezy and mild, hovering around 75 degrees.

"Girl, where do I begin?"

"From the beginning!" Dana was up to hearing anybody's story but her own.

"Well, I'm homegrown, a true Georgia peach. Single, no kids. Working on my degree in marketing. That's basically it. Boring huh?"

She was hoping for more because she wasn't up to much talking. Her mind was on the other side of town with 'Dre, Evan, Simeon, somebody.

"So what's the deal with you? I already know you don't have no kids, you ain't married."

"Excuse me Ms. FBI. Let me get this." Dana searched around in the bottom of her purse for her phone, it had been ringing off and on for the last ten minutes.

"Dana!" Hearing E's voice put a smile on her face. That one phone call dismissed any negative and unhappy feelings she was harboring.

"What's good Ma?"

"Just having a little brunch with a girlfriend." She would dare tell him she was so pitiful that her secretary had to come drag her sorry behind out of bed.

"So are you standing me up for the concert this evening?"

"Were we supposed to go?"

"Well, you did not formally accept, but I did leave you a message. As business minded as you are I assumed that you had gotten the message, just hadn't returned my call."

"You know what they say about assumptions."

"Yeah, you make an ass out of you and me." They finished that last part in unison. She had to stop and catch her breath from laughing so hard.

"Damn girl, I'll take some of that!" Alexia blurted out from across the table. It was loud enough just for Dana to hear. She winked back at her.

"So we on or not?"

"Sure big head! I'll do you a favor and come by and scoop you."

"Bet! Don't be late either!"

"And who was that? That brother sho added a lot of sunshine in your life!" Alexia couldn't wait for Dana to end the call.

Déjà vu all over again. Dana did a double take at Alexia to reassure herself that she had not morphed into Melinda.

"It was a good friend, Ms. Busybody. And I do have good news for you too."

"Do tell!"

"You can have the Maxwell tickets and take a friend!"

"You are the bomb girl! That's not merely good news, that ish is GREAT!"

"Don't even think about it. Just remember you owe me one."

"Whateva you need."

Before Dana could go on with what she was saying, Alexia was dialing someone. Dana excused herself to the ladies room to give Alexia some privacy and try to teach her lesson on it at the same time. If there were any visible signs of stress on her face, Dana's next stop was the spa to remedy it all.

Soul on Fire

✍

Dana chose to indulge in an afternoon at the spa anyways to relieve some built up tension and a few extras. Excitement ran through her veins waiting for the evening she would spend with Evan. Being with Evan always made her feel a little younger than what she was, giggling none stop. Unlike with 'Dre, the goofy Dana had to be toned down and more serious. Alexia had spruced up the place more than she realized. Dana made sure not to put anything in a place it didn't belong. Laying back on the couch she smiled at a familiar phrase, *God sends angels just when we need them.* Church had been a place she rarely visited after the move to Atlanta. Her Saturday nights were consumed with getting ready for a night of club hopping. Sundays were usually a day of rest and recovery. If she ever needed to be in Church the time was now. *"Don't call on God when you're in trouble. Call on him in good and bad times."* Dana could hear daddy saying this time and time again. So she called out, "Thank you for Auntie Lois, Alexia, and the temporary sanity for today. May it end better than it began. Amen."

She was running late. Not too late but enough to have Evan call and ask her why she was late? The mirror commanded a few more minutes of her attention. Dana wanted to be jaw dropping gorgeous, even though they had only seen each other a few times. She could find herself really digging this young man with such a bodacious swagger. "You are brilliant, you are beautiful, and you are loved!" Dana proclaimed to in the mirror.

Evan's eagerness wasn't as obvious when she pulled into his complex. She had to walk to the door, come inside, and wait while he found things to do to stall her. He was showing her how it felt to have to wait on someone else. Finally, he grabbed his sports jacket and took her by the hand and walked to the car. Like a gentleman he opened her door.

"You know I don't mind driving."

"I'm good. After all I'm picking you up. Remember?"

"Do your thing Boo!" He stood in the door way for a minute. Dana couldn't tell what his eyes were saying through the shades. But he stepped back clasped his hands together, nodded, and smiled. She wasn't sure if that was a nod of approval, either way it looked good. At the same time she gave him a once over from head to toe. She couldn't deny that he was definitely getting his *grown man* on. His locks were freshly done and she couldn't wait to get her hands tangled in them. He wore a chocolate button down shirt with a tan sports jacket with chocolate stitching and the shoes to match. Dana was pleasantly surprised. Her flesh began to rise and she fought it, otherwise they would be on the side of the road. In the back of her mind she thought the hell with the concert. They could make their own music. This had to be an addiction or some kind of sickness. She was more than ready to drop the panties at a split second notice. Dr. Mitchell would have to help her work on that thing.

"What's on your mind?" Evan asked stroking her arm and thighs.

"Just looking forward to the concert."

"Oh! Really. The same one you almost stood me up on?"

"Yeah that one, but it all worked out."

"Girl you something else."

"No you something else. It's cool she let you out to play." That sounded like something he would say instead of Dana, the insecure side peeked through. Dana had no idea of his status but figured he was too fine to be single.

"There you go!"

She knew that meant let's not go there so she let it go by saying, "I'm just playing big head!"

"I know that it's not full fledged spring yet so I brought the jacket just in case my baby gets cold later on tonight."

"That was sweet."

"That's nothing. Just wait!"

Dana popped in a CD and they rode and listened the rest of the way to the park.

The music could be heard from the parking lot. The opening act was still performing because it was only thirty minutes into show time. Evan opened her door again like the perfect gentleman.

"Don't start nothin' you can't keep up!"

"This is me all the time. I truly understand a woman's worth."

She didn't wait for him to extend his arm before grabbing a hold of it. Evan turned and surprisingly kissed her on the lips. His lips melted into hers like butter. The park was beautiful. Evan must have had the tickets long before or he had a hookup because they were up close and personal to the stage. Dana was finding out along the way that he was very well connected and knew a little bit of everybody. He had several

Soul on Fire

side hustles some she was too embarrassed to know about. Not too surprised about that because most barber shops and salons in the ATL were like one stop shops. On any given day you had someone coming in trying to sell knock off purses and perfumes, swearing that they were the real deal. One woman had the nerve to tell Dana that she could register the Coach bag online if she bought it. Evan had a long list of contacts. Dana couldn't really decipher which was business, pleasure or both. Right now she wasn't too concerned with that because they were both single which gave them a right to do what they wanted and besides she was his lady tonight. This was a true contradiction to her pledge to stop settling for whatever she could get, yet another issue for Dr. Mitchell to help her resolve.

Maxwell had just finished an acappella rendition of his classic song "This Woman's Work" before intermission. Dana excused herself to the ladies room for a makeup and freshness check. The restroom was crowded so she waited by the bar for a few for it to clear out. "I know my damn eyes ain't playing tricks on me," she muttered calmly under her breath. By that time it looked as though the Boyds had ran right upon her, Ms. So damn beautiful she could be a supermodel Boyd and Mr. Please baby, baby help me save my marriage but I do love you Boyd.

Dana jumped into defense mode instantly. She couldn't forget that face even through a bout of amnesia. She had hired a detective to take pictures of Dana and probably looked at her daily. Either way she knew she hadn't forgotten. Who would when it comes down to your man or woman cheating on you? And like most women, we are so ready to jump in the other woman's ass instead of the man. All kind of thoughts were running through her mind as usual. She did not want to start a scene especially with Evan being there. What the hell would he think of her if he found out she was knowingly messing around with a married man? Shit, who cares? She faltered with making her next move.

Dana stepped out away from the bar to make her way to the restroom. Evan was then walking towards her. Putting up one finger, she signaled she was on her way. Just at that moment she turned and bumped into Mrs. Boyd. Actually she was standing in her path.

"He didn't do too badly. I wanted to tell you that at the office. It is truly even more devastating when a man leaves or fucks around on his wife for shit. You haven't done too bad for yourself, Ms. No kids, entrepreneur, nice little portfolio!"

Dana's mouth dropped.

Skyy Banks

"Don't look too surprised sweetheart. I am the good doctor's wife and have access to a many things."

"Baby let's not do this now." 'Dre pleaded.

Baby? Baby? This nigga got some nerve. The sound of his voice infuriated Dana.

"Why not? Lets! We do have unfinished business, the two of us."

'Dre was pulling at her arm with a firmer grip and now Evan was touching Dana's arm.

"Everything okay?"

"Yeah just ran into some old friends."

"Yes indeed!" Mrs. Boyd smirked.

"Evan this is Dre and...." Dana didn't even know the bitch's first name.

"Sambria." She responded while extending her hand.

"Aight! Nice to meet you guys. Mommy the show is starting again. You ready?"

"Yes, just finishing up."

"Not quite, but WE WILL FINISH!" Sambria winked as she turned away.

Dana didn't know if she should be embarrassed because of her young buck or puff her chest up and hold her head up high. She felt strong. She not only maintained her composure but also showed 'Dre that life does go on. The hurt that she felt didn't dominate any other feelings she wanted to show.

"You alright?" Evan asked again.

"Yep sweetie. Will you grab me a martini with a double shot of vodka while I take my behind to the ladies room for real this time?"

"For sho!"

Soul on Fire

∅

Chelle and Russell

Champs-Élysées, the Eiffel Tower, the Louvre, and the Opera and where all places they had visited in the short time they had been in Paris. Lorraine, Alsace, quail, and squab were just a few of the exquisite dishes that they had fallen in love with. It was true that the weather, which seemed to never rise above 65 degrees, and the architect of the towering buildings, which waned between ancient and classic, were just as breathtaking as seen in the movies. Russell lavished Chelle with gifts daily, many of which she didn't know the purpose or could pronounce the name. If her eyes appeared to marvel at anything she saw it was hers.

"You're going to have to quit this Russell. We have so many things already that we are going to have to ship the majority back to the states."

"That's not a problem. Nothing is too much for my Queen."

"I know, but....."

"But what Chelle?"

"Nothing baby. Whatever you want!" Chelle responded with an awkward smile.

She had so much nervous energy. One of the happiest events in her life was taking place *right* now and she could not share it with her best friend. She wanted so badly to talk to her before she left. Chelle had a way of being over the top with surprises. Paris was the perfect place to tell Russell he was going to be a daddy. The overwhelming feeling of impending motherhood was countered with a little hostility towards Russell. She knew that he loved her but needed concrete reassurance. Chelle needed it on paper more now than ever. They have had a good thing for a long time and the issue never had to be pressed. It was inevitable, after all, they were now cohabitating, something she said she would never do.

"Are you excited about meeting the manufacturer tomorrow? As elegant as this city is I'm sure you will be able to find some beautiful fabric as well as sell the design of your new bags."

That's one thing that she really admired about Russell. He was interested in her and wanted her to prosper as he has done over his

Skyy Banks

years as being an investment banker. If Chelle needed to know more about the financing or marketing side all the tools were available through Russell. Not knowing was not an option as a final answer. He found the answer. With the start up of her own fashion house, Dana would be or was the accountant of choice. She missed her friend and worried about her situation at the same time.

"With my level of talent...fabric from Paris or not...I'm still gonna make it do what it do!" Chelle responded with so much arrogance that Zack Posen would have to take a bow.

"We've only been here a week and my baby already bourgeois!"

"You know I'm kidding. I am ecstatic baby!"

"That's what I like to hear."

They had now made it to a little village outside of the central business district. The streets were narrow and were cobblestone instead of paved with cement, which made it even more beautiful. They stepped inside an establishment that was a winery, restaurant, and art gallery all in one. The walls and ceilings were covered with cherubs, flowers, and brilliant colors.

"Reservation pour Grayson."

"Oui monsieur Grayson, Je me souviens de vous d'hier."

Speechless, Chelle grinned. She knew Russell was educated and seasoned but unaware he spoke French... fluently.

"Cette voie."

"Merci."

Before they were seated, Chelle squealed in sheer excitement. "Oh baby! This place is immaculate. Just beautiful! How did you? When did you find this place?"

"Just enjoy the moment baby." Russell halted the questions.

"I didn't know you spoke French."

"German and Spanish as well."

"The learning never stops."

The hostess served red wine. Chelle declined and asked for water and lemon instead.

"What's wrong?" This was a red flag she wasn't quite ready to raise. She was not quite ready to tell Russell about the baby. It had to be a special moment.

"Nothing, I just have a lot to prepare for tomorrow and you know how wine does me?"

"One glass?"

Soul on Fire

"No baby, maybe tomorrow."

"If you insist."

Russell gave up without a fight and sent the wine back and ordered a glass of water as well. Shortly afterwards appetizers arrived. Not until then had Chelle, realized they had the place to themselves and that Russell had already planned this. She began to get a nervous feeling in the pit of her stomach. This was the perfect scene for something amazing to happen, something that could be life changing. They sat quietly and gazed into each other's eyes. She was too anxious and afraid to say anything. The second course was now being served. The lights had been totally dimmed with just a glimmer remaining on them. Jazz was playing in the background. Jazz? He had brought his own music as well. This man had more than momentarily swept her off her feet. My Cherie Amore was the next song she heard. Russell extended his hand towards Chelle and stood. She stood but her legs felt like jelly. Russell pulled her close to him and they danced. He squeezed her tightly.

"Chelle, you have brought me so much joy. Just when an old man had given up on love, you reassured me that it still exists. Do you remember when you told me that age was just a state of mind and that you were mature enough to handle this May-December love?"

"Yes." She whispered. His tone had further confirmed what she had expected.

"Baby, I love you. I truly do. And I have known for a long time that you were my wife."

The tears began to roll down her face and her body trembled against him. Russell dropped to one knee. "With the blessing of your parents and Dana, will you be my queen, my wife, my everything?

"Yes, daddy!" Chelle moved his hand to her stomach. "Yes, daddy!" He hugged her waist and buried his face in her stomach and not only cried but sobbed. Chelle ran her fingers through his curly locks. "Today is a day that will be just as memorable as the day of our wedding and the birth of *our* first child."

Skyy Banks

∅

Dana's morning was off to a slow start. She had spent the night at Evan's after the concert. He made fun of the fact that she kept a booty bag in the trunk. A booty bag was for those unexpected overnight visits consisting of the basic toiletries, panties, and an outfit for the next day. No need for PJs because they wouldn't be on for long if you were really having one of *those* overnight visits. She lay in the bed for as long as she could. It didn't help that Evan had a way of snuggling right under her. That snuggling was like a remote control. It turned her on. She moved her hips in closer to him so she could feel his manhood against her behind. It grew and that made her move more. Evan was soon after inside of her. The bed rocked from side to side as she gripped the sheets. The alarm clock sounded as they both reached their peak. Dana had impeccable timing when it came to the morning sex. She always seemed to wake up and get enough before it was time to really get up. He lay inside of her for a few more minutes, kissed her shoulders, and stroked her hips. She considered the possibility of seriously dating him.

"Good morning girl! Alexia bumped her out of that state of bliss that morning sex gave you with her burst of energy. "I can't thank you enough for the Maxwell tickets. He made me fall in love all over again."

"Didn't you just tell me you were single? So who are you falling in love with all over again?"

"Me, myself, and I"

"You crazy girl, but I feel you totally. It's not enough of that going around."

"By the way, you had a message from one of your clients. Simeon something... anyways I called him back and squeezed him into a spot right after lunch. He said it was urgent."

Dana didn't want to cause a scene. Alexia was oblivious to what had taken place between the two of them, so she rolled with the punches. Maybe she would call and cancel. This one hit her deep in the gut. "That's fine, and I'm delighted you enjoyed yourself. Hold all calls." Glancing at her watch, "Looks like I will be right on schedule."

"No problem Dana, just doing my job. And oh yeah! I stopped by Teavana in Lenox and picked you up something. It's brewing now. I'm sure you'll like it!"

"Thanks again!"

Soul on Fire

The aroma from the tea was sensuous. The can read Jasmine Dragon Phoenix Pearls, a tea that was for rest and relaxation. Calming and soothing was what the label read. Dana could believe that. This has been a true affect of teas since ancient Chinese time. She had a session at the end of the week with Dr.'s Mitchell and Hogue. Her journal had not been touched since the last session. She had a lot of catching up to do. While she waited on her first client she pulled Mya's journal from the desk and began reading. The more she read the more conscious she became of the troubled life her sister had.

The title of the poem Mya used in this entry was *The Dynamic Black Woman*. Dana knew that it was chopped up to fit how she was feeling. She took only what she needed from the poem to meet her where she was within that particular moment in time.

While struggling with the reality of being a human instead of a myth, the strong black woman passed away. Medical sources say she died of natural causes, but those who knew her knew she died from being silent when she should have been screaming, smiling when she should have been raging, from being sick and not wanting anyone to know because her pain might inconvenience them.

Dana sat upright in the chair, back straight as a board, reading those few powerful lines over and over again. Could she be that black woman who has passed? Dana became literally afraid to read what was scrawled over the next few pages.

I am a dead woman walking. My spirit is broken. I don't believe that people can wrap their minds around the fact that some of their actions could damage a person beyond repair. Who will listen? The constant scrubbing of my skin does not erase the filth that covers my body. I'm not sure how much more I can take? The embarrassment I feel and the dark cloud that could loom over my family won't let me speak against something that I have been taught since a little girl is wrong. Good touch...Bad touch...

Momentarily, Dana traded places with Mya. She knew just as the same blood that ran through Mya's veins ran through hers as well as all she had felt and thought. It hurt deeply. The thing that tortured her so was that she hadn't named names. Did the same person or people that misused and abused her do the same to me? A part of Dana didn't want to know, but her knowing would somehow affect her healing.

Skyy Banks

Simeon was a near memory. She still couldn't fathom that a brother that was so fine, professional, and seemingly mature ran game on her. That old saying "game recognizes game" was some bullshit, or at least for her because she had slipped a couple of times with the same kind of shyster ass Negroes. Lunch had come and gone. Her nerves were in overdrive. He was fifteen minutes early and she made him wait those fifteen minutes and then some.

"Dana." His voice was somber as he reached out to embrace her. She pushed him away and extended her hand.

"Simeon." she nodded. "What kind of nonsense are you bringing to me this time?"

"You have every right to be mad. Our encounter was yes for me to get close to you, but I never expected things to move that fast or get that serious."

"What did you expect with all the charm and romance?"

"Again you have every right to be mad but please allow me to speak my peace and then you decide if you want to deal with me."

"Shoot."

"Well, I am a business owner. I am a private investigator in the financial field, working to stop fraud, embezzlement, mismanagement of funds and the like. My clients are other business owners with substantial assets. I said all that to say I was hired by one of your clients. This person has been doing a little record keeping of their own and the numbers have been skewed for the last few months. This doesn't mean that it is you because they have another financial services company they deal with also. Obviously this is a little different than the norm, but with such short notice, I needed to get in and get in fast."

Dana didn't know whether to be mad at her quote unquote client or at Simeon for staking her out, then playing her, fucking her, and what looks like playing her again with the sob I didn't mean no harm story, just doing my job. "Who is the client?"

"Dana, you know that information is privileged."

"Yeah so was my pussy, but you were all in it! Did you tell your client about that?"

Soul on Fire

She could hear the childishness in her voice, going tit for tat with him instead of at least letting him speak his peace as requested and then taking his sorry ass on.

"Just know that I apologize for using you and in hindsight I could have taken a different approach and gotten the same results. My client is very fond of you and is pleased to know that your business ties won't be severed. I know that is probably no lenity to you. We both know honesty and integrity are the premises for all relationships, professional or personal."

Simeon had very valid points and Dana appreciated his honesty, but she could never look at him the same. On the other hand she had to remind herself that no other being can do more than a person allowed them to do. She took the bait, she accepted the date, she let down her guard, and she surrendered to a night of clue, only to lose the game in more ways than one.

"You don't have to say anything. Again I apologize and maybe one day we can start with a clean slate. I think you are a very special person."

"Thank you." Extending her hand as a way of calling a truce, she smiled and opened the door to let him out. She was going to keep him wondering like she was, wondering about everything including her client.

ℒ

"Dana can you stay and help with putting up equipment?"

"Yeah, just need to call home and let my mom know to pick me up a little later."

"You can use the phone in my office."

The heavy breathing on Dana's neck alarmed her. She placed the phone on the receiver and paused before turning around. His hand slid around her waist and rested just below her navel.

"Don't be afraid, baby. I'll be gentle."

He turned her around slowly to face him. The face was now covered with an orange mask. He had taken his shirt off. The muscles twitched in his arm. Her shoulders began to buckle from the weight of his arms pressing on them. Kissing Dana's forehead he made his way to her mouth. She stood stiff and emotionless. There were several attempts to pry her mouth open with his tongue. She didn't budge.

"It's okay. I've been watching you blossom into a beautiful young lady and waiting for the day to show you just that."

He attempted to kiss her again while applying more pressure to her shoulders. The pain forced her to comply. His mouth not only felt dirty but reeked of cigarette smoke. Pulling her shirt over her head, he touched Dana's small breast. From touching them he began to suck on them slowly. She didn't move fearing that her rebellion would lead to his aggression. He continued to suck her breast until they began to throb. He lifted her on the desk and continued to suck. With one hand under her behind he parted her legs with the other.

Struggling to catch her breath, Dana rolled over to the alarm clock. Three o'clock glared on the screen. Resting one hand on her stomach, She could feel it quiver then begin to ache. Looking at the phone, she longed for 'Dre. Even after she told herself it was over, even after she saw that he had no intentions on leaving his wife, even after he practically begged her to cover up their affair, Dana sat foolishly and alone wanting him. He was the nightcap that she had gotten accustomed to, the one that could put her right to sleep. Although her rolodex was indiscriminate and it held a number of people that could meet her various needs at any given time, not just anyone would do. Evan was next on the list.

Soul on Fire

"Yeah." Evan answered the phone with an unsteady voice. After all it was three in the morning.

"Hey." There was dead silence in the phone.

"D? What's wrong Ma-Ma?"

"I was just having trouble sleeping."

"You wanna come through?" This was exactly what she needed to hear.

"I'll be there in a bit." She didn't bother about getting all fixed up. In sweats and a tee she headed to Evan's. His phone rang for what seemed like a hundred times before he answered. The door was opened and Dana let herself in. Snuggling up to him, Evan kissed the back of her neck and she felt at ease immediately. How could she be given such comfort at the touch of a man? This was another question for Dr. Mitchell. Hell, Dana was paying her for having all the answers. Just the feel of Evan's body sent chills through her and she automatically begin to wiggle her hips. The movement of her hips led to his arousal as before. Her back was to him ready for rear entry. Evan stroked her hips and pulled her in closer to him. He nestled his face in between her shoulder blades, pulling her into his senses, the senses of touch and smell. Dana pushed into him and sighed. He then tapped her hip.

"Ma. It doesn't have to be about sex all the time when I'm with you."

His breath grazed the nape of her neck. Dana lay quietly waiting for him to tell her more.

"It's okay. I'm here for you. I want to know Dana and what's going on inside Dana, her head and her heart. Most women don't get up in the middle of the night saying that they can't sleep. Something's wrong and I definitely don't want to be the one to take advantage of you when you are not feeling well. I want you to not *need* me to make love to you but I want you to *want* me to make love to you. And right now I'm feeling like this is one of those need moments. So be easy Ma."

Her heart sank because it hurt. If it had never been true before it was true right now. The truth hurt so badly. Dana cried softly. The tears rolled down her face onto Evan's arm. He turned Dana to her stomach and rubbed her back. She was in admiration that in this short period of time of knowing him, he continued to show himself approved in both action and words. Dana still had a void because she craved him sexually and missed Chelle. Sex and her girl were two constants in her life. She needed both. Chelle had not called and Dana wanted her to go to counseling with her, to be there for her every step of the way. Pride lands a many on their face and she did not want that to happen to her. They were so much alike if either one of them waited on the other to make the first move, that would be the only thing happening...waiting.

Soul on Fire

ℒ

Dana jotted down a quick list of things to discuss with Dr. Mitchell while she sipped tea.

Why am I so needy, insecure, unlike many women who find comfort in food, why do I find mine in men? The park incident!! She wrote, definitely up for discussion. There were really no lines that were too sensitive to cross these days. Dr. Mitchell had seen the most intimate, vulnerable part of her.

Her private line rang. Only a select few had that extension. It was definitely someone of importance.

"Dana baby."

"Hi Mommy."

"I hadn't heard that one in a long time. Are you okay? Lois told me you called her all upset and was going on and on about something."

"I told her..."

"Before you say it, you know she's just worried about you and has a right to be. You more like a daughter to her than a niece. You know there were times I was a little jealous of you two."

"Mommy. There is nothing wrong. Chelle and I had a fight and my secretary quit on me. So I am just having a little blue in my life with a hard time handling it."

"Well you need to get some yellow because brighter days are ahead and a little red because we got nothing but love for you."

They chuckled. Momma was still sharp and quick witted for her age.

"Now Dana don't go getting mad at your Auntie for calling me, she means well. At the same time I'm just a phone call away too. Damien's been asking about you. He says he might be coming to Atlanta on a business trip sometime soon. I'm not gonna hold you too long. You know true friendship lasts a lifetime. Don't go waiting to you get grown and start acting brand new. You and Chelle have been friends too long for that. Nothing could be that bad that you two can't work it out."

"You're right and I'm going to work on it."

"Okay baby. Call me if you need me...anytime..."

"Momma?"

"Yeah baby."

"Where you really jealous of me and Auntie Lois?"

Skyy Banks

"A little bit, but I always knew you were her favorite and as long as you were talking to somebody that would give you strong, solid advice even when you couldn't talk to momma, it was okay."

"I love you."

"Love you too baby. Have a great day at work."

Dana bit her bottom lip hard to keep from crying. The truth of the matter was that she couldn't always tell Aunt Lois everything. She was her rock but she did not have enough confidence in her to tell her she was being hurt. That's where momma had it all wrong. She didn't have anybody to confide in, neither did Mya.

She died from hiding her real feelings until she became embittered and unchangeable, enough to invade her womb and breasts like a cancerous tumor. She died from never being enough of what men wanted, or having too much class, cash, and sass for the men she wanted.

Picking up Mya's journal, she began to scrutinize the words on the page. Dissecting the lines word by word, she asked herself out loud. "Are you dead Dana?" If she believed what the poem was saying she was spiritually dead, her true feelings being bottled for years all the while sharing this same repression that her sister had miles away. "Are you dead Dana?" She asked again more emphatically. Today she could admit that she was not dead but dying, not in the natural sense of the word but she lacked emotion, her love life was stagnant, she was insensitive to other people's needs, the zest for life she once had was almost extinguished. Her feelings mirrored a poem she had read by Edwin Arlington Robinson when she was in high school titled Richard Corey. Richard Corey was a fine man who seemed to have everything according to the townspeople. They often wished they were in his place. One day Mr. Corey went home and put a bullet in his head.

This reminded Dana of the life she was living, a total lie. To the outside world it would appear that she had it all together. No one could have guessed that she slept only three or four hours most nights, that she was not happy unless she was fucking somebody, or that a woman of her "strength" wouldn't demand anything from a man but happily took whatever was thrown her way.

"Dana call on line one. A Mr. Duncan."

"Thanks." Dana had him wait on hold for a few more minutes before she answered.

"Ms. Taylor."

Soul on Fire

"Hi Ms. Taylor this is Carl Duncan. It's been a while since we last spoke. How is everything looking?"

"Good morning Mr. Duncan. It has been a while. I've not had the chance to run reports yet but the next quarter isn't up until next month. So we should know then." She played the game because she knew damn well he wasn't calling about that. Dana saw Carl as well as her other clients on quarters or as needed to have financial disclosures meetings. Maybe this bastard was the one that hired Simeon to set her up. She sure wanted to know.

"I see."

"Okay, thanks and you have a great day."

"Dana?"

"So the business is no longer business. I did hear you call me by my first name."

"Yes. I was truly calling to say that you have been on my mind since I last saw you. I need you. I need to feel you, smell, you, taste you, hold you. Excuse me for being frank but grandmamma use to always say that *a closed mouth don't get fed.*"

Dana laughed to herself on that one and thought you right baby a close mouth sure doesn't get fed thinking back to their encounter and how she gave him a mouthful.

"Carl, I thought we have traveled down this road before?"

"Wwwwe have?" He responded stuttering and questioning what Dana had just told him.

"Yes, lest not forget the prelude to our encounter. I don't have personal relationships with my clients."

"Let's consider this a work-relationship."

"You are a funny and the answer is still no. Have a good one. I have a client waiting." Dana lied. She was going to give him a chance somewhere in the near future for a few reasons. Her main motive outside of money was to find out if he played her. Then she was going to play him, break him, and dismiss him. He was sure to call again. She gave him two or three days.

Skyy Banks

Ø

Dr. Mitchell's office was colder than usual today. Dana sat in the lobby looking over the notes she had made in reference to her erratic behavior. The alarm on her phone beeped reminding her of the scheduled appointment. Touching the screen to cancel the alarm, she started scrolling through her pictures. There were about 30 or more with her and Chelle and just as many of her, Chelle, and Damien. Tears began flowing before her session even started. This was a sure sign that today would be extremely emotional and difficult.

"Dana, why are you crying?" Dr. Mitchell asked with a tone of sincere concern. She chose to forgo hypnosis and just focus on addressing some of the issues that had been brought to light by the hypnosis.

"Where do I begin?"

"Wherever you feel comfortable."

"I don't have a damn clue. All I know is that I am fucked up. I fucked up and I am fucked up. I bumped into the married man and his wife at a concert. He was holding on to her while she chastised me and the bastard didn't say a word. I was pissed off at my best friend because I wanted her to be down with me if I had to kick the good doctor's wife ass. She told me to grow up and I basically told her to go to hell. I-I-I..." Dr. Mitchell stopped her mid sentence.

"That's good. Let's address these issues first. Was your father in your life?"

"Yes. What does that have to do with anything?"

"I am looking at how that relationship could have played a role in your insecurity. Insecurity is not the only factor but it is a factor that leads us to cross the lines of infidelity. You are looking for someone else to fill a void. How was the relationship with you and your father growing up?"

"He was a preacher, a strong faith filled man that loved and supported all of his children. I can remember running to him and asking him most things that I knew my mother would say no about. It was always yes with him. I was his sunshine. He would always say "come give daddy a little sunshine." I would run to him and....."

"And?"

"Nothing much, just crazy childhood memories."

Soul on Fire

"What's so crazy about that?"

"What's so crazy is that, that stuff is gone and we'll never get that back. So what's the use of hoping, wishing, and dreaming?"

"This is where you are wrong. Memories are the things that keep us grounded, keeps that warm spot in our heart glowing, and most importantly shapes us into the people we are to become. Whether good or bad we have control over how they affect us. And dreams what beautiful things, these ideas, emotions, images give us something to build upon and hold on to."

Dana heard Dr. Mitchell but then she didn't hear her. That memory of her, little miss sunshine revealed something about daddy that she had locked so deeply away. "I understand."

"I want you to write in your journal a daily positive devotional to you. We have to recondition the way you think about yourself and the world. It's not going to be roses everyday but I guarantee you that it can be *most* of the time. So now that you have finally met his wife, how do you feel? Are you angry, hurt, bitter?"

"I am more hurt than anything because it wasn't like I didn't know about her. It's like I was living in a fairytale and wanted it to never end. Then the way Andre totally dismissed me as though I never meant more to him than some new pussy."

"Rightfully so to be hurt but is this something that you could have avoided? Is this not a heartache you could have saved yourself from?"

"Yes in hindsight."

"And your friend. That one is a little less complicated. Just pick up the phone and apologize and thank her for the lesson in maturity. I know it was a hard lesson but a good one I do believe."

All she could say was "yes" while fighting back the urge to get an attitude. Dana hated when people told her shit she didn't want to hear but needed to.

"Look at the time. Our hour is almost up."

"I'll pay you for another."

"I agree we do need that time but I am running a tight schedule today. I do however want to touch on some things from the past sessions. It should be fully apparent to you that you are a victim of childhood sexual abuse by several men. Right?"

"Yes", sulking Dana replied. Her throat burned. She resisted anymore tears. Dr. Mitchell delayed speaking to give Dana freedom to cry if she needed. Cry, scream, shout, or just fall out if this was the need. "What now?"

"Now we need to find out who these men are. You never revealed a name but you gave very vivid descriptions about them, body shape, voice tones, things they were wearing including the color of the masks that hid their face. We have transcribed the sessions into manuscripts. Take them home and make notes. We need to find out who they are and then take it from there whether it is prosecution or confrontation or both. Either way we need to do something with the information than just knowing. It is true when they say knowing is *just* half the battle."

Dana took all that she said and put it in reserve memory to digest later. Tucking the papers in the side of her purse, she prayed that her legs would hold her up as she walked to the car. "Lord, I know that all things happen according to your will. Give me a sound mind and body to make it home safely."

Soul on Fire

ℒ

Dana was not in the mood for tea, jazz, or phone calls, but a mood to do something, anything to get her mind off of herself and the events that hit her like a train wreck, leaving her heart mangled. Even though she didn't feel like phone calls, she played her messages back in hopes that there was something going on or someone calling to cater to her nonchalant vibe. The first message was from Alexia wanting to hang out at Sambucas, a restaurant downtown that was known for its live music and great food. That would have been a good idea but she wanted something a little more. Alexia was cool as hell to hang out with. Dana knew if they put both their heads together they would come up with something wild and crazy. The next message was Jay and then Damien. Now that was a thought. Maybe she would hook up with him and let him fuck her brains out. She didn't immediately return his phone call nor did she dismiss the idea.

After a few hours of sleeping, she felt a lot better or at least rested. The manuscript that Dr. Mitchell had given her to look over lay on the night stand. She declined to pick it up trying to avoid anything that would dump negativity into her spirit.

"Hey chick! I got your message. So you tryin' to hang tonight?"

"Finally you call a sista back. You know I missed talking to you at the office today. That Mr. Duncan called you back. All he did was leave a number for you to call him at. So you want to go to the spot?"

"Let's do something a little more up tempo. I don't feel like jazz or blues tonight. I want do some mixin' and minglin'."

"Sounds like my kinda party. I only said Sambuca cause sometimes you get a little bourgeois on a bitch."

"Lexi, you stupid girl! But I'm down for whatever tonight."

"Cool, just get dressed and I'll be through about ten to get ya."

"Let's make it do what it do."

Dana had a couple of hours left before it was time to go, wine and a long soak would do her good. She soaked until the water turned cold, but it was okay. Her mind was in a faraway place.

The door bell buzzed just as she was moisturizing the last leg. Knowing it was Alexia she answered the door in her robe. She held it closed with one hand and opened the door with the other.

Skyy Banks

"What's up girl?" Alexia greeted her as always with that enthusiastic about life tone. Alexia's attractiveness wasn't noticeable until Dana saw her in her nightlife attire.

"Give me a sec. I spent a little extra time soaking in the tub."

"Not a problem." She followed Dana to the bedroom and perched herself at the foot of the bed.

"Damn. Just make yourself right at home. Why don't cha?"

"Thanks."

"Better yet, make yourself useful and grab us something to drink." Pointing towards the bar adjacent to the kitchen Dana directed her. That was her way of getting some privacy without just acting ugly since she acted as though she didn't know.

"Sure."

Hurrying to get dressed, Dana saw Alexia's reflection in the mirror while pulling her panties on. She was standing in the hallway watching. Dana ignored her and continued to get dressed. The black corset always needed two people to fasten. Before she could ask for her help, Alexia was standing in front of her holding a glass of a blue concoction she had made. She sipped and smiled.

"This is good." Smiling, Dana savored the taste of pineapple.

"Secret from a long time ago, watch out though. You know how those sweet drinks sneak up on you."

"You ain't lyin'." They snickered. "Can you assist me with this please?"

"No problem." Alexia pulled the strings from the bottom and worked her way up. She was standing so close Dana could feel her breathing. She stepped forward a little. As she made her way to the middle of her back Alexia reached around and cupped her breast.

"What the hell you doin?"

"Trying to lift you so you can sit upright in this thing."

"Well damn, a little warning or perhaps just asking would do just fine."

"Excuse me. Will you hold up your tits so I can finish lacing you up?"

"That's better." Dana responded a little confused. She had already peeped how she was watching her from the hall. Even though she was caught off guard, she kinda liked the touch. Dismissing the thought she pulled her jeans on and finished the drink.

"One more for the road?" Dana lifted an empty glass to Alexia.

Soul on Fire

"Let's do this instead. Alexia emerged from the kitchen with two jell-o shots."

"Ummm uumm good."

"Yeah I know."

Alexia decided to take her to a spot called Taboo, a bistro and bar with live entertainment. Sitting in the driveway they watched men file in the club. The whole atmosphere around spoke of distinction, class, and swag, just where Dana wanted to be. They valet parked and made their grand entrance. Her goal was to always stun the crowd. She seemed to hold up well in public settings regardless of what was going on.

They danced a few songs and found their way to the bar. There was much more action at the bar than having a private table. Hopefuls would be bold enough to come by and spark conversation or perhaps use a more discreet approach and send the bartender with another round of whatever they were drinking. These men were called hopeful because they often hoped that after some polite conversation and a few drinks that the rest of the night was theirs. Never trust a big butt and a smile was the motto she had recently adopted after being fucked over too many times.

"Damn I have never seen a woman get as many free drinks as you two."

"Oh really?" Dana flirted back at the bartender. His rich, Jamaican accent turned her on.

"Yeah sweetheart. What's your name?"

"What's yours?"

"You can't answer a question with a question."

"Who says?"

"Oral says."

"So your name is Oral?"

"You're pretty sharp."

"I've been accused."

This went on for a little while. The libations she had thus far had her thinking all kinds of scandalous thoughts, one being how she could get her hands tangled in those brother locks while his face was buried between her thighs.

"So whatcha doin' after you leave this place?"

That Jamaican drawl just drove her insane.

"I might be doing you." It sounded like a classic good girl gone bad line. Her many nights of club hopping and flirting never led to a one night stand. That was something she said she would never do. The good girl image that most women hid behind to allude to the fact that we were closet freaks would not be tarnished by a one nighter.

"Feisty too huh?"

"A little."

"We will see."

"No you ain't girl. I can't let you go out like that." Dana couldn't tell if Alexia was in her best interest or if she was just interested in her. All and all she was right because she had a few pieces on call and most of them were damn good.

"Hell, I'm just having a good time. No worries mon." They danced a little while longer. Dana was too drunk to drink anymore. That was the weird thing about her, she could be almost to the brink of passing out but was still aware of what was going on, unsteady on her feet but able to make pretty decent choices.

The taxi ride home found her and Alexia practically wrapped up with each other. She rubbed Dana's back as she lay across her lap. Dana began to rub her legs. She smelled so good. The taxi pulled up to the driveway. They sat on the steps for about twenty minutes while Dana looked for the house keys. That was one of the disadvantages of having a suitcase for a purse. So much shit could be found and lost in it at the same time. Dana's body fell at the first convenient spot. That spot was the living room sofa.

"Please give me hand with these straps." She pointed at her shoes.

"Hell I'm just as out of it as you. But I'll be more than happy to oblige."

Dana raised one foot and held her thigh up with both hands. Alexia had finally undone both shoes. She kneaded the soles of her feet with her fist. Dana swore the people at Solace did not have anything on Alexia. The sounds of her moaning filled the room. It was just that good. The more she moaned, the harder she squeezed. She found her way under her jeans to massage her calf muscles.

"You know I could do this better if you take your pants off?"

Dana followed through. Alexia excused herself to the bathroom and came back naked with massage oil in her hand. She had a beautiful, curvaceous body, void of stretch marks or dimples. The lights were dim as Dana watched her every move.

Soul on Fire

"Lay down on your stomach and get comfortable." Alexia asked in a commanding but soft way if there was such a thing for both of those emotions to be exhibited at the same time. She started at her feet, again to the calf muscles, and then to her ass. The stroking turned into biting. Dana was trippin' because she knew she wasn't attracted to women, but she couldn't or didn't want to resist what was going on. She nudged her to indicate she wanted her to turn to her back. Dana turned to her back. Her nipples were taut. Alexia teased them with her tongue and made a trail of kisses to her navel. Finding Dana's thighs, she bit and sucked a little harder than before. Dana could feel her own juices escaping. Alexia spread her legs more with her elbows and found her way to that spot. Dana shuttered with delight and grabbed her head, guiding it a little deeper.

The morning greeted Dana lying on the sofa covered with a blanket. There was no Alexia. Her body ached as she sat up. Her thighs were covered with passion marks, something no man had ever done. Replaying the night's events over and over, Alexia could never replace what she yearned for *all* the time, a man.

Skyy Banks

⌀

With a long day ahead of her, Dana mentally prepared herself for what was to come. Her number one priority was to read through the transcript of her therapy sessions and do exactly what Dr. Mitchell had suggested. She was to piece together the details to find the perpetrator. Although the paper was illuminated by the light from the table lamp, a dark shadow was cast over it. She sat in bed very reluctant to unmask the unknown. It hurt so much to remember, but it hurt even more to keep it tucked away and allow the feelings of inferiority, insecurity, hopelessness, and finding comfort in anything that had a sexual connotation control her very existence.

Initially she skimmed through the pages in disbelief of not only her actions/reactions but in utter terror at what she had gone through in such a short time period. She was just a little girl. Every development stage in her life was marred by abuse. Laying the pages across her lap, she randomly pulled pages out, read, and made notes, diamond ring, musty scents, tones, familiar phrases, teeth, gnarled hands, dry hands, rough hands, cigarette breath...the list was endless. Afterwards she made a list of all the men that she had known growing up. There was her daddy of course, Jay, Uncle Willie, really good family friends like Uncle Harry, a few cousins, and her athletic coaches. The name was followed by all the things she could remember about them. Uncle Willie was at the forefront of her mind. He smoked, had rough hands and his chair was a reoccurring image in her dreams. Dana thought back to when she was there for Mya's funeral and how frantic she was after being in the chair. The chair was evil and had been the comfort spot for evil. The diamond ring was flashy. She could remember the way the light hit the diamonds and bounced off of her eyes. The man who wore that ring made sure everyone saw it because he had a way of sticking out his pinky finger when talking. He sipped from a coffee cup with his pinky out. This man was Uncle Harry. Most people called him Reverend Harry. He was a pimp in his own right, self proclaimed preacher, talked fast and slick and always had a joke to tell. The only person that laughed at his jokes was him. Cigarette breath and rough hands? It wasn't too hard to figure out who this was. She had stared at the ugly, stained teeth a thousand times over. The hands that often rested on her shoulders after a game felt much differently on her bare thighs. They were rough as sandpaper. The

Soul on Fire

breath was atrocious. His skin and clothes reeked of cigarette smoke. Coach Gilliam's violation had pushed her into a deep place within herself. Dana believed this was the point where her alter ego emerged. This person didn't have a name but she was different than Dana. She was wreckless and ruthless. She sat on the edge of the bed trying to make sense of all she had concluded. How could it be that the men that mattered in her life, who had a hand in shaping her, cheering her on when she was about to give up and drying her tears when she hurt, devastate her life in such a way?

The task that was yet to be done was to reveal the faces behind the masks. The red was Uncle Willie, the blue was Uncle Harry, and the green belonged to Coach Gilliam. There were masks and men remaining. She was too overwhelmed physically and emotionally to concern herself with more. There was much more work to be done, but Dana had reached a point where she didn't want to know anymore. She now knew something and that was just half the battle as Dr. Mitchell said.

The phone rang. Dana let the answering machine pick it up.

"D." She immediately knew the voice on the other end.

"This is Damien. I'm going to be in Atlanta on some business in a few days and was wondering....well I have been thinking about you a lot since I last saw you...."

There was a pause after that. She only had a few seconds left before the recording time would expire and the call disconnected.

"I got your number from Auntie Lois. I guess we were too caught up in the moment to think past that... it was good seeing you again...."

Jumping from the bed, she picked up the phone just as he was hanging up. The click and then silence in the line compounded the pain she was feeling.

"Hey daddy." This had started to be her pet name for Evan and he was sure to follow with Mami.

"Yo, what's good? What's going on?"

"Nothing much."

"You always say that. Something's got to be going on."

"This is the weekend. What you got planned?"

"I had a helluva night last night so right now I am just trying to recoup."

"Get it girl, I didn't know you get down like that."

"A little something like that."

"I was just calling to see what you were into."

Skyy Banks

"Grindin' baby girl. I'll call you later. Aight?"

"Ok."

"Yep!"

Dana was falling for him hard in the little time that they had spent together. For him to not only remember that she was interested in a piece of artwork and to buy it was icing on the cake.

The phone rang again. She waited to see who the caller was before answering. "Dana? I know your ass at home and you probably just sitting around for whatever reason. This Alexia...as though you didn't already know. Just wanted to say that I had fun last night and I can't wait until next time. Call me back or I'll be all up over there like Rambo on your ass. For real...Call me...smooches."

That was the same way she and Chelle ended their calls to each other. Dana though about calling her, she needed to with all the shit that was going on in her life.

Soul on Fire

∅

The weekend had come and gone and Dana was a tad disenchanted by the occurrences of the weekend and even more so thrown for a loop by Alexia's call. She didn't mention the sexual encounter that happened the night before but there was a subliminal message to her saying that she *couldn't wait until next time.* If she said anything Dana would definitely have to check her. There was no ambiguity to her sexual identity. She loved men, always have and always would, maybe a little too much.

"Good morning Dana."

"Hi Alexia, how is everything this morning?" The energy in the room was crazy. Dana was on edge and was sure she could sense it.

"I have tea brewing, here are the messages from Friday and I put the files on your desk."

"Thanks."

"Sure."

The atmosphere was so thick that you could cut it with a knife as her momma use to say. Dana pushed that to the back of her mind and tried to focus on work. Her first appointment wasn't until afternoon. This would give her time to hopefully get into a better disposition. The last thing she wanted was to lose clients by allowing her personal life to spill over into the business.

"Dr. Mitchell's."

"Yes, this is Dana Taylor is Dr. Mitchell available?"

"She's in session."

"I can take your number and she'll return your call by the end of the day or would you like her voicemail?"

"Voicemail please. Hi Dr.Mitchell. Dana Taylor. Just wanted to let you know that I have identified some of the men who abused me. What's the next step and I need to change the dosage on the prescription. I need something a little stronger. Talk to you later."

Four out of five messages on Friday were from Carl Duncan, this was the move Dana had been waiting for. She would give him another week before she responded. Carl had definitely met his match, he had already underestimated her to fall for entrapment with someone as fine as Simeon.

"Knock, Knock."

"Yes Alexia."

"Here's your tea. What's up with you today? You PMSin?"

"I'm good. Why do say that?"

"I don't know. I'm use to folks calling me back and then...."

"I'm listening."

"You came in here with that strictly professional attitude and it's just us. So you tell me what's up?"

"Girl, stop taking shit personal. I've just had a rough weekend and right now being at work is the last place I want to be."

"Ok, here's your tea."

"Give me a minute." Dana was relieved that the discussion hadn't turned into talking about what happened. The office phone ringing was the interruption she needed just in case the conversation was headed in that direction.

"Call on line one. It's a Mrs. Boyd."

"Put her through." Dana took a deep breath and shook her head. Damn. How much more? She thought. How much more bullshit am I going to be subjected to? What if I just ignored the call? The questions were semi valid and she knew the answers to both. She put herself in the predicament. This was a bed she made and ignoring the problem wouldn't make it go away.

"Ms. Taylor."

"This is Mrs. Boyd and I was wondering if we could meet over lunch and talk."

"About?" The defensive side of her was emerging."

"I do believe since you have devastated my marriage that you owe me that much."

"That's where you are mistaken. Andre owes you."

"You know, I'm not going to do the back and forth thing with you. Either you will or you won't."

Sighing, Dana responded. "I can't meet today but call the office this afternoon or in the morning and my secretary will let you know the time and place."

"I will."

They hung up the phone simultaneously. Her head hurt so bad that all she could do was lie on the desk and take slow deep breaths. She willed herself not to cry, not today.

Soul on Fire

ℒ

The night was a long one. Dana took a "sleep aid" and rested throughout. She was very apprehensive about the meeting with Mrs. Boyd. It still bothered her that she knew so much about her and she didn't even know her first name until the meeting at the park. Dana left directions for Alexia for when Sambria called, to schedule a late lunch, 2 o'clock to be exact and that she didn't want anything larger than a small coffee spot. This would avoid upsetting her stomach any more by eating anything other than a cob salad or deli sandwich. Afterwards, she could go home digest what they talked about and hopefully relax.

The scenic ride to work cleared her mind. The downside to the medicine Dr. Mitchell prescribed was that it caused her to be on edge and fidgety the next day. Dana's cell phone rang as she pulled around to the back of the office. This parking arrangement worked very well for her, it prevented others from randomly stopping in just because they saw her car.

"Good morning Dana. How are you feeling sweetheart?" Dr. Mitchell asked with concern.

"I really don't know. I just feel...."

"Feel what?"

"Detached."

"That's natural. This is what we call shock and disbelief. What we have ascertained is that you were traumatized as a child through sexual abuse by the misconduct of people who were charged with caring for you and guiding you. You have been carrying this weight around for a long time. You will go through many stages before you come to terms with what has happened. Coming to terms is not the same as accepting, but it does mean things will be more bearable."

"That does make sense. What do I do now that I know some of the abusers?"

"You have to decide whether or not you want to confront them. Often times when things happen years before, the perpetrator will also prohibit those things from surfacing or being remembered, especially if no one is around to continually abuse. I believe in making people accountable for their actions, if nothing more than acknowledging and apologizing. I know that is little commiseration for you and that you probably at this point are feeling like causing great harm to those individuals. But confrontation is a very viable option. Of course we will continue to work through the counseling process in an effort to make you whole. What are you thinking?"

"I'm not sure. Everything is just too much right now. I will let you know."

"In the meantime, do you need to come in for a session?"

"I'm sure I do if not more than just to vent. Dr. Boyd's wife called and wants to meet. I agreed."

"I really want you to be careful about putting yourself in stressful situations right now. I don't want to alarm you but too much in a short period of time....for a lack of a better phrase... is a disaster waiting to happen."

"Dr. Mitchell, I agree, but also feel like this is something I need to do, if not for anybody else, but Mrs. Boyd. She needs closure and in a strange way so do I."

"Be careful, Dana and don't hesitate to call me if you need me."

"Thank you for everything."

Sitting in the car, Dana tried to make sense of everything, even the comments that she made to Dr. Mitchell about Mrs. Boyd. Dana couldn't will herself to believe that she owed her anything, even if she wanted to. The dark side of her wanted to dismiss the Mrs. and save all the explaining and apologizing for the good Dr., in which he probably spent the last month or so doing. Her life had turned into a smorgasbord of nothings. Tapping on the driver's side window, Alexia broke the silence and the hodgepodge of thoughts.

"Hey lady. I saw you pull around to the back. After an hour passed I thought I'd come out and check on you. I thought somebody had come and carjacked you or something."

"Shit! It's been an hour?" Hurling the door open almost knocking Alexia down.

"Slow down, I got you. Your first appointment called and rescheduled. Mrs. Boyd called and I gave her the info and she said she'd see you then. All the files are ready and I picked up a new tea for us to try. By the looks of things you need something to calm your nerves too." She winked and nodded.

"Thanks girl, hold this." Dana grabbed her briefcase and shoved it at her real hard. Alexia was sending cues so Dana thought she'd do the same, a cue that she wasn't playing about that shit either.

Soul on Fire

Ø

Dana made it to the coffee house before Mrs. Boyd which was her very intention. This allowed her enough time to try to figure out her demeanor before they sat down to have *the talk* together. Dana would be able tell if she was coming to fight or have a woman to woman talk just by the briskness in her walk and the look on her face. The coffee house was quiet. The vibrant painted walls covered with beautiful art was refreshing. Hidden beach music played in the background. If she wasn't already calm, hopefully the ambience would have some affect.

At that moment, Mrs. Boyd strolled through the door and looked around briefly before her eyes caught Dana's. Standing up to greet her with and extended hand, Dana looked past her face. Mrs. Boyd noticed the avoidance and shook her hand firmly enough for Dana to look her in the eyes.

"Hi Dana."

"Hello Mrs. Boyd."

"Call me Sambria. I think we have shared enough intimate moments to be on a first named basis now." She smirked.

Dana refused to let her get her out of the box into a defensive, rolling her neck, smacking her lips kind of mode. "I agree, Sambria. Now that we are here, where do we start or what do you want to know? Your idea, your call."

"First of all I want to say that I don't blame you wholly, but I do hold you responsible to a certain degree. Andre's commitment and vow was to me but you knew he had that vow and still purposely disregarded that for your own selfish pleasures. You know Andre and I have dated since college. I believed I was the model wife and did everything to make sure he was happy, from keeping up appearances to being a good mother, friend, and lover. Not just his one thing, but his everything."

Sambria paused and her bottom lip shook. She bit down on it to stop from crying, fighting back the tears that welled up in the corner of her eyes. Dana looked away, hurt, angry, and bitter. She sympathized with her. Understanding how much she loved her husband.... Because she loved him too.

"I am not sure what you want from me. I think it would be unfair to both of us to rehash events and details on the times Andre and I were together. I can't lie to you, Sambria. I knew he was married. I knew from day one, and made the choice to get involved. He is a good man, I know. I am sure he did almost everything in his power to keep this from you. I actually broke it off, shortly before you found out."

"All I really want to know is why?"

"That's a question I can't answer. Be honest with yourself Sambria, whatever I say isn't going to change the fact that it happened nor will anything I say ease the pain that we, Andre and I, have caused. Again, I apologize and I wish you the best."

"Wish me the best?" Sambria's eyes went from tame to wild. "Wish me the best? How can you fuckin' wish me the best when you have crossed the line?"

Dana looked around to see if anyone was watching and sure enough all eyes were on them. "You know what? This conversation is over. I don't know how I convinced myself to take time out of my schedule to rectify a situation that needs to be rectified by someone else."

"You owe me too!" Sambria yelled.

Dana pushed the chair out to stand. Sambria came across her face with an open right hand. Dana's mouth flew open and she paused for a minute. She had too much at stake to risk getting an assault charge because she knew the impending *nati ass whipping* she was about to give would have landed her ass under the jail. Standing up slowly, Sambria took a step back. The sudden anger had evolved into fear. She didn't know which way Dana was coming. She stepped directly in front of her, so close that Sambria could smell her breath.

"Bitch, if it wasn't for me just loving me and my freedom. I would beat your ass so bad that your kids wouldn't be able to recognize you. This is the end of the fuckin' conversation like I said and if you have any more questions, I am telling you, not asking you.... Call your damn husband. Lose my number and forget my work address because if I hear from your ass again you're gonna wish I did more than fuck the shit out of your husband."

Speaking confident and cruelly, Dana added insult to injury. "How does my pussy taste?" Sambria knew exactly what she meant. Dana left her standing, holding her breath. She walked out heated and face still stinging.

Soul on Fire

ℒ

Dr. Mitchell was right about staying away from stressful situations. Dana was boiling. Sitting in her car, she grabbed the steering wheel so tight that her knuckles hurt. This wasn't the first time, but she knew that pain would take her mind off of the issues at hand. Dana called Evan to see if she could drop by. He had become the Dr. Feel good that 'Dre used to be. When the reality of what had transpired hit her, she couldn't help but feel both ashamed and disappointed. She was disappointed that she had let her emotions get the best of her which immediately relegated her into the category of a typical angry, black woman.

"Hey big head."

"What's good?" Dana hadn't gotten use to the way he spoke. She was more accustomed to men speaking to her in complete sentences. Asking her how she was doing just sounded better than *the what's good* lingo. She knew they were one in the same, however perceived differently.

"My day has been ridiculously crazy. Just wanted to stop by and unwind if you're not busy."

"I'm cutting late, but you can come through when I'm done."

"What time is that?"

"In a couple of hours."

"Call me."

"Yep."

She would rather see him now than later. Maybe it was a good thing, giving her time to calm down. Her indicator light was flashing on the answering machine. Pressing the play button, she kicked off her shoes and headed to the kitchen for a glass of Moscato or two.

"D. This is Damien. I'm not sure what's going. I thought we were cool when you left. I'm coming to Atlanta and I really want to see you. Either way, I want to hear from you even if you don't want to see me."

"Dana. I just wanted to know if things were okay.....between us. Call your favorite executive assistant." That Alexia was a trip. Dana shook her head and grinned. This was her first smile all day.

Admiring the picture Evan bought, she sipped wine and thought of him. It was a lovely piece of art. Did she hold the key to her happiness or did she allow men to hold the key? These were the kind of questions that she asked herself every time she looked at the picture while trying to find the little girl that was lost years ago. Wine had a way of putting her in a place where she didn't worry, a good place. She showered and lie on the bed waiting for Evan to call.

Soul on Fire

Chelle and Russell

"Breakfast in bed? What did I do to deserve this?"

"Made me the happiest man on earth. Who loves you baby?"

"You, Russell Grayson." Chelle smiled half heartedly.

"What's wrong sugarplum?" Russell was never short on showing his love for her. She believed in actions speaking louder than words and he reassured her time and time again that this was real. Chelle couldn't wait to be Mrs. Michelle Grayson.

"Just thinking."

"A penny for..."

"I know...my thoughts."

"I'm listening." This was another attractive trait of Russell's. He was a great communicator.

"Russell, I'm just sad about Dana. You know we have disagreed many times in the past but never to the extent that we were angry at each for this length of time. Well, I am not angry, just hurt that she reacted that way. Gone are the days when I act a fool with her when she's in the wrong." This was her way of validating that she had done nothing wrong.

"Baby, I do understand. But have you not expressed that Dana was having a difficult time. She's also grieving the loss of her sister. So be patient with her. You two have so much history and I know you know her better than to maliciously do something to hurt you or jeopardize your friendship. Will you do something for me?"

"Yes daddy?"

"Call her. You be the bigger person. You have a wedding to plan and I know you want her there every step of the way."

"I do."

"That's my girl." He smiled, kissing her on the forehead.

Skyy Banks

ℒ

"It's me." Dana yelled into the call box at Evan's.

He didn't respond but opened the gate. She spent a few minutes in the car prepping in the mirror. The wine had her feeling good. She wasn't in the mood for much talk, yet wanted to be in a place where she wasn't alone.

"Hey mommi. You look good."

"Thanks." Mumbling while following him upstairs.

Evan was tying up loose ends and getting ready for the next day so she made herself comfortable on the sofa.

"Give me a sec. Do you want anything to drink? A blanket? Or you can get in the bed and wait for me."

"I'll have some water and the bed sounds like a good idea."

Not long after, Evan slide in the bed beside her. His body was warm against hers and she snuggled in under him. Why couldn't she have this all the time? Lately she felt like she walked around with a magnet on her forehead that said she was taking applications for a man, any man. It seemed as though to get the ideal man she would have to take four different ones and try to package in one, financially, spiritually, and emotionally stable. Not forgetting the cake topper, banging in bed.

He kissed her on the back of her neck. She rolled over to her stomach. His hand massaged her lower back and she was comforted. Evan drew all the negative energy from her body with a simple touch yet she wasn't a person that was big on karma or astrology, signs or energies. This was so evident in her past behavior. If she believed in karma her future outlook for love was doomed. The other two, signs and energies seem to make a little more sense to her now, especially with the dream book. If she didn't feel the immediate release of tension from that one touch, she wouldn't believe that energy thing either.

Dana continued to struggle with her flesh and her emotions. Her body suspired sexual intimacy with Evan. He was sure to remind her that it wasn't about sex and that every time they were together, it wasn't going down like that. Tonight had to be different. His hand moved to the small of her back, gently massaging her inner and outer thighs. She was going to let him have control and ignore the urge to pull her panties off and straddle him for as long as her legs could hold up. In a reverse move, Evan straddled her from behind. Pulling his shirt over his head, he

Soul on Fire

concurrently planted kisses on her back. Her panties soon followed his discarded shirt. Soon after, Evan buried himself deep inside of her. Dana gave him as much as he was giving her, slow and rhythmic. She became conscious that he wasn't wearing a condom, she was too far gone to object otherwise. The music had long stopped playing. Her body was weak from multiple orgasms. Evan kept going and going. Too tired to move, he washed her off. For one night, she was going to rest well. It had nothing to do with sex, but a sense of security.

The sunlight peaked through the blinds awakening Dana who was not ready to get out of bed.

"Ma. Today is my off day. Stay with me for a while?"

"I'll see." She would make it happen one way or the other. Sending Alexia a text-message to let her know that she would be in at noon, Dana turned to face Evan.

"A penny for your thoughts?"

"I've heard that one before."

"Okay. I'm listening."

"It's too early." She turned her back to him, pretending to be asleep.

"I'm ready whenever you are."

She was thankful he didn't force the issue. She was also thankful for the day they met on the street. It was a classic right time, right place situation. She just hoped that it wasn't too good to be true.

ℒ

"You got that glow girl! Wonder why someone called in this morning?"

"Alright Alexia! That's what got my other secretary dismissed." Dana winked at her.

"I'm not a secretary. I'm an executive assistant and we betta than that!" She winked back.

Dana knew exactly what she meant. She definitely blurred the line between personal and business. "Okay chica. Hold all calls until after 3."

"Sure thing…. and Dana."

"I like it when you smile."

Dana flashed an even bigger one going into the office. Work was the last thing on her mind. She scribbled all the names of the men who had hurt her as a child in a notepad. Uncle Willie's was first. It was her hit list so to speak. She had resolved in her mind even though she hadn't spoken to Dr. Mitchell that things would not be better if she didn't confront those she could. No explanation could mend this broken soul, but at least they would know that she knew.

Calling her home phone, Dana checked to see if she had any missed calls from the evening before. Sure enough, there were 6 missed calls from Damien. He was in town already without a word from her. She listened attentively and thought about what to say when she returned his call. He had been attempting to reach her for over a week now. Sad to say that the feelings that she thought she would have after seeing him were not there. She had at least hoped to long and want for him just a little while. Too much time had passed and they weren't the same people they use to be. …..at least she wasn't. Dana blew out a long breath and picked up the phone to return Damien's call.

"Hey!" Putting as much enthusiasm into her voice as she could muster.

"Don't hey me. I've been calling you. You could have at least picked up the phone to say you had somebody, stop bugging you, or something. I never pictured you to be as rude as to not return a phone call. That's whack."

"Now, now. Give me a break. It's not even like that."

"Well, what is like?"

Soul on Fire

"Work has had me busy that's all. But you here now I see. Where are you? We can meet after work if you still not too pissed."

"That's cool."

"What are you in town for anyways?"

"I'll tell you over dinner."

"Secrets now?"

"I'd just rather not talk about it over the phone."

"I can respect that."

"You're not going to stand me up are you?"

"Nope. I'll call you in a bit."

"I'll be waiting."

Damn, he had to say that. She really couldn't stand him up. Dana worked quickly all the while thinking about Evan and what he was doing. He could be so passionate at times. The balance to her madness is what he had become.

"Hey chic. Let's grab a cocktail after work?" Alexia peeked her head around the door.

"Sorry ma'am. I have plans." The disappointment on her face was obvious. "Maybe tomorrow?"

"Sure thing."

Dana pulled Mya's journal from the desk. Skimming through the pages, Dana could clearly see how tormented she was. The thing that struck her most was the direction Mya's life was headed. She had been in a steady relationship after she left and had hinted to the fact that she wanted to share these details of her life with her significant other. Maybe that was the beginning of her healing. That was something she was never able to do. The journal was very compelling with the moods changing from one page to the next. Speaking vividly about her pain, she reminded herself that if she continued with "his" acts that "she" could be protected. Who was she? Dana was overwhelmed with sadness and the need to vindicate her life.

"Dana... you still working?"

"What time is it?"

"Time for me to go!" Alexia exclaimed.

"Hell no!" It was already after 5. Dana didn't have a set time to meet Damien, but he would be expecting her about this time. She would have to go in what she had on. It wasn't going to be too disappointing because she looked good even when she wasn't trying. Or that's how the men around her made her feel even in sweats and tees.

"You okay?"

"Yes, I just lost track of time and have to meet an old friend after work."

Alexia eyes had a question mark in them. "Good friend, huh?"

"Mind ya business. Just mind ya business." Laughing together. "What's good to eat about this time?"

"What do you have in mind?"

"Steak or seafood I guess."

"Why don't you guys go to Benihana?"

"You are good. I like that."

"So we are on for cocktails tomorrow?"

"Sure." Dana replied reluctantly. She was trying her best to not get in another situation with her.

"Cool, get yourself together. You look a little tired. I'll see you in the morning. Do all the things that I would do." Alexia batted her eyes on the way out.

Glancing in the mirror, Dana spoke a few words of confidence to herself and called Damien.

"Heellloooo!"

"Oh, so we are returning calls now?"

"I said I was sorry. Now what you gonna do? Keep harping on it or get something to eat?"

"Both."

"Well we can't do it like that and besides I'm not in the mood for the foolishness."

"Damn girl, you don't have to be so uptight. I'm just tripping with you. I know you are that independent woman trying to make her mark in the A and I ain't mad at ya. You know that's the thing that I admired about you most."

"No, what's that?" I knew exactly what he meant but I just wanted to hear him say that.

"Now you playing....go-getter!"

"Okay you can finish telling me all that good stuff over dinner."

"Where you taking a brother?"

"Benihana."

"Cool. Just tell me how to get there."

"Peachtree St. See you in about an hour."

"Peachtree okay. That tells me a lot. See you then."

Soul on Fire

Evan had ESP or something. He caught her on the way out. Her heart skipped a beat or two. This young thang was having a serious affect on her. She liked it sure enough but dreaded falling into the trap of being needy or diving into him to avoid feeling lonely.

"What's good Ma?"

"Nothing."

"There you go again. I'm gone have to find you something else to say."

Laughing, "I'm off work."

"That's what's up. What are your plans for tonight?"

"I'm headed to dinner with an old friend here from back home." She totally downplayed the fact that this was her high school sweetheart whom she was once engaged, her first love.

"That's what's up. Enjoy yourself. Holla at me later."

She felt some kind of way about that. She wanted him to be nosey and all in her business just to see what kind of reaction she would get if he knew it was another man. They had come to know each other on so many levels. Everything was happening so fast.

Skyy Banks

∅

Benihana was a louder than usual. The mixture of stainless steel cooking utensils clanking against the cast iron hibachi and the jovial spirits of the guests coupled with life, one that was spiraling out of control intensified the sounds. The acoustics in her head were amplified. Dana was annoyed. Surveying the area, she wanted to be sure they sat in a far corner away from the flames and the people. The essence of grilled vegetables, soy, and ginger filled the room. There were couples of all ages enjoying the quaint ambiance of the Japanese steakhouse.

"Dana?" Damien called out to get her attention. The hostess waited to seat them. Dana quickly referenced in her mind all the dates they had gone on over the years and wondered what she'd been missing now that his status had elevated. Besides premium dining and travels to exotic places Dana was sure she missed how groupie after groupie jumped at the chance to sleep with a member of the Bengals or the next best thing, a personal trainer of the Bengals. The bust downs were probably breaking their necks at a chance while throwing panties left and right. As she thought about it more, Dana was glad she was missing it.

The hostess led them to a secluded booth in a far corner that was dimly lit with candles that illuminated a delicate light. The backdrop was a picture of a Geisha or some beautiful woman that had features of such. Red, black, and gold accents adorned almost everything in the room.

"What does this say?" Damien scrawled a few marks across a napkin. He meant it to be Japanese but Dana pretended to not know.

"I thought you were a physical therapist not a doctor?"

"So what you saying? I thought you had super intelligence along with that beauty?"

"So what you saying?"

"I'm just saying...."

"Saying what?"

Dana playfully slapped him on the back of the head. "I read, write, and speak English only."

"You still got jokes. Well Mrs. Smart Ass, this says I miss you."

Totally caught off guard she picked up the glass of water without thinking and started drinking out of it. Dana never drank out of anything without a straw.

Soul on Fire

"When did you start drinking out of restaurant glasses?"

"I didn't!"

"Looks like you do now!"

Pulling the glass from her lips she dabbed at the water that dribbled down her chin. "Do you forget anything?"

"Yeah the hurtful things. It makes no sense to hold on to the things you can't change. Just kind of eats away at ya."

The conversation had now taken on a serious tone. The sad thing about it was that this was the very thing Dana faced. The only issue was that she wasn't holding on to a damn thing. Hurtful things just crept up on her.

"Mr. Remember It All, Tell me what I was wearing the first time you asked me out?" She put him to the test, trying to change directions before the blame game ensued.

"The first time I asked you out and you said yes?"

"Yes, that time."

Dana smiled inwardly remembering what they both wore. Damien had on what she called the classic RUN DMC jumpsuit minus the gold chain and Kangol. She wore cut off jean shorts that were rolled up and a shiny silver jacket with layered tanks underneath. What was she thinking? She began giggling at herself thinking about how crazy they dressed back in the day. Those were the times, nothing like the eighties. Let momma tell it, there was nothing like the late sixties, early seventies.

"I can't forget the huge doorknocker earrings you rocked. But I have to be honest, I can't remember exactly what you had on but I do remember what you said."

"I'm listening."

"Persistence pays off! Whew, you know you had a smart mouth to be so young."

"And it still does and I still do." She replied.

"Any more questions lady?"

"What kind of business that's not football related brings you to Atlanta?"

An inscrutable expression came across Damien's face. It was clear that he had something to tell her but didn't know how to begin.

"So Mr. Professional?" Dana prodded a little. This kind of reaction spiked her curiosity. The hostess approached the table with drinks, ready to now take their orders. After all they had sent her away at least three times before.

"Saved by the bell!" Dana laughed it off while hurriedly looking through the menu.

"Order for me?" Damien asked.

"What do you like?" This was a rhetorical but Dana wanted to be difficult.

"Surprise me!"

"I will have the filet mignon and salmon. He will have teriyaki salmon and shrimp."

"That was a great choice." Damien put his stamp of approval on his upcoming entrée. Dana waited for him to tell her what his trip was all about. Sipping her tea, she bluffed as though she had forgotten about the conversation in progress. "Have I told you how proud of you I am?"

"A few times." Short on words, Dana wanted him to see how anxious she was to pick up where the conversation left off.

"I'm here in Atlanta....." Damien's words dangled and he cleared his throat. Dana's attention was drawn away from Damien by a vibrating phone with a text that read, *you look just as beautiful as the last time I saw you*. "I'm here in Atlanta for a paternity test."

"Really?" She heard but she didn't hear.

"Yeah, I was seeing this girl off and on a few years ago and she just hit me with the.... you have a son thing. Better yet she had me served with child support papers."

Dana wanted to be sympathetic but a feeling of hurt wouldn't concede it. What if it really is his son? Wasn't I supposed to be the mother of his child? All kind of questions ran through her mind as she searched for a sensible response. Dana's phone vibrated again with the same message as before now with a little more information. *Your hair pulled away from your face is very appealing.* She tried not to be obvious as she looked around the restaurant for a familiar face. It could be only one of two things, either Alexia was playing a trick on her, because she was the only person that knew where she would be having dinner or someone that knew her and had her number was there as well.

"Really?" That was the only thing she could say being distracted and a little unnerved by the text message. Another message came across. *Now, Now we will talk. I just think it's a little rude to come over and speak while you are entertaining your male friend.*

"Is that all?"

"Damien, I'm not sure what you want me to say or do?" She maintained her composure while speaking through the hurt. "This

Soul on Fire

happened years after we had separated. It would be foolish of me to think that you would not see anyone else in hopes of us somehow reuniting, as it would be unrealistic for you to think the same for me. I did, however figure you to be a little more responsible. Remember you are the one who has always said that you didn't want children out of wedlock or didn't want to raise a child from afar." Excusing herself to the ladies room, she wanted to give him time to mull over what she said. She would also the privacy she needed to text the mysterious person.

Walking slowly to the bathroom, Dana scoped out as much of the restaurant as she could. *I'm right behind you.* Another text came through. She stopped at the bathroom's foyer too afraid to turn around. The mirror in the foyer revealed who the mysterious man was, Simeon. The brother looked impeccable. Dana knew from past experiences he was not without fault.

"Simeon."

"Dana." He spoke back. They stood for a moment staring at one another. Words escaped her at such an awkward time. She didn't want Damien to come looking for her either. "As I said before you look beautiful. Although things ended in a fucked up way, I want to apologize again. I was definitely wrong for mixing business with personal, but from our first conversation I knew I wanted to get to know you better on that level."

"Well, we have been down that road before. I can't say I agree or understand. But hey that's the nature of the beast in business. It was good seeing you." Dana extended her hand. She was not going to let him get close to her again. He extended his, they shook hands civilly. Dana stepped into to the ladies room to collect herself before returning to the table.

Damien stood as gentlemen do when ladies return to table. "You okay baby?"

"I'm good." The food had been served yet Dana's appetite had long been gone. She ordered an apple martini and nibbled.

"So how is business?"

"Business is good. My clientele is growing at a steady rate. Looking for ways to expand or offer different services."

"Sounds good." The air was stale. Dana ordered another drink and looked around for a glimpse of Simeon. She started not to care he betrayed her trust. Tuning Damien out, she wished he would say he was finished eating. "You're not hungry?"

"Not too much. I think I will grab me a carryout box."

"For what it's worth, I hope this doesn't change our friendship. I know we were disconnected but after seeing you.... feelings I thought no longer existed re-emerged."

She heard him but was not listening. Her mind was somewhere else and she was ready to go home.

"You know, I can't be upset. I just wish the best for you and your situation. You'll be a good father if that is the case. Have a safe trip and I'll be in touch." Dana placed sixty dollars on the table, stood up, kissed him on the cheek and exited the restaurant. Indeed this was a difficult thing for her to ignore but she wouldn't let it show.

The phone rang about 5 or 6 times before going to Evan's voice mail. She sat in the parking lot for 5 more minutes hoping that he would call back soon. Even though she saw him the night before, she was so rattled by the news Damien had laid on her that she didn't want to go home alone. Just as I she had placed the gear in park, the phone rang and it wasn't Evan.

"Dana?"

Holding the phone, she contemplated on whether to answer or hang up.

"Yes?"

"This is Simeon. Do you have a minute?"

"What's up?"

"I'm not sure where to begin."

"It's late, you've already apologized."

"Did I tell you how beautiful you are?" He dismissed her attitude and continued to try and talk his way into a situation she didn't want to be in. She was the self proclaimed recognizer of game, yet she went through the same motions with men time and time again.

"Yes."

"Did I tell you I have thought about you since the first and last time we made love?"

"No, but it's interesting how you would think more about that than the fact that you used me!" Anger arose in her voice.

"I respect that...."

In the midst of his sentence someone tapped on the passenger side window. It was Carl Duncan. He tapped again, louder. Letting down the power operated window, Dana spoke. "Hi Carl."

Soul on Fire

"Good evening Ms. Taylor. Please don't let me interrupt your phone call, I noticed you sitting in your car on my way to mine and deliberated on whether to acknowledge you."

"Simeon, I will have to call you back." Dana hung up without a response.

"What a gentlemen you are!"

"I've called you several times. Either you are telling me to get lost or you are extremely busy. But you do know I pay by the hour." He winked.

She didn't know whether to be insulted or turned on. This was just the bait she had been waiting on. He was already on the chase.

Flirting, she responded. "Well I think we will have to discuss those hourly rates sometimes."

"How about tonight?"

"Not tonight. It's been an extremely long day for me and on top of that I went into the office late."

"I will make it worth your while. I don't live far from here, near Roswell. Will you follow me?"

Looking down at her watch, the long hand had just struck eleven. "An hour?"

"If you say so, but I'm sure you'll want more."

"Are you going to stand there and talk or put your money where your mouth is?"

"I'll pull around in a sec."

Damn, she thought to herself as he walked off. Short, round, bald, what the hell can I do with that?

Skyy Banks

℘

The drive to Cabriolet Drive was short. Dana was feeling discombobulated. She could be having extraordinary sex with Evan right now or continued being used by Simeon. Bill Withers was right she had to admit, if it felt that good being used...then keep on using me, until you use me up. She cracked herself up at the absurdity. Dana letup on the accelerator before following Carl through the wrought iron gates. Water erupted from the fountains arranged on either side of the sprawling doors.

Carl came around and opened the door for her. She left the booty bag in the car knowing she would not stay for more than the hour. It had been long conjectured.

The spread was absolutely majestic, any woman's dream house. The sparkles in Dana's eyes were overt to Carl. There was no hiding how impressed she was. "What would you like to drink?" Anything less than vodka wouldn't do.

"Vodka and cranberry."

"My kind of girl."

There was a bar off to the side of the room, a replica of many club bars. The marble black countertops were spotless. Mirrors lined the shelves and the wall. Knowing Carl, they were two way. Premium liquors and vintage wines were the only beverages available for tasting. While pouring the drinks, Carl pointed Dana in the direction of the bathroom to freshen up, not before waiting for him to mix the drink to take with her. The drinks at the restaurant had long worn off and if she was to survive the hour, liquid courage was needed... fast.

"If you could... Make another one for me? Please."

"Anything for you."

Uuuugghh. Dana was sick thinking about the decision she had made. It was the underlying sexual dare not really the money that had enticed her. If there wasn't something filling the void between her legs, she didn't feel right. She never considered herself promiscuous however the person she was involved with was going to put in overtime in the bedroom. The bathroom was just as magnificent, a complete marble design with gold faucets. Dana spent a few minutes snooping through the drawers which turned up nothing. She swallowed the last corner of her drink and stepped into the shower. Hitting the sweet spots, under arms and down

Soul on Fire

below, she made it quick. Drying off, she put on a plush robe from the closet and a matching pair of slippers. It was just like a spa experience without the massage. Carl had dimmed the lights and lit candles all around. A screen had been lowered from the ceiling and Sparkle was playing. Easing into the room, Dana found Carl just as comfortable on the sofa that appeared to have been converted into a bed of some sort.

"Hi baby." He beckoned for her to come.

The drink she consumed had to have been ¾ vodka and ¼ cranberry juice. The buzz kicked in right on time. This man must've been some kind of psychic because Sparkle was one of her all time favorite movies next to Lady Sings the Blues. Carl handed her another drink. His moves were subtle. First stroking her thighs and then her breast, not playing back, she let Carl do his thing. Strokes turned into kisses from top to bottom. He slowly parted her thighs and bit softly on the inner part. His tongue found a familiar spot and teased it. Her back arched and fell, arched and fell with every stroke across her clit. Digging his tongue deep inside her, she moaned louder and rubbed her hand across his bald head. She took it a step further and raised her legs to expose more of herself and he followed suit by circling every orifice with his tongue. Her stomach began to knot up as she approached her first orgasm. Feeling her body become rigid underneath his hands, he sucked her clit until she came. Dana's legs shook and he continued to suck. He kissed her inner thighs, down her legs to her feet.

"Lay on your stomach baby and take off the robe." She did as he asked catching a glimpse of his penis in the process. It was a very nice size to be an older man. The warm oil on her back was a pleasant welcome. Carl stroked her back, her ass, her thighs, her everything in just the right way. When he finished, her pussy spasmed, wanted him inside of her.

"Well, my hour is up and I know you have to get home to prepare for tomorrow." That's it? Dana asked herself somewhat confused. Carl got up and began to blow out the candles. She turned over to give him a full frontal view of her glistening pussy. He continued to clean up as though she wasn't there. She asked herself again. Is that all? Damn, he was good. But she was better. She put on her clothes and made her way to the door. Carl handed her the same kind of envelope as before. Dana refused it.

"I pay by the hour remember."

"Yes you do!" She smirked and took it.

Skyy Banks

Pulling into her driveway, she sat in the car and popped the gold seal on the envelope, twenty 100 dollar bills exactly.

Soul on Fire

♌

The matching pink shorts and tube top I wore was my favorite spring time outfit. The shorts hit mid thigh with ruffled edges. Many might say it was quite juvenile for a pre-teen. My birthday was in three days and I was extremely excited. Aunt Lois would be taking me to the store to shop for party stuff. Her plan was to pick me up around three after her 6-2 shift at the hospital, but I woke up earlier than usual, got dressed and begged momma to take me over there so I could wait.

Dana sat on the edge of the sofa, wringing her hands vividly remembering the details of the day. Dr. Mitchell sat quietly, looking at her and then away, jotting down notes. Pausing before she continued, Dana let out a long sigh. She spoke in a monotone voice, short, simple, and without emotion.

It was almost one when I made it to Aunt Lois' and Uncle Willie's house. Uncle Willie was sitting in his favorite chair watching an old movie with Richard Roundtree. That was his favorite actor.

"Hey Sista-n-Law." He called out to momma. For some strange reason he always called her that instead of by her name.

"Hey Willie. I see you watching your main man."

"Shut yo."

"Mouth!" Momma finished the line and they laughed together. "Well Dana wanted to come on over. I know Lois still at work. She promised to take her shopping for her party."

"Yeah, I know." Uncle Willie said without blinking an eye or taking his eyes off the TV. "She'll be fine."

Momma had barely made it out of the drive way when he called out to me. "Somebody's birthday is coming up. If you are good to me I'll buy you those concert tickets you've been asking about." I knew what Uncle Willie's good to him meant.

Skyy Banks

He asked me to take off my shorts and then my panties and lay on the couch. With his penis in one hand he rubbed his penis over the inside of my vagina. The wetness came from his penis oozing pre-cum. It wasn't long before his body shook violently. There was a wet spot on the couch.

"Go clean up."

The party was cancelled. Looking down at her hands, Dr. Mitchell passed her the box of Kleenex to dry her eyes. Dana grabbed her purse and walked out the office with Dr. Mitchell calling. The outer body experience occurred again. How she made it home, only God knew. Dana sat on the edge of the bed holding Mya's diary, too drained emotionally to read yet she had found many of her entries therapeutic. Turning towards the end, she read a quote that was written inside a heart: *"No man is worth your tears and the one who is won't make you cry."*
Tears streamed down Dana's face as she cried for Andre, Simeon, Myles, and the countless others that weren't worth her tears. It sounded simple, but what woman doesn't cry when she's hurting or has been hurt by a man?
A tap on the French doors leading to the outside patio from her bedroom startled Dana. She knew it wasn't a booty call signal. That hadn't happened since she stopped seeing Allen, which was another story. Shaking her head thinking about all the times that boy lied and still was able to get in with just a tap on the window, she peeked out to see Alexia.
"What you doing back here?"
"Well, I saw your car in the driveway, but you wouldn't answer the doorbell or your phone."
"How you know I wasn't in here getting busy?"
"You must have been getting busy by yourself 'cause I don't see another car, I don't hear no music, and I don't see no candles."
Dana couldn't help but smile at her list of observations.
"Anyways, what's wrong?"
"Girl, I'm just tired! It's been a long day."
"Long? Hell. You left most of your work at the office." Offering a folder to me she continued, "I thought you might need these for tomorrow. Now that I am here I see you might need something else."

Soul on Fire

"Don't even try it!" Dana laughed again.

"Girl, please! You are looking too pitiful for me to hit on you right now. I actually feel sorry for you!"

"Don't feel sorry for me. Hold a sista up!"

"Well I think I could do a better job if I knew exactly what I was holding you up for," Alexia joked as she made her way past Dana to the kitchen. "I'm going to fix us some wine and you just put whatever you reading to the side. Come on in the living room because that bed sure looks tempting," she winked.

"See there you go. I'm going to put your ass out in a minute."

"Come on girl."

Alexia poured two glasses of Merlot, that was all Dana had left. Seemed like these days she drank more and more. Her fully stocked cache of wine and other spirits was gone. "Truth or dare?"

Whining, Dana responded, "Truth?" For some reason, she figured a dare would put her in a compromising position with this chick.

"Why are you single?"

"We have discussed this or so I thought. But anyways, I am single by choice. Right now my career is my focus. Once I get settled into this thing, then I will have time to devote to a relationship."

"You said truth. Stop giving me that same old rehearsed bullshit answer that you give everybody else."

Dana gulped the last half of the glass of wine down and advanced it for a refill, all the time calculating a truthful response. This heifer had seen right through her and her comeback to her quote-unquote bullshit hit her right in the throat.

"Don't hurry, I'll wait." She expressed amusement while pouring Dana's second round.

"Truth?" Dana asked. Sitting up straight, she stared past Alexia. The truth caused tears to fill her eyes. "Girl, I got too much baggage and wouldn't know where to start or how to keep a relationship. I have been dating off and on but it's been either somebody else's man or some sub standard bullshit that I allowed myself to be subjected to."

The tears flowed effortlessly and the room became exceptionally quiet. Alexia sifted through the music program LimeWire. She looked for a song to touch Dana where she hurt, or so she assumed.

"If you know this, then what's the problem?"

Skyy Banks

"I'm not sure." Partly lying, Dana shrugged. However, she was not about to reveal to Alexia her dirty little secret that seemed to be the very root of the issues. "Your turn. Truth or Dare?"

"Truth!" Alexia was more than eager to give her spill. In the background Confunkshun's Love's Train filled the room. Dana's question for her departed her mind and full attention was on the song. "Damn girl! You didn't have to do that to me, raising her glass for another round. Swaying her head from side to side, Dana sang along.

"If you are that special lover
Love keeps you tied to another
That's the way it goes on love's train
Sometimes heart strings can be broken
You've just got to keep on goin'."

"Start it over!" Alexia didn't say a word she hit replay and continued browsing LimeWire. Dana laid back in the corner of the sofa, swaying and crying. Alexia came over and rubbed her head. She gently stroked her hair to the back without speaking, letting her have that moment. Dana yearned for Chelle. The playlist streamed from one song to the next and they were all sad but true. Music had a way of telling a story and it always seemed to be your story. "Okay! Now you have me feeling worse than I was before."

"That was not my intention at all. I just figured hell if we had good music and good wine then we, no you...could cry it all out because I don't have nothing to be crying about! Thank God for small favors." Alexia nudged Dana.

"You are right about that. That one song took me back for a minute. Damn he was good, it was good." Dana giggled.

Alexia prodded, "Who was that and what song?"

"That was Damien and the song was......" Dana stumbled over the words and couldn't remember the song.

"Any day now?"

"Well, you know the song, you played it. Some love shit but anyways it was good. He was good. That's who I went to dinner with the other night. He was my high school sweet heart. The bastard was here for a paternity test. I was supposed to be having his baby." Dana let out a long wale. Alexia stood up in front of Dana and pulled her to her feet. She hugged her tightly.

"Poor baby." She said while rubbing Dana's back. "Let it out mama."

Soul on Fire

Dana cried for a moment and pulled back wiping her nose with the back of her hand. "Girl you crazy." She tried to dismiss her roller coaster emotions.

"Yeah to be here dealing with you and your issues. That's why I don't do men."

"That brings me to my question."

"Well save it for later. You feel like getting out? It's still early?"

"Aren't you the one that brought me work over for tomorrow and aren't you one that has gotten me a little too drunk to move?"

"I am guilty, now tie me up and whip me!"

"On that note, bye Alexia and I will see you at the office."

"So that's how you do me? I let you cry, curse, wallow in self pity, and put snot on my shirt and you kick me out?"

Holding the door open, Dana mumbled "Yep!"

Alexia let out a sigh and put her head down as though her feelings were hurt. "I can accept rejection."

"You too much."

"I know." She smiled back walking out the door.

"Alexia."

"You changed your mind?"

"No, but I do want to thank you for taking the time to listen." Dana reached out for a hug.

"Girl, you gonna be alright."

"I know."

Alexia pushed Dana back and looked her straight in the eyes. "Dana, you are gonna be alright. Women have been through worse than you and endured."

Dana hugged her for the last time. "Thanks and I'll see you tomorrow."

Sitting on the couch Dana thought about Alexia's last words. *Women have been through worse than you*...she didn't even know her worse but she knew she was right, it just made sense. Sense because history had shown it to be true. She picked up the phone to call Chelle and hung up before she dialed all the numbers.

Skyy Banks

Right there baby. You know how to do it. Don't act like you scared. Squeeze it. The masked man squirted more baby oil into the palm of Dana's hand and guided it in and up and down motion over his penis. Just like this. He leaned back in the chair and propped his arms on the wide arm rest. His breathing was heavy and his body trembled from time to time. Harder, he demanded. Harder baby. Sit up here and do it. He patted at one of the arm rests. She moved to where he asked and he parted her legs and began to rub between them. Dana stopped. Don't stop! Don't worry about me just keep going. He rubbed between her legs so hard it began to burn. Harder baby! She squeezed hard just to get it over. He left out a snarl like a bear and his stomach shook.

       Dana's pajamas were drenched with sweat. The ritual of the clock glaring 3am continued. This time she didn't get up to shower, instead lied back down and stared at the dark ceiling. "Lord take this pain away from me. I don't think I can take anymore." She cried out literally. Her eyes were swollen almost shut. Without thought, she rolled over and paged Andre. Not until he called back had she realized she made such a move.

       Staring at the phone, Dana let it go to voicemail. Andre called back three times. She picked up on the third.

"Dana?"

"Hi 'Dre. Didn't mean to disturb you."

"No, that's fine. Are you okay?"

"Yeah, I'm good."

"You don't sound like it. Your voice is a little hoarse. You need some medicine?"

"I've been in meetings all day and talking a lot. I just need some warm tea and maybe some lozenges."

"Ok, you know I am always concerned about you."

"I know." Hearing his voice put her in another state of mind.

"You need me to come over?"

       As bad as she *needed* him to, she couldn't continue to engage in things that were detrimental to her emotional well being. "No, but thanks for asking."

Soul on Fire

"You know I am always here for you. It's just that I'm stuck between a rock and a hard place as the old saying goes. You have always been good to me and good for me. You definitely deserve better and more than I could give. If I were a single man, I would grab you in a heartbeat."

"But you are not single and I do understand. Thanks again 'Dre. Take care of yourself."

"You do the same."

She willed herself up and to the kitchen. Either she was all cried out or didn't give a damn anymore. She was okay. He sounded great on the phone and she knew he looked and felt even better. Her mind wandered to Evan. He hadn't called in a couple of days. That wasn't strange because he wasn't the kind of guy to just let a girl know he was feelin' her. He was more into being chased instead of chasing. Sipping on her tea, she took a deep breath and read through the reports Alexia had brought over until she fell asleep.

✄

"Good morning, Dana."

"Good morning Dr. Mitchell."

"How are you feeling this morning?"

"I don't."

"Why is that?"

"I had what you would call a meltdown last night."

"Dream?"

"It started before then."

"Have you been taking your medicine?"

"When I feel bad."

"At least you are honest, but that's not how it works and that's not going to get you to feeling better. I need you to take it as prescribed, once a day. If it makes you sleepy during the day, once before bedtime. Try to take it at the same time daily. You will be able to handle your emotions better. I know it's not the answer to all, but it's part of the process."

"I know and I'm working on it."

"I need you to not just work on it, but ascribe to it. You have so much to look forward to. Now it's like you are stuck in time but once we accept what has happened and deal with it, we can then move forward."

Tears welled up in her eyes again. "I know but it's so hard right now."

"Dana, I don't want you to get upset before you go to work. I called to have you come in and see me within the next couple of days. You have been on my mind heavily since we last spoke. I definitely don't want to blur the lines between doctor and patient relationship, but God spoke to me concerning you. He showed me that you were hurting badly and that I have been charged to see you through. I'm not going to say that it's going to be easy or even after we have gone through the process that you won't have thoughts. That too shall pass. I know that these sessions have been a bit costly. Please don't be deterred by that either. Everything from this point will be at no cost."

"Thank you Dr. Mitchell." Dana bit her bottom lip hard to keep from crying.

"Don't thank me baby. I was getting tired and God sent you to my office just so I could be reminded of why I am here. I want you to

Soul on Fire

have a wonderful, productive day, filled with smiles. Can you do that for me?"

At that moment a text message came through. It was Evan. "Yes and I will see you in a couple of days."
Dana read through the text message and smiled to herself. Maybe today wasn't going to be so bad after all.

She pulled into the office parking lot and noticed a flower delivery van leaving. Dismissing it as something for the office next door, Dana looked in the visor mirror before going in. Her makeup was still fresh and in place. Her eyes were still a bit puffy. She pulled out her caffeine stick and dabbed under her eyes. The claim was to eliminate under eye puffiness. She didn't know if it worked but it made her feel better to think so.

"Hey chica." Alexia greeted her grinning from ear to ear and a hug. "You look fantabulous!" Dana knew she was lying but it made her feel good. "You ready for your meeting?"

"Kinda."

"That's okay because I pushed it back an hour and a half for you. I also scheduled you a lunch. You are supposed to be at the Cheesecake Factory at one. That's all I know!" Alexia hurriedly interjected before Dana could ask her anything else. Dana knew she was up to something. It was written all over her face. "Oh and your tea is ready."

Slowly nodding her head as to say yes, Dana watched her until she walked into the office. Alexia was acting utterly strange.

When Dana opened the door to her office a vase of white calla lilies waved. She looked around the room and four more vases did the same dance. It wasn't a mystery who they were from. She had just seen Simeon the other night and this was the same way he got her the first time. It did make her smile however. Sitting at her desk, Dana opened her files to quickly brief herself for the meeting. Alexia had laid the card from the flowers on her desk. The handwriting was very familiar which prompted her to take a look. Her assumption was wrong. Andre had sent the flowers. It was a sweet gesture but left a bitter taste in her mouth. He was playing unfair. *Hell hath no fury as a woman scorned*. The quote brought tempestuous thoughts to mind. Andre' wanted to play mind games and manipulate the situation from the call last night. She could send the card to his wife. Dana could call her up there to see with her own eyes or she could call 'Dre up here and get him in a compromising position, all caught by the web cam. There were a number of things she could have done, but none of it made sense.

"Alexia."

"Yes darling." She playfully answered back.

"Will you please come and discard these lovely flowers?"

Bursting through the door, "What's wrong?"

"Everything's right. Just opens my mind a little more to the extremes men will go to try and get you right where they want you."

"Do tell."

"Not right now. But please do take these things away. Better yet take them to our neighbors. They are just too perfect to throw away."

"I agree. They are pretty impressive. You are special to somebody lady. And all that showing out you did last night!" She shook her head in shame.

"Don't remind me. Enough small talk, take them please and shred this. Don't be nosey either! That's what got the other chic gone."

"I think I have earned that right. I don't think the other chic knew you like I do." She licked her finger.

Dana rolled her eyes. "Keep it up and you will be getting that pink slip today!"

"Dang, I'm just playing." She grabbed two vases and walked towards the door.

"I am too! And oh! I thought I was special too."

"See that's why I don't deal with men!"

Soul on Fire

ℒ

Lunch was an even sweeter surprise. Evan was the secret person at the Cheesecake Factory. He stepped in the room with his grown man on again. Nicely dressed in slacks and a button down shirt, Dana was bubbly. He stood to greet Dana with a warm smile and a kiss on the lips. That took her aback. Although they had been seeing each other frequently, she didn't know they had made it to PDA status. It felt good nonetheless. Although her day had gone pretty well, she wasn't very hungry or talkative.

"What's on your mind?"

"Not too much. You look really nice." She wanted to avoid this conversation all together.

"Thanks babe. Now what's on your mind?"

"I've just been a little swamped at work that's all. Not getting the rest I need."

"Well you should come over and let daddy take care of that."

"I should." she said flirting back. Her phone vibrated with a text message. It was Alexia saying she had more flowers at the office and that she would get rid of them. But she would keep the card. Before Dana could slide the phone back into her purse another message came across the screen. This time it was Damien saying that he was leaving today and he would like to see her to clear the air before he left. Lord knows she didn't need anything upsetting her today. So, she pushed Andre, the flowers, Damien and anything else that was not conducive to her mental health to the back of her mind. "What time is your next appointment?"

"I'm done for the day."

"So am I?"

"Is that right? Looks like you got the hotline over there."

"Just my secretary keeping me informed on what's going on at the office."

"What you want to do?"

"You want to come over to my place and watch a movie?"

"I thought you'd never ask."

"I think you've earned that privilege."

"Privilege?"

"And don't you forget it." Dana rubbed his thigh under the table and she could feel him growing.

Skyy Banks

"I see someone's about ready!"

"I was born ready!"

Soul on Fire

It had been a week since she last saw Evan. Dana had attempted to call Chelle again but hung up the phone before it could ring. The early morning flight to Cincinnati was what she needed. It was quiet, no children, and only a few passengers. The entire row was hers. Meditating on the events that had transpired to bring her back to the city within a year's time, Dana looked through the dense clouds. Maybe an angel would just appear and take all her sorrows away and she wouldn't have to face the unknown of what awaited. No one knew she was coming home, it was the opportune time to take care of unfinished business. There was even some left with Damien. The more Dana reflected on the conversation she had with him, she found no reason to be angry. Their time had come and gone.

"Skies are clear, 72 degrees, landing in 28 minutes"...the pilot gave his usual spill before they touched down on the runway. Dana's stomach was entangled already. As soon as the pilot stated it was okay to turn on cell phones and other electronic devices she reached for hers and called Dr. Mitchell.

"Hi Dr. Mitchell."

"Hi Dana. How are you? Did you arrive safely?"

"I did and now I am looking for any sign to tell me that I shouldn't be here."

"You have every right to be there as you do every right to confront your abuser. I'm not saying you have to go back and forth or get into a heated argument either. This person might even decide to not know about anything you are saying. That's okay as well. Just maintain your dignity. Say what you need to say and leave. That's the reason why you are there."

"Well, I'll give it my best shot. Talk to you soon."

The streets were littered with trash and young boys hung on the corners of the local mom and pops. The radio was barely audible, which was fine because she had tuned everything out. The chime of the low fuel indicator prompted her to pull into the nearest gas station. It was not until then did she recognize she was about 100 miles south of the city. She had driven aimlessly off the path. After refueling, she headed back to the city to check into a hotel. Her flight was scheduled to leave on tomorrow morning. So it was now or never. Her stomach hurt, but her head hurt worse.

Dana noticed she had four missed calls, one from Dr. Mitchell. She didn't know how to take her concern. She really wanted Dr. Mitchell to trust her to handle it the best way she could but her persistence felt as though she was forcing her into something that she didn't want. Strolling through the call log there was a call from Russell and two from Evan. It was unusual for Russell to call. Dana was sure Chelle informed him about the issues surrounding their not speaking to one another. Maybe something was wrong, it had become second nature for her to think the worse of any situation. She contemplated calling Russell back for 30 or so minutes.

"Russell? This is Dana."

"Hi girl. I know your voice. How have you been? It's been a while since we've seen you."

"I've been well and yourself? How have you been?"

"Busy as a bee with work." There was a pause in the phone. He hadn't mentioned Chelle and she dared to ask. "You know this thing with you and Chelle has to stop. I'm not sure of the ends and outs of it all, but I'm certain it's not serious enough to ruin a friendship of all these years. The problem is you two are too much alike. Stubborn. Just plain old stubborn."

Dana listened and laughed inwardly at how old fashioned Russell was. "Well, she can call me if she wants to talk. My number hasn't changed." Dana was definitely being stubborn, although she missed Chelle.

"That's what I'm talking about." Russell interjected before Dana could get into full rant mode. "I can hear it in your voice, you don't mean it. She is miserable around here. Dragging and moping when she gets in from the office. I can barely stand it. She needs you as a friend in her life now more than she has before."

"What? Is she sick or something?"

"No she is actually healthier than she's been."

"Well, why does she need me so bad?" Dana's mouth fell open. The scene from the night they had their argument that put them in the present predicament began to replay itself. She could see Chelle standing in the living room and her saying she couldn't and wouldn't behave the way she did when they were younger. She was on her way to

Soul on Fire

motherhood and marriage. Motherhood? "You know Russell you don't have to answer that question. I will think about it and thanks for calling?"

Dana ended the call before Russell. There was nothing to think about. She was wrong and Chelle was so right. She would have been a fool to jeopardize the health of her baby and more so she would have been a fool to fight another man's wife. All of it made sense and cut her deep. "She's pregnant." Dana said out loud and Sambria is someone else's wife. The whole thing was crystal clear to her now. She was dead ass wrong. Amends would have to be made and she would have to be the bigger person as Chelle was that night. Dana needed her now as much as Chelle needed her. Can a person really be all cried out? Maybe so, even though she had a lump in her throat and a saliva filled mouth, nothing came out. The only thing that was absolute was the pain, unbearable. Dana took two instead of one of the prescribed sleeping pills. The sooner she could get to sleep the better.

Skyy Banks

Cincinnati would have to see her for another day. Dana overslept with not enough time left to accomplish her mission and arrive on time for her flight back to Atlanta. Her stomach was still in knots but her headache was gone. Using the hotels' computer she searched the white pages for Harry Dewbar. The last name was not common so the listings were short. Dana jotted down the two addresses for Dewbar and mapped quest the unfamiliar one. The other was the same as it had been when she was a child. Dana figured it wise to go there last, feeling it would be the obvious place to find him. She drove past the map quested address twice before her phone rang.

"Dana, I know you not in the city?"

"Damn Jay! Can anything get passed you nosey ass people down here? Anyways you off in college. So where you get that from?"

"Tony said he saw you yesterday driving pass the corner store on Langford."

"His ass should have been working somewhere and not hanging on the corner."

"Momma didn't say you were there. I just got off the phone with her."

Trying not to get a bad attitude with him, Dana coolly responded. "Momma doesn't know yet. I hadn't made it by there. I'm in town on some quick business, in and out."

"In and out my ass. You know that's foul if you don't get by there and see Momma and you right in the city."

"I didn't say I wasn't going by there. You just don't call and tell her I am here before I do. Tell them nosey ass friends of yours to get a J-O-B and stop worrying about the next man."

"They are trying to get it together. What kind of business are you there for?"

"None ya! And don't be taking up for them. They had the same opportunity you did. If they did less smoking and tail chasing then they wouldn't be on the corner being bums."

"You cold girl!"

"Nope, just brutally honest!"

"That too!" he laughed.

Soul on Fire

"You crazy boy. Trying to act like my daddy. How's school going?"

"Nope, just your big, baby brother. School is good. You know I am almost finished."

"I do know big, baby brother and how's momma?"

"She is good. I know she's going to be happy to see you and go by Aunt Lois too. Uncle Willie has been sick lately."

"I can't promise that one but I will get by there to see Momma."

"Well let me let you get back to your business. I love you and be safe out there. You know those Nati streets are real mean!"

"Yeah, your thug friends terrorizing them! Love you too!"

The conversation lightened her spirits but she wasn't prepared to go see Momma. Dana had inadvertently parked in front of the Dewbar resident while on the phone. A couple of teen girls sat on the porch in their hot shorts and tanks, cackling like hens. Dana built up the nerve to roll down the window and ask for the person she was looking for.

"Hi ladies, is there a Harry Dewbar that lives here?"

"You talking about Mayne or Granddaddy Harry?"

"Your grandfather."

"He don't live here. He lives over on Shallowford. You know how to get there?"

"I do. Thanks."

"What's yo name?"

"I'm an old friend."

"You look too young to be an old friend of my granddaddy."

"He and my father were friends. Thanks again." Dana lied, rolled up the window and drove off before declaring another word. She pulled over at the next street and cast the driver's side door open before she threw up in her lap.

Stopping at a corner store to use their facilities, she splashed her face with cool water and placed a cool, wet paper towel on her neck. Looking in the mirror, she took slow, deep breaths. "Girl, get it together! You have come too far to freak out now," she told herself in a non convincing voice.

The Harry Dewbar that she sought did not live very far from the younger one, his grandson, she had discovered. Pulling into the driveway with a renewed sense of confidence, she could see an old man sitting in a rocking chair on the side screened in porch. She studied him from the car before fully approaching the porch. He was frail but still sat tall. His skin wrinkled and loosely hung around his neck. A wooden walking cane was propped against his thigh.

"Girl why are you just standing there? Who you looking for?" He asked in a low but powerful gruff. That voice stopped her in her tracks and her feet suddenly became immobile. "You deaf?" He called out. Dana opened her mouth to speak but nothing came out.

Damn Willie you got this little thang over here scared. She gone be something else when she grows up. Come over here and give your Uncle Harry a hug. You know I'm just like your Uncle 'cause me and yo' Uncle been friends, like brothers all our lives. Come on over here. I don't bite.

Dana had been taken back in time just by his voice and she remembered. She remembered all the times he touched her. She remembered that big ugly ring and the smell of his Oldsmobile from the rides to get ice cream after he violated her. Tears flooded her eyes. Her mouth was dry and stomach hurt badly. She forced her way to the doorway.

"Oh hell. Is that you Dana? Lois and Willie's niece?"

"Yes."

"I'll be damned! What you doing here? What you crying for?"

"I'm here to see you Mr. Dewbar."

"What for? What's wrong with you? You got a wild look in your eyes. You still pretty though."

"I'm here to see you Mr. Dewbar."

"You said that already. Here to see me about what?"

"You remember when I was just a little girl? When I visited my Uncle and Aunt quite a bit? I was just a little girl. You hurt me. You touched me inappropriately. You watched Uncle Willie do the same. Do you know what that has done to me as a grown woman? Do you?"

"I don't know what you talking about girl. You can get your ass off my porch with that foolishness too!" He responded with anger.

Although Dr. Mitchell said this is what would possibly happen, Dana was not prepared and she became angry. Just as fast as the tears came they had dried up. She stepped close to him, so close that her knee touched his. Dana bent over, staring him directly in his eyes.

"You can sit here and lie and deny what you did to me until the day you take your last breath. I know and God knows. You took something away from me that I will never get back. You have broken me emotionally and spiritually. You took advantage of me and did things that are unspeakable. I remember and I want you to know that."

Soul on Fire

Dana stood up and backed away. As she turned to walk out, he called her name.

"Dana. I'm just an old man who trying to live out the rest of his days. That was so long ago."

She waited for an apology, but nothing. "Is that all old man?" He dropped his head in silence. "You don't have to atone for your sins against me. Live out the rest of your days old man because the rest of them will be spent burning in hell."

Sitting in the car Dana let out a sigh of relief followed by a scream, no tears just a scream. Thinking about what Alexia had said. She boldly spoke. "You okay girl."

Skyy Banks

℘

Alexia had really taken care of things while Dana was away. She was a special lady with unhealed wounds of her own. Dana didn't have the necessary courage to even go there with her considering her own baggage. She had resolved to hire her full time although she couldn't offer benefits.

"Hi chica you want to hang out tonight?" Dana asked.

"Not you boss lady? You must be up to something."

"No, I think you deserve it. Hell I deserve it!"

"You only saying that because it's the weekend."

"It doesn't matter. I'm saying it so what you gonna to do?"

"I guess I'll go."

"You guess huh? Why you smiling from ear to ear if you just guess?"

"You coming to get me?"

"Why sure. You always come out this way. See you in an hour, hour and half latest."

"Smooches." Alexia flirted with her through the phone.

Dana pulled up at Alexia's in exactly one hour. She had been by her place before but never inside. The complex was very nice with a gated entrance. Dana chose to dress a little sexy tonight. She had only been back in town a few days and tried to do any and everything to keep her mind occupied. She had not called Dr. Mitchell either. That conversation would have to wait until another time. Playfully ringing the doorbell, she could hear Alexia bouncing across what sounded like hardwood floors to the front door.

"I'm here in all my grand and splendor." Alexia stepped back and allowed Dana to pass her high stepping. She handed her a bottle of Moet and surveyed her living space. The girl really had some class about herself. Her music collection ranged from Mozart to Meshell Ndegeocello to TI. Her walls were adorned with small but elegant pieces of art. It was simple but classy. Dana loved the mismatched furniture, not only colors but fabrics.

"So do I get your approval? I see you checking out my place."

"Just admiring the view, that's all."

"Well if you are admiring then it must be okay. You brought the good shit I see." Alexia marveled.

Soul on Fire

"Maybe. One drink and then we should be heading out."

Heading in the direction of her bedroom, Alexia yelled out "That's cool. Let me finish my makeup."

"So what's your story?" Dana ventured off into a place that she said she wasn't going.

"Story? Where do I begin?"

"Anywhere you want to, but you know what they say everybody has a story."

There was silence and then she emerged from the bedroom. "Girl, I ain't got no story. I told you the biz at Milans. Just a bunch of shoulda, woulda, couldas and you know how that goes."

Dana stared back at her. She was hiding a lot of pain behind that beautiful smile. "If you say so. You ready lady?"

"Yes ma'am. Let me get another one for the road."

They came to an agreement to go to a lounge off of Luckie Street. The line wrapped around the corner and down the sidewalk. "Great choice, but I don't stand on lines." Alexia smirked.

"I don't do lines either. I guess having the owner as a client has it perks." Dana gloated.

"Well let's make it do what it do girl!"

The lighting inside was damn near perfect. The dance floor and eating area were dimly lit with hues of pinks, blues, and purples offset by the brighter lights on the bar. There was a wall length fish tank filled with exotic species illuminated with orange and red. A packed sushi bar was adjacent to the VIP. Bouncers clad in black form fitting button down shirts could be seen throughout the place directing the flow of traffic and making sure that the few people that were on the verge of having a little too much to drink wouldn't get the Spartan attitude and do things they wouldn't otherwise do.

They found a comfortable spot at the bar and on looked just as spectators would. There was so much to see, beautiful women, underdressed women, scandalous women in their "fuck me" clothes, thug wannabes, pussy starved men, and well dressed men. The DJ was on point.

"Let's get a shot of Patron and hit the dance floor."

"Let's." Dana second.

After about ten minutes of waiting they were on their way to the dance floor. It was too crowded to move and Dana began to sweat before the first song was finished. She motioned to the bar again. Alexia pushed her on and stayed behind on the floor. Dana had a few more drinks and waited for her. Drinking always made her horny. She looked through her phone of possibilities. Her list was short now. This was by choice however. She called Evan to see if she could come over. No answer. This was unusual. He answered almost every time she called even if it was to say he was sleeping. Dana waited another fifteen minutes and called again. No answer. She didn't know whether to be concerned or keep looking through the phone. She couldn't trip because they weren't officially dating.

"I'm back." Alexia reappeared from the dance floor with a sweaty face and back. The curls she came with were long gone.

"I see someone's having fun."

"A little bit."

"You good?"

"Girl do your thing. I'm a lady. I don't do sweat. Not that kind anyway." They laughed.

"You nasty! Let me get one more dance and then we can go. Maybe two."

"Go on. I'll be right here."

Dana sat on the barstool with one leg resting on the floor and scoped the scene while sipping on a martini. Looking straight ahead she saw someone who she thought resembled Evan. The build, the dress, and the hair was unmistakably Evan. She forced her way through the crowd to get a closer view. Sure enough it was Evan dancing in a well drenched shirt. Making a bee line around the crowd that formed around him, she walked towards him just as the song was ending and he was leaving the dance floor. She purposefully stood in his walkway. Dana opened her mouth to speak at the same time a young lady who was about his type came from the side and took his hand.

"What up D? I didn't know you hung out here."

"Hello Evan. I don't, just thought I'd bring a friend out for a good time."

"Cool. Oh Tika this is Dana, Dana- Tika."

Not wanting to appear angry Dana extended her hand in a cordial manner.

"Nice to meet you." Dana looked her up and down. She was a very attractive girl. Didn't know who she was and what she was to Evan. She wasn't even sure if she wanted to know.

"Be easy and be safe."

Soul on Fire

"You do the same." Dana responded rolling her eyes like some high school kid.

Making her way back to the bar, Dana selected a shot of Patron this time. Vodka and Tequila. She knew her night was over.

Skyy Banks

✄

Abilify for the road home was the last thing the lady in the commercial said. Abilify was for adults that were diagnosed with major depressive disorders according to the television advertisement. Dana didn't fall into that category but felt on the brink. She thumbed through a few pamphlets, played with her phone, and popped her gum while waiting for Dr. Mitchell to call her back for their session.

Hey D. Sorry about the other night. Call me when you get a chance. Read the text message from Evan. She hit delete. Hell what was there to be sorry for. He wasn't hers and she wasn't his.

"Dana, I'm ready." Dr. Mitchell beckoned for her to come back.

She found a comfortable spot on the sofa and kicked her legs up and crisscrossed her arms across her head. "You know, I'm really not ready for this."

"Who says? Is that why you have been avoiding my phone calls and sending me to voice mail?"

"I guess."

"It's not an I guess. You are an adult and will speak on those terms. The issues are what they are and how you handle them will determine how you will be... mentally, physically, emotionally, and financially. Contrary to what you believe, it has a domino affect in your life."

"So, I ask you again. Is this why you were avoiding my calls and sending me to voice mail?"

"Yes, that is why I was avoiding your calls and sending you to voice mail. I'm checking out. I don't want to deal anymore. You know it seems no matter how nice I am to people, I still get dumped all over." This time she was referring to Evan. What was that bullshit all about?

"Checking out is not an option for you. Explain, dumping all over you."

"It's just that no matter how nice I am to people. It always ends up being lies told, deceitful acts, and bullshit."

"Did something happen?"

Obviously something happened but Dana wasn't going to tell her. It was just drama, nothing favorable to her well being. She let out a sigh. Hopefully she would catch on and know to move to the next topic.

Soul on Fire

"That means yes, but you don't want to talk about it. How have you been doing with your meds?"

"Fine." Short and to the point.

"What happened when you went to Cincinnati?"

"Nothing. The bastard was dead." Dana was untruthful.

"Dana, if you are going to reclaim your life and move past the trauma of this childhood sexual abuse you have to be honest. I know that Mr. Harry Dewbar is alive. He resides in the same home as he always has. He is not in the best of health, but he is alive."

Dana sat up on the sofa, eyes wide in shock. "So you are playing private investigator now? You send me on a wild hunt for some sick in the head pervert and you have all the answers there?" Pointing at her file.

"It's not about being a private investigator. It's about making sure you find your way on your own. But in the meantime, I have to do checks and balances on my own, confirm you are doing what is needed, and are safe doing so."

"Lies and deceit. Well since you have all the answers right in front of you in that damn...that damn manila folder, you find them all, call them all. Tell them you know that they are child molesters and that one of their victims' hopes they rot in hell. No, better yet, tell them that if she could she would blow their damn brains out." Dana was too angry to cry.

"Calm down Dana. There are no lies or deceit. I'm doing what I need to do for your protection as well. What if you went there and confronted him and things became violent on either your end or his? Have you looked at it from that perspective?"

Dana lay back down on the sofa with her arms folded across her chest. Although she didn't want to hear it, Dr. Mitchell had a very valid point. What if things took a turn for the worse? "I understand, but it would have been better if you just gave me the information and let me take it from there."

"Yes it would have been easier, but this is your journey. Now what happened when you saw Mr. Dewbar?"

"Exactly what you said would happen. He denied everything in so many words."

"How did it make you feel?"

"Angry and sick...then...but as I thought about it especially his last words. I knew that he would never admit to hurting me, but at least he knew that I knew and remembered after all these years. I'm almost certain that he won't be able to sleep after my visit. He probably had buried those things along with many other secrets. Just as I did."

"What were his last words to you?"

"I'm an old man trying to live out my last days. That was so long ago. Let it go." Her voice weakened.

"Dana, do you realize that he acknowledged what had happened, by omission. I say that because he didn't come out and say I did X, Y, or Z but did infer by saying that it was so long ago. Maybe it was just as painful for him to remember. No, they won't all admit to wrongdoing. Which is okay? But some kind of acknowledgement is better than none."

Whatever, Dr. Mitchell was saying, went through one ear and out the other. It was okay. It was over and that is all that mattered to her. She gave a damn about his apologies or any excuses that he could have made. It was over. She lay silently on the couch while Dr. Mitchell waited on a response.

"Acknowledgement? Well, if there is nothing else...."

"I'm not going to force the issue. Dana, know that I'm proud of you. I am so proud. Don't become consumed with bitterness or blame. And checking out is not an option."

"Thanks Dr. Mitchell." It really didn't feel sincere but Dana owed her something.

Soul on Fire

✍

Mya's journal held so many secrets to her life that Dana did not know about. She had pondered suicide on several occasions. One of them Dana prevented her from. For that she called Dana her guardian Angel. Today was definitely a better day. Evan's calls were still going unanswered. Dana was really tripping which made her conscious of the fact she was into him more than she thought. It was wrong to act that way. She had her own indiscretions but who sees that when they are in the middle of doing their own dirt. Not until it comes down their street anyway.

Chelle's phone rang three times before Dana hung up. She had finally gotten to the point where she could dial the whole number and let it ring, but always hung up before she answered. That girl was definitely stubborn because she never returned the call. Holding the phone in her hand, Dana thought about the things she should be doing but didn't want to do any of it. She needed a vacation.

"Alexia, I need you to pull the calendar for next week and see what I have scheduled."

"Okay, but what happened to hello- how are you? You call and start with your demands. What's up?"

"Nosey. Just let me know and then I will let you know."

"Give me a few." Dana could hear her shuffling through the appointment book. "You are in luck. There are no meetings. You do have some deadlines and reports due but no one scheduled to come in."

"Perfect! Well send me a quick email on the reports due. I will try to do as much as I can here but I might have to come into the office."

"Okay, now what's up?"

"You feel like a trip?"

"You paying?"

"I wouldn't ask if I wasn't! Remember I cut your check!"

"So where do you propose we go?" Alexia asked with excitement.

"Not sure yet. Somewhere fun and loud! That will be your assignment while I work on the other stuff. When you come up with something let me know."

"Tootles!"

Skyy Banks

"Bye chic." Dana looked pleased. Alexia could be a good friend, but never Chelle. Looking at the phone, Dana thought about trying one more time but decided otherwise.

Soul on Fire

✍

America's Favorite Playground is what the brochure read when describing Atlantic City. Alexia thought this would be a fun place to vacation or for her to have a pay-cation. They had just arrived and the sun was beginning to set. She was ready and raring to go. The weather was favorable considering it was early fall and they were up North, which was known to have cold weather around that time.

"Okay let's get checked in and head to the Boardwalk for some food and sightseeing!" Alexia sounded like a kid in a candy store.

"That's fine. Can I change first? You don't know who we might see. This is Atlantic City, baby!" Dana responded with as much enthusiasm to match hers.

Dana wore one of her long form fitting dresses with a light sweater. She slipped into her metallic gladiator sandals and put on the matching accessories. A little touch up on the face was sufficient. She didn't wear makeup, from time to time some light foundation, a hint of brow powder, mascara, and Mac lip gloss. Mac went solo often. Alexia preferred a nice pair of skinny jeans, a tank, and a half sweater with gladiator sandals topped with matching accessories. The more Dana hung out with her she wondered why she preferred women. She was amazingly beautiful, flawless skin, not a dimple or hint of cellulite on her body with a toffee complexion. Knowing how superficial men could be Dana couldn't understand why she couldn't have found one. She appeared happy with her situation and at the end of the day that's all that mattered.

"How do I look?"

"Do you have to ask?" Dana responded trying not to sound envious.

"Well you look sexy as hell. Look at those hips!"

"Thanks for the compliment or are you trying to flirt?"

"Both!"

"Well you can cancel that! Quick!"

"Come on." She scooped Dana's arms into hers and pulled her towards the door.

The Boardwalk was every bit of 5 miles long, adorned with shopping, eating, and people. The lights were spectacular, even after the sun had gone down it still appeared as if it were setting. They continued to walk arm in arm over the worn planks of wood until they found a cozy spot to dip inside and eat.

Cuba Libra was a nostalgic restaurant that reminded one of Old Havana. It served up Cuban cuisine in the open air. It also offered Latin dancing as the night progressed.

"I would like to start with a Mojito and beef empanada as an appetizer."

"I'm going to have the same." Alexia stated handing her menu to the server.

"Thanks for coming chic. I needed some companionship. I'm sure if I went anywhere alone, I would be wallowing in some form of self pity."

"You know I gotcha. What's up with that anyway?"

"I've told you enough about me. Now it's your turn to tell me something about you."

"What is there to say? I live a stress free life."

Dana wasn't going to let Alexia off like that. Obviously it was stress free. She was single with no children, no sig other, and had a full time job. It wasn't much but it was enough to allow her to take care of herself and any little extras.

"Stop the madness please! Tell me something I don't know. Where's your family? Do you have any family? Why are you a lesbian? Anything? Hell, what you know about Parliament and the Funkadelics?" Both having a fit.

"P-funk? Girl, I grew up on all that. That was my Saturday morning ritual, starting off with Johnnie Taylor and by the end of the day The Gap band. Family...huh..well they still living.... doing what they do back in Missouri. I'm the outcast now since I'm quote unquote a dyke."

"Family. They can be something else. But you don't seem to be bothered."

"For what? Everybody has an opinion, doesn't mean their qualified. I am the one that has to deal with the stereotypes, judgments, and not being accepted. I can't be concerned with how anyone else views my life. When it comes down to it, I will be the one that has to answer for whatever...yada yada yada...blah...blah..So forth and you know all that other bullshit."

Dana gestured to the server for another drink for both of them. Alexia was candid and free, but Dana still wanted to know more about the other thing.

Soul on Fire

"Okay after this we are going to be done with the serious talk. We came here to have a good time."

"Shoot?" Alexia was prepared.

"Why..."

She stopped me mid question. "You want to know why I prefer women?"

"Yes."

The server came over with the second drink and Alexia took it straight to the head. "I'll take another and so will she." Clearing her throat, she continued, "I really can't pin point the reason why I prefer women. I know we can be drama and come with some bullshit but it's less complicated dealing with someone that has the same desires and wants as me."

Listening attentively, Dana asked her to elaborate.

"For example we know that we want to be spoiled, we like long walks in the park, candlelit dinners, just romance. We know we like the way our skin feels from our own touch. We know when we don't want to be bothered. Those are just a few things that give me a strong attraction to a woman."

"So you've never been with a man?" The server approached with their food as Dana posed the question. He directed his attention to Alexia as though he wanted to hear her response as well. "uum hmm." Dana denounced his rudeness politely.

"It's not a problem girl. I have been with a few. Some not worth mentioning, but I have a few. Now you can give her that plate and I will take mine." He was speechless.

"I can understand your rationale but I will not say that I agree."

"I can respect that! Let's eat so we can dance and finish that drink. I got you two to one right now."

Skyy Banks

⌀

They drank and did the Cha cha cha, Rumba, Samba, Salsa, and whatever else they thought they could. They were so drunk that there was more falling than the usual fast paced rhythmic groove that was usually accompanied with Latin music.

A taxi was called to drive them back to the Casino hotel. They whooped all the way to their destination. Dana probably overpaid the driver but it was probably worth it with all the noise they kept up.

"Okay heifer, I know you drunk but you gone get us killed out here leaving the door wide open like that." Alexia slurred.

Dana was too busy wrestling with her dress and trying to avoid peeing all over herself rather than closing the door behind her. Turning the shower on, she stepped inside while the water warmed. The initial cool water felt good to her body and helped lowered her current state of inebriation. Pressing her back against the ceramic tile of the shower wall, she inhaled the steam and relaxed before moving towards the multiple shower heads that spew different pressures of water. The water poured over her head, into her mouth, and down her body. The soothing spa quality of the multiple shower heads was even more reinvigorating as she squeezed shower gel into the sponge and began to wash her shoulders. She didn't hear or see Alexia come into the bathroom until the shower door squeaked opened. She didn't speak, instead removed the sponge from Dana's hand and began to wash her back in strong circular motions.

Dana stood silently as she washed her from head to toe. They faced each other, both standing and anticipating the move from the other. She then did the same thing to Alexia, not as sensual as she had her.

"You want to?" Alexia asked.

Dana's body moved in agreement towards her. The role of aggressor had now changed. The first time Dana shared herself with Alexia, she didn't know if it was the alcohol or her emotional needs that released her. One hand stroked Alexia's face and the other held her waist. She leaned into her and they kissed, soft, long, and passionate. Dana could taste the alcohol that lingered on her tongue. Her mouth was warm and sopping. There was a distinct difference from kissing a man and she liked it. Alexia placed her arms around Dana's waist and stroked her back. They continued to kiss and the water continued to flow. Dana

Soul on Fire

began to kiss her on the neck and slowly licked and sucked her nipples. The move was overpowering.

"Let's get out of here. My feet are getting wrinkled." Dana suggested. She really wanted to feel her body next to hers. Stepping out of the shower, they moved to the bedroom. Alexia had booked a stay at the most expensive Casino overlooking the city. The bedroom's fire place was blazing. Alexia had already turned it on. Dana toweled her dry and began to massage her body. Every spot that she massaged was followed by a kiss. "You relax and let me do this."

"Where do you want me?" Alexia didn't protest.

"Right there, just lie on your back."

She turned over to reveal a neatly trimmed vagina that only had a little tuft of hair in the middle. Dana began at her feet and massaged all the way to her thighs, she took her hand and ran across Alexia's clit. It was soft. Not that she expected anything different but to feel another woman.... Alexia spread her legs wide. The invitation was accepted. Dana wasn't sure of what to do but thought about how 'Dre use to do her and used that as a guide. Kissing her inner thighs and then her belly button she played all around the sweet spot. Alexia's body shuddered and she moaned softly. She pulled Dana in closer by her head. She wasn't forceful but wanted Dana to know where she wanted her to be. Dana kissed the center softly. She smelled good. Dana licked the center up and down and then kissed her thighs again. Alexia could sense the awkwardness.

"Come here girl."

Dana crawled on top of her and they kissed deeply. Alexia shifted her weight and Dana was now underneath. Alexia kissed her neck and made her way down to her vagina. For a minute Dana thought she was Carl, 'Dre, Evan, Damien or one of her past lovers that ate pussy proudly. Dana's hips moved with Alexia's tongue. She played inside of Dana with her fingers and let her tongue do the rest. She moaned and rocked. She continued until Dana reached her peak. When she was finished Alexia sat at the edge of the bed with her legs spread and vigorously brought herself to a climax.

Skyy Banks

ॐ

What happened in Atlantic City stayed in Atlantic City. Alexia and Dana were only together the first night. They never spoke on it again. It was an experience that she valued because everything Alexia said was true as far as a woman knowing another woman's needs and desires. She almost made Dana feel sexually as good as a man could, but her needs ran deeper than sexual healing. The dreams were becoming less frequent, she couldn't decipher if it was the medicine or her actually coming to a place of acceptance.

"Hi Dana." She looked at the caller ID after answering the phone to make sure the voice she heard was actually the person on the other end. It was and her heart fluttered.

"Hi Chelle." They both held the phone waiting for the other to speak.

"How have you been?"

"I've been up and down. More up lately than down."

"How is Ma and Jay?"

"I went home a few weeks ago. Mama's doing fine. Spending a lot of time at the Church and working with the local youth ministry. Anything to stay busy. I asked her to move down here. But you know she wasn't hearing that. Jay is Jay. He's almost finished with school."

"That's good to hear."

"Did you say you were preggers?"

"Four months now!" Chelle exclaimed. "And Russell popped the question when we were in Paris."

"I knew he would."

"How?"

"Well he called when I was in Cincinnati and asked for my blessing. He knew how much you meant to me."

"That man never ceases to amaze me and you with your sneaky behind didn't say a word."

"Yes ma'am. I am guilty."

"What kind of ring did he get you?"

"You will have to wait and see. I'll say this bring your stunna shades."

Dana screamed. "Stop playin'!"

"Your boy showed out Ms. Dana."

Soul on Fire

Dana held the phone in elation. It felt so good to hear her voice, to talk to her and be genuinely happy for her.

"I got to see you girl. I am behind. I have so much shopping to do for my little niece or nephew!"

"There you go! Well chic, let's do lunch tomorrow." Chelle extended.

"Sounds great! I'll text you a time and place."

"Talk to you later."

"Chelle."

"What's up D?"

"I love you."

"Awe ma! You know I love you too and when I have this baby I'm going to kick your ass."

"I deserve it!"

"See ya later."

It couldn't have been better timing. Alexia buzzed on the intercom to say that Dana had a visitor. He didn't have an appointment but was sure she would see him anyway. Dana rang her line and asked her to come to the office.

"What's up?"

"He didn't give a name?"

"No. He just continued to say it's cool and that you would see him if you were free."

Dana knew she was talking about Evan if he spoke like that. "Young, goatee, dark smooth skin, shoulder length locks."

"Fine is what I call the brotha. What's the deal?"

"I know who that is and it is no deal. Let him wait for another 15 minutes and send him in."

"Will do, but you know I gots to know."

"You gots to know?" Remember my last assistant.

"How can I not? You always remindin' me. But you know what the deal is." Laughing Alexia pointed at Dana and then herself.

Looking in the mirror, Dana told herself, "you are bold, you are beautiful, and you are loved." She felt good and ready to face Evan and whatever excuses he felt like dishing out, although she wasn't asking for any. He didn't owe her anything. Alexia sent him in exactly 15 minutes later.

Skyy Banks

Dana stood up and walked from around her desk to greet him. Kill them with kindness is what her father use to always say about the people around the city who treated him unkindly.

"Hey bighead."

"What's good ma?" Pulling Dana into him, he hugged her around the waist tightly.

"Don't be hugging me like you miss me."

"I do. You put me on ice. Won't answer my calls or text messages. You mad at me?"

"You put yourself on ice. What you doing here?"

"I couldn't get you on the phone so I figured I'd just come down here. Then you would have to talk to me. I came by a couple of times last week but the office was closed."

"Yeah, I took a trip to Atlantic City, needed to just get away. So is there something you want to say to me?"

"Well, I just wanted to apologize about that night."

"No apology needed. If you feel comfortable with seeing multiple women at one time, that's what you do. But I won't have any parts in it."

"I respect that, however I'm a single man."

"That you are, as I am a single woman. But it all comes down to choices. Who in the hell in their right mind assumes that just because a person is single that they are loose and fancy free?"

"I don't think it's about that."

"Then what is it?"

"I think it's about being free to see who you want when you want without any strings or stipulations."

"I think it is all about respect and giving me the option to decide if I want to be number 2, 3, or 4."

"You think I'm doing it like that?"

"I don't know but it is more than me."

"Tell me what you want D?"

"Honesty and the option."

"Well right now I am single and I do have several friends. Some closer than others that I do spend a little time here and there with. But I am diggin' you."

"Oh! That's sweet." She responded satirically. "But you know I'm a one man woman. When you decide you want to seriously court me, then date me... let me know. I can see you from time to time. You know maybe

Soul on Fire

for a dinner and a movie but we can't get down like that." She was giving him a bunch of double standard bullshit, just like they do. She knew damn well she liked to do her at all costs but it felt a little different being on the other side of the coin. Hell, she accepted this whole situation with a married man, whom she knew loved his wife and gave her the business on a regular regardless of what he told her. 'Dre was keeping the Misses happy in more ways than one.

"It's like that?"

"Yeah, no pressure. I'm diggin' you the same but I don't like the extra. You on your way to a full grown man, you know I can grow with you or reap the benefits of everyone else's hard labor down the line."

"You tough. I didn't think you had it in you. I hella respect that and don't be surprised. I might be ready sooner than you think." He grabbed Dana again and kissed her on the forehead, nose, and then lips. She couldn't deny it was sweetness about him that she truly adored.

After Evan left Alexia couldn't wait to stick her nose in.   "He is sexy girl and I don't even like men."

"Yeah I know. He's alright." She downplayed it but he was something serious in and out of the bedroom. "We were just kickin' it. Nothing serious. I chose to nip it in the bud after I saw him out with another woman."

"You not talking about down on Luckie? I saw you talking to a guy and a girl. I didn't recognize him as being the same dude though. That's foul."

"It's cool. We have an understanding now."

"Understandings. They are always good."

"Now you being funny. Don't you hear the phone ringing?" Dana closed.

"I guess that's my cue to leave."

Dana pointed at the door. "Yes ma'am."

Skyy Banks

✍

The patio was bustling with people. Dana was concerned with it being a little too cold for Chelle, although heaters were strategically placed around to disburse just enough warmth for everybody. She couldn't imagine what Chelle looked like pregnant. Was she all belly? Had her hair grown? So many questions ran through her mind while she waited.

Answering the phone, Dana yelled. "I know you not standing me up?"

"No girl, I'm just stuck in this dang traffic over here but I should be there shortly."

"I can't wait! Hurry up and get here."

"On my way babes."

Dana beamed at the thought that they were speaking again. She definitely had transitioned in many ways. That would be her project tonight. Make a list of things to do in her personal as well as professional life. She did have quite a bit of unfinished business with unfinished people in her unfinished life. Her goal was to have it all hammered out by the end of the year. She could not possibly see taking any of this baggage into the new one. The countdown would begin tomorrow.

"Why you look so sad?"

She looked up to see Chelle standing in front of her. She looked absolutely astonishing enveloped with that pregnant glow. "Well if you must know. I've been sitting all alone for the last..." taking a glance at her watch... "Twenty or so minutes waiting for my best friend."

"She's not too good of a friend to keep you waiting. Poor thing." Chelle poked her lip out.

Dana jumped from her seat almost knocking it over. "Come here girl and let me check you out." She embraced Chelle and then stepped back. Tears begin to form in her eyes.

"Don't start." Chelle wrapped her arms around her again. "Don't start that mess." She hugged her even tighter and Dana did the same. They must have embraced each other for a while because Dana began noticing other patrons on the patio staring at them. She didn't care.

"I'm not going to or at least I will try not. I have missed you so much."

Soul on Fire

"I have the same but hey we are here now." They hurriedly placed their orders so they could get caught up on things. "So you still running from that girl?"

"You got jokes I see. For your information I was never running. I just don't have time to be acting all alley and ghetto with other folks. But no, it is resolved kinda."

"What do you mean kinda? Either it is or it isn't."

"Okay let's come back to that?"

"Are you still having those crazy dreams? You still going to that shrink?"

"The dreams are better and Dr. Mitchell, the psychiatrist is great! Now quit making all this fuss about me. Let's talk about you all grown up bout to be a wife and mother. Speaking of wife let me see that rock."

Chelle held out her hand and Dana almost died. The ring was so damn big and gorgeous. It was a platinum double Pave of at least 4 carats. "That's what I call flawless. Damn! I didn't know you were doing it like that to the old man."

"You stupid girl! I'll take that as a compliment though. I'm going to ask about you. After all the nuttin' up on me you did. Don't you think I have not thought about you one single day?"

Tears welled up in Dana's eyes again. She tried to dab them away before Chelle could notice. "To be honest there has been a whole lot of nothing going on. I have been seeing Evan and of course am done with 'Dre."

"Not Evan down on...on...on..." she snapped her fingers in the air trying to recall just exactly where his shop was.

Snapping back at her, Dana smirked. "Yeah that Evan!"

"Hell naw, you definitely have to tell me about that one. What happened to that damn fine as twin?"

"He was just a decoy. Enough about all this and that. I want to take you shopping." Chelle was extremely happy and Dana definitely did not want to put any unnecessary stress and strain on her talking about all the chaos in her life. Dana decreed she would open up to her when the time was right, which would be after the baby or some time when she was *well.*

"I know when to leave well enough alone. I'm here when you ready though."

"As always." Dana nodded. "You want to go shopping today?"

"Why not?"

"Not a problem boo."

Soul on Fire

Their first stop would be Lenox mall. There were several baby and maternity stores that carried the cutest things. Chelle pulled Dana into Mimi maternity, apparently she had been a frequent shopper there since she became pregnant. Dana marveled at the clothing for pregnant women. Some of the styles tempted you to buy them even if you weren't pregnant. She stopped at a rack that had the matching baby doll top and leggings. Turning to get Chelle's attention, she bumped into a familiar face.

"Dana."

"Sambria." She acknowledged.

"Are you expecting?"

It took everything in her to maintain self-possession. This wench was speaking to her as though they were old friends. First of all it wasn't any of her damn business. What? So she could run back and tell 'Dre. Secondly, Dana was in awe as she looked at her perfectly rounded stomach that appeared to be due any day. She completely ignored her, walked away, and called out for Chelle.

"Girl, that is Andre's wife right there."

"Don't start nothing, please." Chelle begged.

"It's not me. She had the nerve to speak then ask me if I was pregnant. How about I haven't talked to Andre in months except for the other night when he asked if I wanted him to come over and on top of that he sent about 5 vases full of..."

Chelle interjected. "Calla lilies."

"Yes, well as long as you know you are not dealing with him anymore. She's doing that to rub in the fact that she is pregnant."

"I know but the thing that pisses me off is that Andre is still on a trip."

"Let them both be on that trip. Happy thoughts girl! What you think about this?"

Chelle had a way of bringing Dana to her senses most of the time. Dana looked around. Just as fast as Sambria had appeared' she was gone.

"I love it! Get it!"

Chelle and Dana shopped and talked until after dark. Russell called about four times checking on her and he called Dana to make sure she was taking care of both of his babies. He loved her and she loved him. Dana dropped Chelle off at her car shortly past nine.

"Call me as soon as you make it home I don't want Russell coming after me."

"I will! I love you girl."

"I love you more! I'm sorry for everything!"

"I am too. We all have to put away childish things at some point in our lives."

"We do! Now get home and don't forget to call!"

Soul on Fire

♨

The air was still and cool as Dana rocked back and forth on the porch of the log cabin. She had gone into shut down mode for the past few weeks. Her intentions after leaving Chelle were to go home and clean house. She started cleaning house literally until there was nothing else to clean or discard. It was spotless and the scent of cranberry and mandarin bled through all the rooms. A bottle of wine accompanied her to the chaise lounge in her bedroom. Kenny G romanced the soprano saxophone while she gathered her journal, notes from Dr. Mitchell, a writing utensil and Mya's journal. She had been reading her journal more frequently and was near the end. That was the last time she opened it before burning.

The room was dark and I could hear his footsteps moving closer to my room. Hiding under the bed, I thought that if he noticed I was gone then it would be okay. It wasn't okay. He sat on top of the bed and waited. After hours had gone by my light snore let him know that I was in fact under the bed and not gone. A light tap on the shoulder startled me. I reappeared from my safe haven. He began to suckle my breast as though he was angry. I winced in pain. It was barely audible. I did not want anyone to know. I lay on the bed going along with the normal routine. He entered me slowly and began to move in and out forcefully. The door to my bedroom opened. I could see her shadow. She let out a gasp and slowly turned.

Mya wrote as though she didn't want anyone to know but Dana knew. It hurt her so bad to know that the person who had the power to stop the abuse sat by quietly. That was the last night he came to her. She drove down the street to find a metal trash can or dumpster. She lit the journal with charcoal starter and watched it burn until there was nothing left. That one entry had changed everything. She began to regress. She and Chelle were back to their usual selves. She knew something was bothering Dana and she tried her best to hide it. Alexia was the person that suggested that she get away. Work had slowed because it was nearing the end of the year.

"Girl, you walking around here in a daze, you should take a few days off and get yourself together."

"Do I look that bad?"

"Not so much as bad but more like you are just somewhere else right now. You haven't been drinking your tea, taking many calls, and leaving work. You know if you call me one more time to bring a file to your house without giving me something...."

"I gotcha. I hear you and I think I will take your advice. Oh! And your something is this job. Nothing more." Dana patted her on the butt in a flirtatious manner.

"Okay now you wanna play? Aren't you the one that said what we did was what we did. It was cool then but that you preferred that we not blur the lines. Keep it business?"

"I did and I meant that. That was a love tap because you are such a good friend."

"Friend?"

"Yes, you are that and I appreciate you. While I'm gone you can work from home also."

Dana called Dr. Mitchell to let her know she was going to the cabins for a few days. She wasn't at her best and that by the time she came back all would be sorted out.

Looking around at the peace and tranquility that surrounded her, Dana pulled nature deep into her nostrils, closed her eyes, and cried out to God. Her father was a minister and she had grown up in the church. She had not forgotten how to pray, but had turned her back on believing that God really healed. Over the past months, turning to a psychiatrist, a dream book, and people to take away the pain, anything except God. She couldn't understand how someone who was charged with nurturing and caring for another would do anything but that. If she was truly God's child as she was raised in knowing and believing, she found herself questioning if this was how Jesus felt on that fateful day before giving up his spirit. "*My God, my God, why hast thou forsaken me?*" That's how she felt even though the magnitude of what his cause was and his suffering was paled in comparison to her suffering. She was not bearing the world's sins on her shoulders but her own and those that came against her. She even bore 'Dre's sins of adultery along with hers of fornication. That thing rocked her core so violently that Dana thought she would lose her mind.

"*Jehovah Rophe, I come to you with a bowed head and humble heart. You already know my hurts, my pains, my transgressions. I call on you now for deliverance and healing, a sound body, and mind. I'm lost and empty. Guide me to righteousness and salvation. Forgive me of my sins. It*

Soul on Fire

is in your Holy name I ask of these things. You said in your word let my requests be known by prayer and supplication. Continue to do a work in me as I seek your face. In your son's Jesus' name I pray. Amen."

The tears streamed down her face. At that moment she felt a release. The pain was still dull but it was not intense. Retrieving her list, she immediately began to work.

1. Call Andre, Simeon, and Damien.
2. Find Coach Gilliam
3. Give Alexia a raise.
4. Plan Chelle a shower
5. Uphold my end of the bargain with Dr. Mitchell (give her something nice)
6. Talk to Uncle Willie
7. CELIBACY
8. Work things out with Evan, maybe?

Her list was short and powerful. Everything on it was important to pulling all the pieces back together again. Celibacy would be a struggle, but what she needed was to make sure her relationship with men would be genuine and not based on a void she needed to fulfill. If the brother couldn't understand, he wasn't the one for her.

Skyy Banks

∅

Andre' took her decision to cut off all ties with him a lot harder than she thought he would. Dana found herself feeling guilty and missing him. The picture of Sambria's pregnant stomach resurfaced in her mind.

"You know 'Dre if you don't get your shit together, you will find yourself divorced with child support and alimony out the ass. Your wife deserves better but if you don't think she does, maybe you should holla at that fine little pharmaceutical rep that visits you often. It was damn sure fun while it lasted but *our* time is up." He continued to plead his case for a little while. Dana settled to give him a little word of advice before hanging up.

"What do you think the phrase *pay to play means?*"

"That it will cost you money to have your cake and eat it too."

"Sounds like a typical man's response. What it really means is that if you are willing to cheat and see other women that it could potentially be more than a monetary expense for you. The pay could also mean the loss of family, career, status, and the like. So you see my friend it's not always about the money."

There was a short silence in the phone followed by. "Thank you D. I apologize. I never expected it to get this deep and things to fall apart the way they did. I wish you well."

"The same here."

Simeon on the other hand was easy. He respected her decision, although he wouldn't reveal who his client was. Dana had put two and two together. It was no coincidence that he and Carl were at the restaurant the same night at the same time. She figured in the end everyone got what they wanted. Carl got a little more.

Damien's call was painful. She truly felt disappointment in knowing that he wasn't more careful. However, the baby was not his. She felt compelled to tell him about the abortion years ago, but there was no need to open old wounds. He loved her to this day and that probably would have hurt him more than anything. They committed to keep in touch but no need to back track. Whomever, he dated and became serious with would be a great catch, Dana was assured.

"Nuke."

"Oh! Look at you now."

Soul on Fire

"All jokes a side. I am thrilled that we reconnected. You have always been a friend to me first."

"Don't go to getting' all sentimental. You know I feel the same way."

"The next time you in the A call me."

"I will, but expect to be hearing from me sooner and more often than that. Just answer your phone."

"Will do. Love you dude!"

"You too baby."

That was all in a day's work. One down seven to go. Dana was craving Evan and having second thoughts about the whole celibacy thing. She turned over in the bed, popped a pill, and asked for strength. The scoreboard read 7-16. The hometown was up by 9. Benton College was playing tonight. Dana left work early to make the 3 hour drive South of Atlanta and be on time. Coach Gilliam had been the head coach for the past 5 years. She sat far enough but close enough to see him on the sidelines. Not remembering what he looked like, she asked a rooting fan to point him out. He looked to be in great shape. He was tall and slim, with a bald head. From time to time he pulled his headset and ball cap off and scratched his head. Football was one of her least favorite sports but she toughed it out. The game went into overtime before his team scored the winning touchdown. The teams lined up on the field, displayed the final act of sportsmanship before leaving the field. By that time, Dana had made her way near the locker room and lingered in the parking lot.

"Excuse me can you tell Coach Gilliam that someone is here to see him. Dana from Cincinnati."

"It will be about an hour or so. We have film to watch and other stuff before we leave." A player warned her.

"Thanks. Let him know that I will be waiting."

She went to her car and journaled her thoughts to pass time. Rehearsing in her mind all the things she wanted to say as well as the reaction to any ignorance on his behalf. A couple of hours had gone by before she saw him emerge from the locker room to the parking lot. Dana left her car in a near sprint to get to him. As she approached she saw a young woman standing at the back of a Land Rover with a bag over her shoulder. She looked like one of the cheerleaders. Maybe that was his daughter, she thought to herself. The girl's face lit up when she saw him, not giving him time to make it to the truck she jumped into his arms. The players, custodians, and any other students were gone. Dana was the lone witness to what was going on. As she watched their interactions with each other, it was evident that it was not a father-daughter relationship. They carried on like they were having a teenage love affair with no cares in the world. She had driven too far to let this silliness deter her from the mission. Walking towards them, she stomped hard as to be heard. She definitely did not want her to think she was the other woman to cause confusion between them. Dana's issues were strictly with her man, the coach.

"Coach Gilliam. How are you? It's been a long time." Dana smiled and reached for his hand.

"Dana Montgomery. Girl, look at you. You have not changed a bit."

"You don't look too bad yourself old timer. You have been true to the game I see." In more than one way Dana thought, looking at the pretty young thang over to his side. She gritted her teeth. One thing that she despised was bullshitting.

"Look at me. I'm being rude. Monica this is Dana. I coached her years ago when she was in junior high. I mean that was years ago, almost twenty if my math serves me right?" He joked stroking his beard and smiling at the same time.

"Seventeen to be exact."

"Wow, that's a long time. You haven't changed very much. Just as beautiful but a grown woman now. What brings you to these parts?"

"I work in Atlanta now. Doing some research about my past led me to you. I called back home at the old school and they told me that you were now coaching at Benton."

"Small world."

"Yes indeed. I would rather speak with you in private. I won't try to take up too much of your time." Dana peeked over at Monica who seemed to be getting a little irritated with her being there and interrupting their post game celebration.

"That's fine. It's getting late and you have a long drive ahead of you. Monica will you wait in my office or Dana is there anywhere you would like to go besides standing out here." He was cordial as always. That's how he got his way most of the time.

"This is okay. I don't plan on taking much of your time at all."

Soul on Fire

He handed Monica the keys and winked at her. She headed off to the office, when she was out of earshot. He began to speak. "I know why you are here."

"How do you know?"

"It only makes sense. All the time in Cincinnati, I never had contact with you or you me when you left middle school. Not for coaching, training, references, or anything. I followed you through high school and knew you would be getting a track and field scholarship. Do you remember how you would have still been playing basketball had I not talked to you in giving track a try?"

"I do, but that doesn't tell me how you know."

"After having no contact in seventeen years and to just show up without a call, email, or anything, it has to be about the things that happened between us while you were at Oakgrove Middle."

Dana's head dropped in disbelief, disbelief that he could remember and acknowledge the fact that some very intrusive and inappropriate things transpired. "I don't recall anything happening between us but I do recall you preying on my innocence."

"That may have been the case Dana. I have been dealing with this thing that I have about young girls and sex for years. I lost my wife over a lapse in judgment a few years back. I'm not perfect by far but I do my best. Now I just have relationships that won't land me in jail. Is this an excuse for violating you? No." He answered his own question.

"Do you know the things I went through then and what I am going through now? We as girls are raised to value ourselves. It is instilled in us early on how sacred that one thing is above everything else. Because in some strange way it helps mold us and bolsters our self esteem."

"I understand, so much power is there."

"Let me finish, please." Dana stood firm and didn't shed a tear. She had no desire to. "I have since then, not been able to hold valid and meaningful relationships based on anything else but that, my self worth in my opinion doesn't compare to the average girl."

"I am sorry baby. I truly am and if I could take it back I would. I'm not saying this just to be saying it. I'm an old man that has a lot of demons, things that I am not proud of. But what do I do?"

"I guess, hope that they don't come back to haunt you." she responded.

"In aspect this one did."

Skyy Banks

"No, Coach Gilliam. I wouldn't call it haunting but just bringing it to light. What you do with it of course is your territory. It's more so for my healing and maybe yours." Dana wasn't angry at all. She was empathetic and sympathetic at the same time, if it was such a way to feel both. He had let her for a brief time, be a part of his world.

"You are right. Had you not come today I wouldn't have known the hurt I've caused outside of knowing that the physical acts were wrong. I apologize. Is there anything I can do? Are you seeing a counselor? I can pay for that as well. I know that I can't right a wrong so deeply rooted."

"I appreciate that and I will be fine." That was the first time she heard herself speak those words. "I will be fine and I do accept your apology you take care of yourself."

"Thank you so much and if you ever need anything....well I've probably done enough already."

"Don't beat yourself up and I will keep that in mind."

He reached out to hug her. She didn't resist. Dana could see Monica standing just outside the gate to the locker room. Maybe she heard everything.

"Thank you again for even having the courage to come to me."

Dana was tender. The drive home would be a peaceful one. An hour to go and she was beginning to get markedly sleepy. Her body was tired. Evan was the first person that crossed her mind as being able to call anytime of the night. She recaptured the last time she tried calling in the middle of the night. He was out frolicking with one of his many women friends. They had past that so she thought with his visit to the office, calling a truce. That was another issue she had however, holding on to bullshit. It's not forgiving if you can't forget. That quote made little sense to her because if you accept and come to terms with something it's okay. It's only human nature to remember which allows you not to do the same thing again. That's what the phrase *those who don't learn from the past are destined to repeat it* means.

"Yo!" she assumed he answered the phone without looking at the caller ID. She could hear a lot of background noise, music, people, and the typical sounds that made a fun party. "Yo!" The sounds were becoming distant as Evan moved to a place where he could hear her plainly.

"What's good D? Sorry about all the noise. I have a few friends over."

Soul on Fire

"The same old. I didn't want anything really. I am just heading back from South Georgia. Got another hour to go and was getting a li'l sleepy. But don't let me hold you."

"You good babes. We just having a few drinks, playing cards, watching movies, eating. Just hanging out really. I can stay on the phone until you get here."

"Get where?"

"You should come on over."

"Those are your friends."

"And you are mine." He insisted.

Dana thought about her little booty bag in the trunk and more importantly how she wanted to feel his touch. "I'll see how I'm feeling when I get closer."

"How much longer."

I was directly outside of the city of Atlanta. "About another 30 minutes or so."

"Cool, I'll see you when you get here. Unless you need me to stay on the phone?"

"Go on and finish entertaining. I will call you when I get closer."

"Yep." One day she would tell him how that really annoyed her.

Turning the radio up almost as loud as it could go and letting the window down for the cool fresh air to blow in kept her awake until she reached the city limits.

"What's good Mama?"

"Just wanted to let you know I made it to the city and to see if that invitation was still open."

"No doubt." There was still background noise but not as loud.

"You sure it's okay with your company and all?"

"Man, come on thru."

"I'll be there shortly."

He buzzed her in the gate on the first ring. She could hear people laughing from the bottom of the stairs. The music was rockin'. Luther's Never Too Much blared from the speakers. The few girls that were there were bopping their heads and snapping their fingers.

"Hey everybody, Dana. She mad crazy with numbers so if you need anyone to do your books." He pointed at her.

"Hi."

"What cha drinkin' girl?" One of the girls asked.

Skyy Banks

Dana looked over at the counter. "I'll take some Hyp and pineapple."

"That's my shit." High fiving each other. The night wore on with them playing cards, singing, and playing a silly game called spoons. The object of the game was to have a spoon in hand after a round of card matching. If not you would have to take a shot of whatever liquor. Our liquor of choice was Patron. Dana was attentive to the game, daring not to be the one that had to take the shot. Cognizant that her vow of celibacy was at stake if she had too much to drink, she slowly sipped the sweet green concoction.

She relaxed and sat Indian style around the table. That was her first mistake. One shot, two shot, three shot, and four. She said her goodbyes and excused herself to the bedroom. Evan soon followed. He came directly at Dana, pulling her jeans down to her ankles, he turned her over and went deep. Her celibacy no longer mattered. This is what she needed. He pounded her. She grabbed his thighs and pushed back with just as much force. She wanted him to hurt her so bad that the other pain would dissipate. Collapsing on the bed, Evan laid on her back. Their shower was brief. Dana curled up beside him and fell asleep on his chest.

Soul on Fire

Watching Chelle's belly grow and to see how happy she was warmed her spirits. They now had weekly lunch dates and talked about everything from business to life. Dana had not had a dream in a few weeks and things seem to be leveling out in her life yet there were so many uncertainties and esteem issues that she continued to deal with.

"Hey chica. I'm going to lunch with Chelle. You want to come?" Alexia had spoken with Chelle over the phone and the two seemed to get along well.

"Sure."

"Good. I think it's about time my two girls meet." Dana had grown very fond of Alexia as a person.

"Yeah! I need to see the other woman that has your heart." She smirked.

Dana pushed her shoulder. "Bring your ass own Miss Messy."

Walking out the door, a young lady walked in. It was Monica, Coach Gilliam's tender roni.

"Hi Dana."

"Hi Monica. What's wrong sweetie." Alexia was all eyes and ears.

"Alexia, will you call Chelle and let her know we will be running late?"

"I really need to speak with you about your visit to Frank."

Not wanting Alexia to hear about what was going on, Dana asked Monica to come into the office to talk. "What's going on?"

"I heard Frank apologizing for something he had done to you as a teenager. What was it?"

"Did you ask Frank?"

"No, but I heard most of the conversation. Do you know how people talk about us or even me? They talk about how I am just another one. I know I'm not the only woman that he is seeing but he treats me good."

"It's not my place to speak on that with you. That's something you will have to deal with Frank about."

"I don't want to be with a child molester. Do you think he would really be honest about that?"

Looking her in the eyes, "Monica, that's a choice you are going to have to make. Those are questions Frank will have to answer. I have made my peace with him about the issues we had."

"So, no response?" Monica asked in desperation.

"You are being concerned with something that happened a long time ago. I'm not sure how long you have been in a relationship with Frank but I am sure you know of his character."

"Well, I am pleased that things are okay between you guys."

"Me too. Think about what I said. You know his character, flaws and all. Do what is best for you, not because he treats you well."

Dana came off like she was offering some motherly advice even though they were less than a decade apart in age.

"You are right. Don't let me hold you up. I guess I'll go shopping while I'm up here. Thanks."

"No thank you and have a safe trip back."

"Don't tell Frank I was here."

"Girl please. I doubt if I ever see or speak to him again." It wasn't a doubt, it was a fact. "No worries." Dana acquiesced.

Soul on Fire

⚘

Lying on the sofa, Dana had a towel on her neck and head. She had thrown up all she had at lunch and was feeling unduly nauseated. This was going on for the last week and she was late. Being pregnant was not an option for her now. She wasn't in a relationship with anyone. She and Evan had been seeing each other regularly, but it wasn't a solid commitment.

"Evan this is D. When you get off work can you stop by?"

Fifteen minutes later the phone rang. She was too nervous to answer. "Hello."

"What's up babes?"

"I just wanted to know if you could stop by after work? Wanted to just talk and see you."

"Yeah I can do that. It's Friday so it will probably be a little late."

"That's fine. I'll see you then."

"Yep."

She was anxious as hell. Journaling would be the only option while she waited on Evan to come over. Before she could do that, she thought back to when and how. She had recently abandoned her morning ritual of taking the pill before brushing her teeth. Hell, she wasn't seeing anybody on a regular nor engaging in unprotected sex. But the last few times she had been with Evan they just did the damn thing. That just doing it was trying to change the whole course of her life.

Day 309

Today brings another challenge for me. Things have been better, but I am still left feeling overwhelmed with sadness, loneliness, and bitterness. I am so good at faking it so much that I sometimes feel superficial to myself. The men that fed on my powerlessness are gone. But I sometimes ask myself are they gone for just the moment or is it always. I am sure that as many men say that they always have that one they could call on anytime, married or single that 'Dre or Damien would be that for me. But we all deserved better. I have found myself feeling sadness for Mya and feeling like I could do something so that her living and dying was not all in vain. The other part tells me that these things should remain as ghosts. Any idea of it happening is long gone anyway. Maybe I am perpetuating the secret that plagues our community, the secret of incest, child molestation, and sexual demons. Could I be giving this thing the centripetal force it needs to spin out of control as with a tire that has lost its secure place on the drum of a wheel. When that tire spins off it wreaks havoc on any and everything that comes in its path. Much like I have done. I am still coming to terms with the root of it all, but we all know time heals all wounds. I think I've gotten myself in an even bigger situation now. I'm mentally not ready for a child if that is the case. The financial part is there. But it makes no sense to impart these raw and restless emotions into my unborn child's soul. Whatever the case may be, I can't and I won't go through with it. I'm torn on whether to share this with Evan. Is he ready? Will he care? So many questions.........

Dana's pen played pickup sticks on the paper and her mind played musical chairs. The thoughts were sporadic as she contemplated her next move. The right thing was to share with Evan but the ultimate decision rested in her hand. She often felt guilty about the situation with Damien and wondered if their lives would have followed a different course if she followed through. The serenity prayer entered her mine... "The wisdom to know the difference." She repeated out loud. Those few lines made all the sense in the world, but were always clouded by the what if's. "The what if's are the things you need to let go Dana." She spoke to herself sternly.

"Dana, I'll be at yo' crib in 5." She looked up at the wall clock and dived off the sofa and peeked outside to make sure the clock wasn't lying. The sun was setting and the skies were blotted with pinks and oranges. She opened the door on the patio to allow the cool, fall breeze to blow through, lit a few candles, and made sure she wasn't looking as bad as she felt. The chime of the doorbell cut that short.

"Hey mama."

"Hi Evan. How was work?"

"Work was good. You hungry? I was thinking we go somewhere and get something to eat."

"I'm not hungry really, but we can order something."

"What's wrong?" Kissing her on the forehead. He held on to her lovingly. She began to cry. Concern was written all over his face. "What's wrong D?"

"I think we messed up?"

"How? I thought we were doing good."

"We are, but I'm not. I think I'm pregnant."

Soul on Fire

He let her go and stepped back. "Serious?"

"Serious."

"How?"

"How do you think women get pregnant?" Her emotions went from sad to being on the verge of pissed off with all the asinine questions.

"No baby girl. I don't mean how like that. First we need to see before anyone of us starts jumping to conclusions."

"Let's do a test."

"Okay, go get one. I'll wait." She plopped on the couch and kicked her feet up. She flipped through the channels while watching him stand and look at her from the corner of his eye. He stood and looked for a few minutes.

"What are you waiting for?" If he wanted to act stupid, she could do the same just a little bit better. All of that wasn't necessary considering the decision she had already made.

"Cool, I'll be back in a few."

Dana nodded in his direction. She felt a certain way about the whole thing, expecting him to respond in a different way besides all the woe is me bullshit. Wanting to pick up her journal, Dana decided it best to postpone any channeling of her thoughts. She was engulfed with so much negative energy. The clock ticked on as Evan arrived back to the house about thirty minutes later with a CVS bag in his hand.

"Let's do it." Were the first words that came out of his mouth. Not a how do you feel? What's on your mind? Nothing but let's do this. Dana snatched the bag from his hand and marched to the bathroom. Laughing to herself at the thought of what she must have looked like. Acting like a kid is not the way for someone pregnant with a kid.

"I can't go." she yelled into the other room. "Can you bring me a bottle of water?"

Evan appeared in the bathroom with two waters instead of one. He propped himself on the bathroom sink while she sat on the toilet. She drank one while they had small talk. After 15 minutes had passed, she asked him to turn on the faucet. A few drops came followed by a light stream of urine. She held the Clear Blue Easy at an angle and allowed every drop to saturate the tip. Dana placed it on the counter and walked out leaving Evan reading the instructions on the box.

A few minutes later, she could hear him walking across the floor towards her. He was holding the test and shaking his head.

Skyy Banks

"Well, it says you are pregnant." He sat across from her still holding the test and looking at it.

Not wanting to get into a long drawn out discussion she looked at him, "I'm having an abortion so no need to worry about it boo."

"I'm far from worried. If that's my seed then I'm going to do what I have to do."

"I hear you now, but we aren't even dating. I don't have time for baby daddy drama or for raising my child in a single parent home. I wasn't raised like that."

"Hold up. No stress, no drama. Whatever I need to do. You know I care for you. Yeah this is a lot for me. But I'm a man about mine."

"Like I said Evan. It's no need to do the back and forth thing. I'm sure you will stand up and do the right thing. Now is just not the right time. I definitely don't want you to feel like you owe me something because I am carrying your child. I'm going to have the abortion."

"I don't know about that just yet. Hold on. We hadn't even talked about anything."

"Really nothing to talk about. I just wanted to show you a little common courtesy and tell you what was going on. I'm tired. We can talk on tomorrow if you would like."

"Can I stay with you?" He asked while moving closer to kiss her.

"Not a problem." The mood had leveled out and she wasn't so uptight. Dana went on to the shower. Evan stayed in the living room made a few phone calls and raided the refrigerator. The last thing she remembered was him rubbing her back until she fell asleep.

Soul on Fire

Two months pregnant and Dana was miserable. Every morning until about noon the morning sickness was debilitating. She didn't have an appetite and was nauseated minus the vomiting. Evan was definitely being a team player, sure to call every morning to check on her as well as throughout the day, asking if she needed anything, if she'd eaten and going through the whole routine of impending fatherhood. It did make her feel better but the fact remained the same, they would just be co-parenting and that wasn't enough.

"Good morning Mama." Evan came across cheerful. They had spoken earlier but she was calling him back with what she knew he would think was unsettling news. "You alright?"

"As well as to be expected. I was calling to let you know I have an appointment for Thursday at the clinic."

"So you made the appointment without talking to me?"

"You know what I wanted to do."

"Yeah, just like you knew what I wanted to do. And you are not trying to find a middle ground."

Dana attempted to not raise her voice. She didn't see a middle ground when it came to having a baby. "Evan there is not one. Either you do it or you don't. I'm not saying that either one of us are not financially stable but when it comes to rearing a child it takes more and right now.... Truth be told that's all I am able to give."

"Let me do the rest." He pleaded.

"It's not that simple. This is what I am doing and you know I don't need your consent. Call it dirty. Call it whatever you like."

"Let's sit down and talk this through."

"Can I come through or you can come through."

"I'll let you know." She was needy right now, but she was not going to let her emotions get the best of her. She was unyielding.

Evan circled the parking lot a few times trying to avoid the chants and shouts of the picketers. They were holding signs with slogans that read choose life, abortion kills, and so forth and so on. Women were out with their babies. All this was occurring in front of the facility.

"D." before he could finish his statement.

Skyy Banks

"You can let me out in front and come up shortly." Dana could see the tension and sadness in his face. "It's going to be okay. I just want to get it over."

The previous night they had finally come to an agreement as to what to do. He really wasn't feeling her decision although he understood. They would continue to see each other and let things progress. His crush on Dana was a long standing one which made his words a little more sincere. Somehow in the back of her mind, she knew she would keep her guard up because she saw what he was capable of.

"I know, but man these people out here protesting and all up in your face makes me feel bad. You know that's my seed no matter how you look at it. What if God does something and I can't have anymore because of this?"

"Look at you! You will be okay. That's why Jesus died on the cross. Now come on. Get that spot right there. We can walk up and get some of this fresh air. Then you can come back around and pick me up when it's over."

"Man, I don't know."

"Don't start." Dana said with an agitated voice. "Park right there and come on." Pointing to the empty space.

She grabbed her bag and headed towards the door without him. It didn't take him long to catch up to her with his two steps to her one. "Young man you should think about what you are doing." One of the protestors called out to Evan. Dana pulled his arm as to say come and ignore these people. "Young lady." The same man called out to her. Her head snapped around and her mouth flew open.

"How can you people be out protesting without knowing our situation? We are the ones that have to answer for whatever decisions we make. My having an abortion is not going to stop you from getting into heaven. Take your old ass home and pray for me. Hell don't you think I feel like shit already without you piling it on?" By that time she was all in his personal space. He couldn't utter a response.

"Damn D." Evan pulled her this time. "Come on."

The waiting room was quiet and not too welcoming. The walls were drab, the chairs were standard with little cushion and the magazines were old. The room was filled to capacity. Could there be this many babies being aborted in one day? She questioned. Dana expected more subdued colors on the walls, with paintings throughout, informative magazines, and to put it way out there relaxing music, something to

Soul on Fire

counteract an already intense situation. She scanned the room looking for someone she might know. Thank God for small favors, but Evan saw one of his friends. He dapped him up and walked to the side for a brief exchange of information, more so, to tell each other about their situation.

The receptionist was very polite. The facility worked on a first name and first initial of the last name basis. Evan had a form to complete as being the person responsible for her after the procedure. "You can go and get something to eat or take care of some business." Dana really didn't want him to be there with her.

"I'm good." Evan reached for her hand and she pulled back. She wasn't in the mood for the caring and sympathy, even though he meant well.

An hour had passed and she was yet to be called to the back. She couldn't help but notice a lady beside her wiping at her eyes and sniffling. There was a young girl beside her that didn't look much older than fifteen or sixteen. Soon after they called for a Cynthia L. The two walked through the door leading to the back office area. Thirty minutes later the woman reappeared without the girl. This time she was crying harder and from time to time she let out a low sigh. Dana's natural instinct was to comfort her.

"Can I do anything for you?"

"No child. I think enough has been done."

"Can I get you something to drink?"

"No thank you."

Dana didn't think she really wanted to be bothered, but she felt bad for her. She continued to cry. Evan reached for her hand again. Dana pushed him away.

"I just don't understand why people are so cruel." She spoke out loud enough for Dana to hear and to elicit a response.

"I've asked myself that same question over and over again still with no answer."

"Why, why, why." She cried out again.

Dana could tell whatever grieved her. It ran deep, almost unbearable. "Is the girl your daughter?"

"Yes. She's a good girl." The lady added.

She must have assumed that she thought otherwise because her daughter was a minor and she was having an abortion. "She looks like it." Dana didn't want to say anything that was inappropriate.

Skyy Banks

"Do you know after being married for twenty three years that I had no idea that my husband was abusing my daughter? Now she's pregnant."

Instant déjà vu. Dana searched for, if there were any, the right words to console her. Dana knew however that her words wouldn't be able to take away the pain and the guilt of not protecting her child, as a mother is charged. "That has to be tough." Evan acted as though he wasn't listening but she was sure he heard. This complete stranger opened up to her. Dana owed her more than a *that has to be tough*. She took one hand and rubbed her back.

"What I do know is that you are going to have to be there for her more than ever. Prayer does make everything better and you both should seek counseling." Dana wanted to say more but didn't want Evan to know that this was a situation similar to her own. She fought hard not to cry. This time when he reached for her hand, she didn't resist.

"Dana M." her name was called.

Evan stood to walk her as far as he could go. She held on tightly. "I'll be right here." He looked Dana in the eyes and stood strong. She nodded in agreement.

After they went through the technicalities of the procedure, blood work, ultrasound, and the like she was led to a waiting room where she undressed and waited to be called back. There were many women waiting. It was like a chop shop, get them in and get them out. The room was cold and everyone was quiet. A few talked amongst each other as though this was a casual meeting. She overheard one person saying that this was her 6th abortion. Dana tried to distance herself from them by thinking about things and places that made her happy.

The room was cold and she lay on the table. The anesthesiologist asking her to count to ten was the last thing she remembered. She awakened in utter confusion, sitting up and crying uncontrollably. Shortly thereafter Evan was at the door holding her by the waist and escorting her to the car. The ride home was quiet, no music, no conversation, just Dana staring out the window.

Soul on Fire

ø

Fried turkey, dressing, macaroni and cheese and the traditional Thanksgiving fixings filled the room. The football game was on and all eyes were glued to it. They all converged upon Chelle and Russell's place because it was large enough to accommodate everybody, even the occasional house hoppers. Momma and Jay had picked Atlanta to spend the holiday this year. Dana was feeling better these days but more anxious to resolve the last few issues before the New Year.

"You think I can get an edge up while I'm here?" Jay asked Evan. They had been hanging tough for the past few days.

"No doubt."

Dana looked in the room at Evan who looked back at her and smiled. They were now at a different place in their friendship. This had a lot to do with her seeing him as who he was and not who 'Dre, Simeon, and the other ones were, even Carl Duncan. The kind of men who played games and their only conquest was to get what they wanted at whatever cost. 'Dre's cost was his family, Carl's cost was his money which he had plenty of and Simeon's was his credibility. Dana asked herself so many times if she was falling in the same trap, if she was being naïve, if she was perhaps feeding the emotional connection that she was starving.

Dana thought back to Evan being what she couldn't be, honest with himself and her. He stepped out of that comfort zone to say *D as long as I am single I'm free to see whomever.* This totally debunked the stereotype that all men are no good. She had a warped since of security due in part to spending countless nights over there, receiving frequent phone calls, and just because gifts. She would have appreciated knowing beforehand. Truth be told no man really comes out and gives you a choice without being confronted with a situation. She, Dana, on the other hand wanted to have her cake and eat too. The very thing women loathed men for.

Dana now believed that the decisive moment in their friendship was several days after the abortion. They had agreed not to speak about it. She left Evan to heal in his own way and his own time and he did the same for her. On this particular evening, Evan in what had become usual routine after work was very attentive, making sure that she had eaten, was in no pain, rubbing her feet, and bringing things from the office if she needed. If she didn't know any better she would have thought she had instead delivered a baby. He laid his head on Dana's lap and conversation flowed. In the middle of the impromptu conversation he became quiet. She looked down to see tears roll down his face. He grabbed her hips and buried his face in her lap without vocalization. At that moment, she knew he was sincere and truly bleeding on the inside for their child.

"Watch out now!" Dana heard momma tell someone. She walked to the family run to see her joogin' to whatever was blasting from the radio. All eyes had gone from football to her. Evan was holding one hand and they were tearing the floor up.

"Go head Mavis." Momma was referring to Mavis of the Staple Singers. She felt very warm by the playfulness of the two. Evan looked at her and winked. Dana winked back. Chelle, looking as though she would burst any moment pulled her by the arm, indicating she wanted some alone time, if only for a little while.

"Hey baby girl." Chelle reached out to hug Dana as tight as she could without putting undue pressure on her protruding stomach. "How have you been?"

"I have been doing well. Business is good." This was a move to evade any questions about her personally.

"There you go again. I think the last time I asked this question you responded the same way. I'm not letting you off that easy this time. Now how are you lady? Are you still reading that crazy dream book?" She laughed.

"Actually, I am not. That's why I have Dr. Mitchell!"

"Yes. So tell me."

"I have not had any dreams in a while. We have gone through a process to determine the origin of it all. Now that we know, I've been laboring to reconcile or find peace with it."

"What's the issue? It's like you are going around in circles to just say what it is. Our bond, our friendship runs deeper than that. How can I be there for you if I don't know what the necessity is?" Her plea was urgent.

"Chelle, it is so complicated, it's like an intricate web of people and the situation is so delicate that I don't want to open up a sea of emotions by pulling other people in. Trust me on this....please." Dana pleaded.

"I do trust you. But please know there is nothing that you can't tell me. Especially if it hurts you the way this has been."

Soul on Fire

"Chelle you are one of the kindest people I know. I have the utmost respect for you."

"Why thank you ma'am. You not too bad yourself!" They embraced again and let out soft, nervous giggles, the kind that worked hard at preventing an impending cry.

Dabbing at the corners of her eyes, Chelle continued with her insatiable curiosity. "So what's going on with you and Ev?"

"We just kickin' it."

"It's more than kickin' it. I see him too often, I hear about him all the time. Now he's spending family time. You must forget who you are talking to, someone that has read your book and knows your story. The Dana Montgomery I know doesn't bring the people she just kicks it with around the whole family."

Dana's infatuation was written all over her face. "At first I thought he was the typical game spittin' Negro, but he's proven himself to be a little more. So to answer your question, we are trying to build something." Dana smiled.

"I knew it! I knew it! Good for you! You know we still have a baby shower and wedding to plan. So don't go getting too serious on me and become M.I.A. All booed up and shit!"

"Did I hear you correctly? Miss I always want to be politically correct all the time." Dana couldn't resist that one. "I got you boo. Just let me know what I need to be doing."

"Don't worry!" Chelle jumped up from the couch almost losing her balance. Dana turned to see what had caught her attention so quickly while putting hands up to her back to help brace her. "Aunt Lois!"

Dana echoed her. "Aunt Lois! What are you doing here? Has somebody died and we don't know about it?"

"Girl you a mess." She tapped her on the face and squeezed her cheeks. "Come here! Both of you!" She wrapped as much of her arms around Dana and Chelle as she could. "How are my two favorite girls? Let me look at you."

She stepped back to face Chelle first. Dana started crying. She was simply overjoyed with having her family there with her. "Girl, you are absolutely beautiful. More beautiful than in the pictures you sent me."

"Thank you!" Chelle acknowledged with grace. "I'm so happy you made it where is Uncle Willie?"

Skyy Banks

"He's not feeling too well. It was safer that he stay put. I will only be here for a few days." She turned to Dana. "My baby. Look at you. Auntie misses you so much."

"Okay, now! It's a family reunion!" Dana looked up to see Chelle's parents singing and waving to the crowd. This caused her to run and damn near jump into her dad's arms. Looking around she saw Alexia's face in the midst of family.

Evan had made his way to Dana and put his arm around her shoulder while kissing her forehead. She could admit without any reservation that she was happy. She later found out that Chelle had not only orchestrated Momma, Jay, and Aunt Lois' coming down but paid for their airfare as well. Russell's gift to Chelle was having her parent's come down.

The dinner table was loud and jovial. Childhood stories were told of course they focused on Dana and Chelle. Russell was the perfect host. He toasted Momma and all the adults and commended them on raising beautiful and intelligent women. "Thanks for allowing your baby to come to Atlanta. I would have missed my shining star." Russell raised his glass.

A little cynicism tried to creep in as Dana looked at Mr. Davison and then at Russell. They looked almost like twins. She wondered what Mr. Davison thought about Chelle being with a man his age, old enough to be her father. She quickly dismissed the thought. She knew the answer to that question. As long as his baby was happy and Russell treated her well it would be fine. Although they would have preferred her married before pregnant, but Russell wasn't going anywhere.

Momma looked so peaceful across the table. Dana caught her a few times staring at her as though she wanted to ask her something or perhaps just trying to discern something. The last times their eyes met, Dana blew a kiss across the room. She reached up and made a motion with her hand as to catch it in mid air. Instead of placing the invisible kiss on her cheek, she put it close to her heart. That simple gesture almost made Dana cry. At that moment, she knew that if she didn't know about her or Mya already. She was not going to know.

Dr. Mitchell's couch was a recluse, a safe haven of some sort. Their sessions were down to an as needed basis. When Dana did come in, she blocked off the rest of the afternoon, allowing her a notable amount of time to be candid about her emotions. The majority of the time was spent lying on the couch and breathing. Her dosage had been lowered to 5 mg and she was on her second journal.

Soul on Fire

The event that brought her to the office today was a call from Aunt Lois saying that Uncle Willie had taken a turn for the worse and that she should come. Dana hadn't gotten all the closure she felt necessary for her to move to a healthy place in her life. The only thing that was missing was her encounter with Uncle Willie. She took his not being at Thanksgiving dinner as a sign of something positive. Her stress level soared from non-existent to migraine immediately.

"Dana, don't be dismayed by this. You have achieved great strides in coping with these malicious acts against you. I don't think there's anything wrong with not wanting to go."

"The uncanny thing about all of this is that I still love my Uncle."

"That's understandable."

"But how could I love someone that has hurt me so badly?"

"You know that's a question that the most brilliant psychologists can't answer, similar to children who love their absent fathers. However, Dana we can't go back and forth and you get entangled in your emotions. Our goal is to progress and not be stuck in a time zone."

"I know. I guess I have a decision to make."

"Yes. Whatever you decide, I will support you."

Dana was still not at the point where she could just be a river and let every obscure detail about her life flow. Sometimes, she felt this was hindering her, but on the other hand if it wasn't bothersome, she tucked it away in her secret place.

Skyy Banks

The room was quiet and cold. Uncle Willie lay with oxygen in his nose and tubes protruding from what appeared to be every vein in his arm. His breathing was shallow. If it was such a thing as death in the air, it was evident in the room. Dana approached him slowly. Aunt Lois did not want to leave his side because she knew death was imminent and wanted her hand to be the last he felt and her voice the last he heard. Dana begged her to give her a few minutes alone with him.

"Remember I'm his favorite niece as I am yours." The use of reverse psychology at a time like this was a low blow, but it was necessary.

"Go on baby. I know he'll be happy to see you."

Dana watched the heart monitor and prayed that a flat line would not come across the screen while she was with him. Holding his weak hand firmly, she placed the other hand over her heart.

"Uncle Willie?" She called out. He couldn't speak, but turned to look at her. "I remember. I remember all the things you did to me when I was little girl. I don't need to ask you why. I know you were a sick man, you and Uncle Harry. You hurt me." Dana clenched at her heart. "You broke me and I'm still broken. I want you to know that!" Tears flowed from her eyes nonstop. She could feel a slight tug at her hand. Looking down she could see tears streaming down the sides of his face, he pulled at her and made inaudible sounds. She leaned in closer.

"I'm sorry."

Dana buried her head in his chest and sobbed uncontrollably. The machine above his head sounded with a long beep. She knew what it meant. Nurses rushed in along with Aunt Lois. Dana continued to cry as they pulled her back.

"Dana, it's okay baby. He's gone home to be with the Lord." Aunt Lois stood stoic in the corner. "Father, I just want to thank you." She walked around the room while the nurses and doctor's frantically worked on him, not knowing that the tears Dana cried where tears of anguish and despair from being hurt by the hands of her precious Willie. Dana gave a damn about him dying and the cruel part of her wished she had doused his ass in gasoline before wishing him well in the fiery pits of hell.

"I'm Sorry Mrs. Roberts. He's gone." The Dr. said holding Aunt Lois' hand.

Soul on Fire

"I will praise the Lord at all times and his words will continually be in my mouth. Thank you. Thank You." With every thank you her voice grew louder and louder. She broke out in a shout. Dana stood in the corner watching and crying. After about five minutes of shouting Aunt Lois walked over to her, pulled Dana to her, and rubbed the back of her head.

"You okay, baby?"

Dana shook her head yes. Her mouth was too dry to speak and even more so she was at a loss for words. "You know your uncle loved you? You were his favorite. I always wondered what made you so special to him. I knew why you were special to me."

Dana looked through swollen eyes. Aunt Lois asked again or made the same statement again. "I always wondered what made you so special to him." She said it as though she wanted her to say something or perhaps answer something she should have asked of him. "But you Dana, I hope you spoke your peace. I pray that you have the answer that you need. I know. Willie has had a lot to say to your Auntie these past few months. I've been too hurt, angry, to say anything to you or your momma. I didn't know." She shook Dana hard and cried. "I didn't know and I'm so sorry. You know we take secrets to our grave. Your Uncle told his. I don't know if it changes things for you or will I have guilt the rest of my days because I could have done something."

"Shhhh...we not gonna do that Aunt Lois. How could you have known? I loved you like you were my momma and I still do. I'm not mad at you and I don't want you blaming yourself." Things had changed. The thing that changed was that she knew and Uncle Willie knew. He had confessed on his death bed one of many things to her and apologized to her.

Dana looked out of the window of the Cardiovascular Intensive Care Unit to see Evan standing near the nurse's station. When she asked him to come with her, the only question he asked was when he should be ready. Dana felt like she was having an outer body experience. Everything around her moved in slow motion, the voices sounded distant, and everything in her field of view was doubled.

"You okay, mama?" Evan asked with concern. Before she could answer he took her face in his hands, kissed her lips, nose, and each eye. Just like the first time she spent the night with him, his touch seemed to extract everything that was bad out of her. He softly brushed her face with his hand. Holding her close, he gave her all the security she needed.

Skyy Banks

"I'm okay." she repeated. She heard Alexia's voice in the background. *Girl you already okay*. She finally knew it to be true in her heart.